Five Bullets

BY LARRY DUBERSTEIN

Novels

The Marriage Hearse
Carnovsky's Retreat
Postcards From Pinsk
The Alibi Breakfast
The Mt. Monadnock Blues
The Day The Bozarts Died
The Twoweeks

Stories

Nobody's Jaw
Eccentric Circles

Five Bullets

two interlocking novellas by

LARRY DUBERSTEIN

BRIMSTONE CORNER PRESS
HANCOCK, NEW HAMPSHIRE, 03449

for all of them

ISBN: 978-0-692-25508-7

BRIMSTONE CORNER PRESS
Hancock, New Hampshire

"The missionaries of Christianity had said in effect to the Jews: 'You may not live among us as Jews.' The secular rulers who followed them from the late Middle Ages then decided: 'You may not live among us,' and the Nazis finally decreed 'You may not live.' ...And the 'final solution,' you see, is really final, because people who are converted can yet be Jews in secret, people who are expelled can yet return. But people who are dead will not reappear."

—RAUL HILBERG, IN CLAUDE LANZMANN'S *SHOAH*

Summer, 1936

They were barely three kilometers from the Convent and even closer to the confluence of this small unspoiled stream with the Vltava. From here, on a windless day, they could hear the band playing at the riverfront pavilion, well enough to sort out the sweet scrape of violins from the melodic exhale of accordions. Even so, even if Karel could start running and be standing on the dancehall terrace 20 minutes later, they were alone here and quite private.

So private that they always swam naked. One could do that anywhere, of course; it made sense to keep everything dry except for your skin, which dried soon enough in a summer breeze. Even on the outskirts of the capital, at certain places where the Vltava narrowed, people swam naked at lunch hour, returning to work afterward dressed and dry.

But Mila was shy. She did not like appearing naked before strangers, and at times could even be shy with her husband. While this made for a pleasant joke between them, Karel never understood it. Women far less attractive would display themselves proudly, some enjoying the simple power of sexuality as they shed a dress and flashed to the water, others oblivious to the matter and merely practical. Mila did not lack confidence or pride in herself, she was just shy—whatever shyness was, wherever shyness came from.

Though they had to walk a short forest path to get here, the site itself stood in the open, in knee-high field-grass that 40 years earlier had surrounded a wooden cottage whose four stonework corners remained. Those corner supports, standing seven meters apart, made the vanished cottage easy to imagine. A nearby pile of flattened, rotting debris indicated the way its boards and battens had looked. They had never been painted, so that even the color, or lack of color, was knowable.

They considered this place their own. Not that they held the deed. The fact was that no one else ever came here—not the owners, not the gypsies, not so much as a pack of youngsters. Someday, when they had the means, Karel and Milena hoped to buy it and rebuild the cottage exactly as it once was, or exactly as it was in Karel's rendering. He had sketched it in pencil, added pastel colors, and had taken the further liberty of adding a barrel-vaulted dormer which accommodated two casement window sash. Why not, if the whole thing was fantasy? His drawing was pinned to a kitchen wall in the flat where for now they had just enough money for rent, food and clothing, and perhaps, Mila had begun to argue, a second child.

The blue duvet had been spread over trampled grass and as soon as Benno was enveloped in its folds and sleeping, Mila eased into the river to cool off. Now she stood in the sun, brushing water from her belly, impatient to get back into her dress. In that regard, she and Karel were at cross-purposes. Each time she was nearly dry, he would splash her and laugh, so cheerfully that she could not quite be annoyed with him. She could pretend ("Let me dress, you naughty boy") but she was laughing too.

"Let me help you," he said, gently brushing water from her breasts, both at the same time, to see if it held true (as it always did) that her left nipple grew and straightened before the right one. He never ceased to wonder how something so pale and soft could sprout from its middle such vivid rose-colored thimbles. But then her hand dropped, touching him lightly, and he was sprouting too. Mila tried to retract it, both her hand and the invitation it had sent, saying again, "No, no, Karel, let me dress."

"He is sound asleep, Mila. You know he never wakes up quickly."

"What if he does, though?"

"All right then, what if he does. He will wipe the cobwebs from his eyes"—he passed a palm over her eyes so they shut and then re-opened—"and behold something so ridiculous he will laugh his famous gurgle-gargle at the people doing such silly things. And he will laugh all the more," he said, now pulling her close and lifting her buttocks, "when he sees that the people are his own silly loving parents. Momma and Poppa! Imagine it!"

"He will be scarred for life," said Mila, altogether joking at this point, for he had persuaded her, partly with his words, partly with his hands, and was lowering her onto the other quilt, where they fell together into what Karel liked to call "God's simplest puzzle, with just two pieces to solve." They had solved it and celebrated the fact with movements which, in a reversal of the norm, he worked to slow down while she aimed to accelerate. Mila always expected someone to emerge suddenly from the notch where the pathway opened out and catch them at it. "Let them look, my love," he reassured her. "Let them have a good laugh, too."

She was not looking that way at the moment; she was not in a rush because of Benno, either. For one minute of her life, Mila was lost to care, elsewhere, and then for what—ten seconds?—she was flying heedlessly past the sun. The instant she landed, though, she was up and stepping into her dress, buttoning it quickly despite his protests ("No, my love, let the sun see your wonders, let your poor husband enjoy them") and fussing with Benno's sunshade in a way that was bound to wake him.

Soon she began fussing with the alcohol burner which, after all, never worked on the first try anymore.

Later they ate the baked fish and drank coffee while Benno mauled his torte. The air was still sultry at six o'clock, when Karel jumped in the water one last time before packing up. He knew how the stream would turn black in the moonlight, how countless stars would salt the blackening sky, and how despite the ravenous insects they would be happy staying all night. He had to be in the office early, though; had to keep earning money if they wanted to buy these four stone corners on the riverbank, or at the very least continue to buy food and clothing.

Fortunately, there would be more Sundays like this one ("Fifty times fifty-two," he promised her by way of consolation, "*thousands* of Sundays") so they dragged themselves away from the shimmering light on the water and started back to Praha, to sleep instead in their small stifling flat.

1947

Certainly it was strange to be "Carl," and to be speaking with Cousin Jan and calling him "John." Not the most difficult thing, perhaps not important, simply odd. They were playing assigned roles in the American show, explained John, who by now had been playing his role for 15 years, to the point where he sounded (to Carl's ear, at least) a native speaker. The flavor of the Czech language has to be wrenched from every syllable Carl utters, where John just rattles on, his accent imperceptible. This, John has advised his younger cousin, is extremely helpful in business.

Strange too is this wasteland where John established his steel fabrication plant. On one side stretches a wide flat barren where a twin propeller airplane is simply parked, like a large mutant automobile. Bordering this expanse is a marsh into which flows a shallow sickly canal featuring, among other unsightly objects, a partly submerged, presumably embedded metal cart with its wheels in the air. And coiling its way through the entire varietal mess is a paved roadway making straight for the gigantic door of what is more a huge enclosure than a building proper, a metal shell large enough to stage football matches. Such is the fiefdom of Carl's American cousin.

But John has made a fortune and he made it right here in this repellent wasteland, at this unashamedly utilitarian facility, whose cinder block and sheet metal façade lacks even the slightest pinch of charm. Minimal daylight sifts inside through high, miserly windows. Most of the ambient light is fluorescent, ample yet harsh. On broad shelving, arranged in endless aisles as if for shoppers, a million lineal feet of steel—sheets, slabs, rods, and blocks of every dimension—are neatly stacked, an inventory John assures him will be completely turned over, every piece sold, by month's end.

"You will see. Money will not be a problem for long, cousin."

"Money," says Carl, dismissively, "is not a problem to begin with."

"Okay, so what is?"

"Everything else. Everything except money."

"So that's good. I mean, what with just *everything* being problematical."

"Czech and double Czech," says Carl, deploying his cousin's catch-phrase. He has found John's humor, the current of merriment flowing through his voice, to be both contagious and familial. This man, whom Carl barely remembered and had hesitated to call upon, is family. He has the Bondy traits, some as superficial as the bat-shaped ears, others as pivotal as the straight-faced irony that fixes itself on any hint of the absurd.

"Listen," says John, his arm around Carl's shoulder, "I want to take you back to the city now, into Manhattan. There are presents I would like to buy you, some clothes to wear in the U.S., for example."

"Clothes are not a problem."

"They don't have to be a problem," says John, lips pursed at the getup Carl has on. "These are just some presents I want to buy, to welcome you. Okay?"

In the dim, narrow tap room on 38th Street, facing a maze of mirrored bottles inside a framework of varnished wood, they raise tankards to the fallen. John has lost countless (literally, as from here in America, he has been unable to count them) family members from every generation, "beginning, or ending perhaps, with my Grandpa Max."

Carl has no need to count; he has lost them all.

"Do you know, I haven't been back since 1932. It has been that long."

"Believe me, cousin, you would not recognize it. It is not there anymore."

"Praha? People say it is the same. Brno?"

"What people? Who are these people?"

"You're right, I may have simply read it somewhere. But Sylvia—my wife, who you will meet tonight—wants to see Brno. She wants to show our children the places I was growing up."

"No one knows. Not so much Brno, or even the capital, but no one knows what went on over there," says Carl, reverting to the Czech language as he will do when laying out more complex matters. "The rest of the world, that didn't see it, has no idea what was going on."

It crosses his mind lightly—to be dismissed as quickly as possible—that in truth John has done well, that the War can only have made him richer.

"Still, it's in the past," says John, motioning to the bartender for two fresh pints. "It will come back to normal in time. This is how history works."

"I am sure the two dozen Jews drawing breath in Europe today will rejoice at your news," says Carl, clearly still agitated.

"Cousin, forgive me," says John at once, laying a hand on Carl's arm and finding it so rigid it threatens to bend the hollow brass bar rail. "I neglected to mention that this process of returning to normalcy might take five thousand years."

The War has hardened Carl, John notes, and naturally enough, just as America has softened me. It will take time, his cousin's transition. Not five thousand years, of course, but perhaps not one year either. At least Carl looks the part now. There was no way of getting a tie around the stubborn mule's neck, but the mule does look better in a brown suit and brown leather shoes. John is not worried. His cousin may be stubborn but he is obviously a smart cookie.

1939

"So look now, Milena. Finally we can say for certain that I am myself and you are yourself."

"Stop being silly, Karel."

"What then? I should be tragic? Because either this is very silly or it is tragic."

They had just acquired (or more accurately, suffered through days of bureaucratic nonsense and stagnant queues in order to have issued to them) their so-called identity cards, papers that ensured the occupying Germans total control over their every movement. In taverns and coffee-houses where semantics had become the national sport, it was being debated whether this added insult to injury or injury to insult. The good old facetiousness would not die easily in Praha, however diluted by an expanding bitterness.

"It's both, of course," said Mila, "and for us it's best to ignore it, regardless. Put the stupid card in your pocket—there's my good boy—and take it out when they ask. Otherwise, pretend it doesn't exist."

"Pretend *we* don't exist, you mean. After all, that's what he wants."

"He, Hitler?"

"Hitler, Hacha. Throw them in the same pot. If Hacha wanted us to continue existing, why give up without a word of protest?"

"Karel, we exist. We simply do. Tonight we will go hear Mozart at the Rudolfinum. Tomorrow, our parents will come for supper. Monday morning you will go to work."

"Where the windows must be shut tight, by law."

"We are being protected, my love," she said, still attempting to steer him toward a lighter view. "By our nice new protectorate."

"As the lion protects the antelope."

"Yes, my jungle hero. But really, right now, today, next week—what is the choice? That we should stop going to work, stop eating supper? Isn't that exactly what you deplore Hacha for doing?"

"You are wise, and right. I agree with you."

"You do?"

"I do. We shall remain optimists. Any day now, God will rise up, take note of what is going on here, and see to it the Nazis all drink poison and die. Before we do."

"You are making fun of me."

"Why do you say that? If your God is good—"

"He has been good enough to give us a second child. A healthy child, Karel."

"A beautiful child. I just didn't know that it was He who delivered her. I had heard rumors of the stork."

"And who do you think gave us the stork?" she said, not yet emboldened to reveal that the selfsame stork would be engaged again in the not-too-distant future. "Do you think storks are made in factories?"

"You are making so many good points today, Mila. Meanwhile, I think our beautiful healthy child has begun to howl. Can you hear the beautiful music she is making?"

Mila had prepared a roast and baked a Russian sponge cake that somehow managed to soak up half a litre of rum. The cake was for Helena's half-birthday, or for those coming at noon to celebrate it: Mila's parents and Karel's, her two brothers, three friends. She had yet to see any evidence the Nazis objected to her cooking the family dinner.

Whatever they wanted—power, land, wealth?—whatever they took for that matter, a government was only a government, life was still life. How often, really, had their private lives intersected with the powers-that-be? Architects and teachers were certified, fees and taxes were levied. If you were fortunate enough to purchase an automobile, one or two petty officials would stand in your way for an hour. No one knew the politicians before, no one knew them now. All that had changed were the bland faces one saw in the newspaper.

"You see how life goes on," she said. "Your son still refuses to wash up or permit me to comb his hair."

"Good for him."

"That's a nice lesson. Ignore what your momma tells you and stay filthy?"

"He has a nice clean shirt."

"Yes, and he has something purple stuck to his ear."

"Let the men take care of this problem. Benno, come with me a minute."

Karel lifts his son onto his shoulders, waits for Mila to sound the alarm ("Watch out for his head!") as they negotiate the arched portal, lowers the boy back down in the lavatory. When the water gets warm, he soaks a fresh cloth and drapes it over his face like a barber's towel.

"That felt good," he says, removing the cloth, "but did I get it all?"

"Get what, Poppa?"

"The jam on my nose. Is it gone?"

"You didn't have any jam. You were clean."

"No, no, you didn't see it is all. Look, you can't even see it on your own face."

Hoisted onto the stool, peering into the mirror, Benno insists he can see it perfectly. He snatches the wet towel and begins to rub. Standing directly behind, Karel ruffles his son's thick hair, playfully pushing it down over his eyes.

"You are the messiest hair comber in all of Praha, my dearest. I am afraid I have failed to teach you the art of combing."

"You did that. You messed me, you know you did."

"Show me then."

It was not perfect, but the attempt itself would suffice. In his clean blue shirt, with his face rubbed red, brown hair parted and the cowlick damped down, Benno would please his grandparents, even if his mother objected to Karel's methods. Don't trick him, teach him. She was the teacher in the family. But wasn't the lesson conveyed? Benno understood he had done well to spruce up, without having lots of rules broadcast at him. So there were more ways through the woods than one.

They were arranged in overstuffed chairs and divans in the parlor. Milan, Karel's father, poured the wine and said little; his wife Jitka said less. They left the floor to Vaclav, for Mila's father was always talking, whenever he was not shouting outright.

"Just look at this big boy," he exclaimed. "He shines like the boy in the soap posters. Milena, what did you do to him?"

"Nothing. He sees to himself, as it should be."

"Well, he is a handsome lad, that's for sure. Which is no surprise—after all, he is my grandson. Benno, do you deserve a gold coin?"

"No, Grandfather."

"No? But you will *accept* one?"

"Yes, Grandfather. Thank you."

"Enough of this," Karel interrupted. "Or the baby will be demanding gold coins too."

"And she shall have them. But at six months? I know your daughter is precocious—"

"Precocious indeed," said Karel. "She has an identity card now, you know, and therefore an identity. She is Helena Bondy, where just one week ago she was nobody."

"I hope," said Helena the elder, grandmother to Helena the baby, "we are not here to talk politics. I hope we are here to eat."

"We are," said Mila, "and the time has arrived. If everyone will come to table, we shall have a dinner every bit as good as last week's. Or last year's."

"The best ever, I am sure," said Karel. "Come, everyone, time to eat."

As they paraded through to the adjoining room, Karel slid a palm over Benno's head and shuttled it just enough to activate the cowlick. Benno wiped his father's hand away and pressed the cowlick back down, with moderate success. Then, while his mother was assigning the seats, he checked to make sure the gold coin was still in his pocket.

1949

"You could live out there, you know," says John. "Save yourself a lot of time."

"Who wants to live out there?" says Carl.

"To hear you tell it, everyone does! Isn't that it, with the population booming?"

"Exactly. Too much cars."

John laughs at the notion. Traffic on the Island? From anywhere in lower Manhattan, where Carl is now living in a small flat, you can see a hundred cars. See them, hear them, and smell them, John points out. "Out on the Island, they still have a little space between the cars."

"Space between? Not on Sunrise Highway, cousin. It's good—not to live there, to build."

All those cars, with however much space between, contain drivers who need to buy gasoline, a newspaper, a bottle of milk, a pound of coffee. They need to wash some clothes. So these little strips of stores—filling station, small grocery, laundry—are welcomed by the towns and are instantly successful. Keep them or sell them; either way it is profitable and each time the profit is larger. Carl explains he has been "learning these ropes."

John gets a kick whenever Carl flings such idioms around. Has he gone to the Berlitz after all, as John advised? Impossible. John knows the man well enough by now to know he would never take advice, never go to the language school. "School!" Carl said at the time. "I am thirty-seven years old!"

Now he is 38 years old and slinging around phrases like "learning the ropes."

"I'm impressed," says John.

"That I can know these ropes? You thought I was a fool?"

"Not at all. Impressed that you keep picking up so much of the language."

"Double features. My school."

"The movies?"

"Yes. In the Village, theaters with double features all day, and cheap. They let you stay, too. Never kick you out."

So Carl has been learning English from John Wayne and Errol Flynn. Learning the ropes from cowboys, who ought to know them, and from gangsters.

"When I hear in English, I understand. Speaking is not so easy."

"Because in the movies, listening is all you do. Maybe you should try talking back."

"This I did," says Carl, shaking his head. "Two of us watching, in the whole theater two customers that day and so I ask him to please explain 'kettle of fish.' And this guy runs away like I will murder him."

John does not trouble Carl with his best guess at why the man took flight. "Did you ever find out?"

"Natural. I ask the girl."

"What girl?"

"At the window. Who earlier I ask why open up when just two people come to watch."

"Good question."

"She says, so you will buy some popcorn. Okay, I tell her, pop it and I'll buy. So it is costing me twenty cents extra to find out. Language tax!"

"That's a fine kettle of fish, cousin. But listen, it is costing you a lot more than that today, because this is your treat. You're buying my breakfast."

"It is my strict pleasure."

"Another phrase! But don't you want to know why?"

"Why what?"

"Why you are treating me to coffee and Danish this morning. It's my birthday, cousin. I am fifty years old today. Can you believe such a thing?"

Not really. Carl Barry cannot believe such a thing, any more than he can believe he turned 38 last month; that birthdays can keep occurring. At first, he failed to register the date, much less celebrate it. When he saw the date that afternoon in the *Post*—his other English language school—he did not think about birthdays or birthday parties, not even Benno's "best day ever" when they went on the night-time boat ride. What hit him like a stone to the head was that if he was 38 today, then in precisely one week Milena would be 36.

Would have been. And he wondered, would her birthday always be his first thought as he continued to age. If he lived to be 50, would his sole response be the sudden awareness that in one week Mila would turn 48?

"Happy birthday, cousin. It is so much my pleasure to be in your company today, I will pay this birthday tax."

"And my pleasure too. It's wonderful to see you thriving, Carl, truly it is."

Thriving. Not a word he knows, though its meaning is clear enough. John is praising him, noting his progress. Carl could indeed afford to buy a small house out on Long Island, if he wished to do so.

"Funny," he says. "Funny like strange, how there is always the birthday, but never the deathday."

"Strange is right. Your mind, I mean. There is no such thing as a deathday."

"The day you die, like the day you are born." Carl shrugs. "Birthday, deathday. Why not?"

"If you did happen to know your last day on earth, you wouldn't know it for long."

Smiling, Carl lets the misunderstanding stand. He did not mean his own deathday, or John's, nor was he concerned for one moment with the *yahrzeit*. He was just thinking of Milena, and bumping up against the fact that as firmly as he knows the date Milena was born, he will never know the date on which she died. She died in a world without calendars.

"Who needs it, right?" says Carl, adopting his cousin's jovial tone. "If you are dead, nothing can be so very important to you now."

1941

Here was Benno again, clamoring to come with him to the office. The boy always enjoyed himself there and why not, with the bowl of hard candy, the bottles of cold juice, and everyone treating him like visiting royalty. Plus, Karel could lose track of the boy's whereabouts, leaving him free to wander the corridors, explore in and out of rooms.

Benno was quite sure he was invisible. Even the beautiful Sonya (who more than once had brushed his cheek with the back of her hand and called him handsome) sometimes failed to register his presence. Though not always. One day last summer, Benno had spotted a giant sea-serpent swimming up the wide busy flood of the Vltava. That time, as he darted from office to office tracking the monster's progress through successive windows, Sonya accompanied him. Taking his hand, she marveled at the monster—which was in reality an oddly rigged Dutch sailboat—and gave him paper and colored pencils with which to draw it.

Karel was at a loss, out of lame excuses. He was unsure what to tell his son, or better, what not to tell. Unsure *how* to tell that he no longer had an office they could go to. He was still at "liberty," free to travel around the city, but he was no longer employed at Pikarny-Kovy. Three weeks ago, 14 Jews were working there. This week, zero.

Karel's initial response was to deride the bald stupidity of the move. Let them see how business proceeds without a Jew around, much less 14 of the best engineers, architects, and draftsmen in the capital. Artur, Bohumil, Karolina, Franta, both Josefs—who would take their places? Surely the work would suffer to the point of incompetence and outright failure.

And failure might be just the thing, considering the assignment he and Artur had been handed. They were to study the Pilar warehouses—assess the economics of demolition versus rehabilitation, evaluate the various proposals regarding fenestration, systems, timetables—for conversion to a museum. But this proposed museum would not house works of art, ancient armor, or dinosaur bones. The Museum of Extinct People, so-called, would recapitulate the life of a Jewish people who had once existed and would no longer exist. "It takes a Jew to embalm a Jew?" Artur spat out, when Petr Kovy outlined the project for them.

Now they were all extinct, at least as structural engineers in the Protectorate of Bohemia and Moravia. When Kovy sat them down to "explain our situation," Karel laughed in his face. The situation explained itself perfectly.

Or it did so to everyone except Milena, who still refused to believe this black joke could be reality. She would not believe what was happening until their skulls were displayed under glass at The Museum of Extinct People.

Nor would she believe they could suddenly disappear, in exactly the way the Lilienfelds and the Poppers *had* disappeared: taken somewhere, who knows where, for their own safety, they were assured. A lie, of course. The only threat to their safety lay with the people taking them away. Tradesmen well known at Pikorny-Kovy had reported being bussed to the fortress town of Terezin and kept there for months, laboring to prepare a "haven" for the Praha Jews. Karel knew the place and remembered it as a perfectly efficient garrison. It was not a place where any of them would choose to live.

No one had told him they were going there, to Terezin. Not yet anyway, though it was hinted that their apartment house might soon be requisitioned for use in the "war effort." If so, the Bondy family could rest assured their new residence would be pleasing to them and that above all they would be safe there.

"Today we are not working," Karel said to Benno, as nonchalantly as possible. "Today we will just have a little fun, you and I. We'll poke around."

In their household, poking around was an honorable activity, of long standing.

"Can we go there anyway, Poppa? I like to poke around at the office."

"Better stay closer to home, save a bit on tram-fare."

"We can drive. Will the car come back today?"

Karel could smile right into his son's eyes, but he could not say the words. How could Benno be expected to take them in? He let Milena do the lying, because she believed she was telling the truth: "They have the car for a while longer. They don't say exactly when."

All Karel could do was hug the boy, and fuddle his hair.

That night, in bed, he was resolved to hold his tongue. To let Mila deceive herself without contradiction. Normally, inexorably as a ticking clock, he would push back against her foolishness with facts. But perhaps foolish optimism was all they had now. To embrace the logic of illogic might be the best strategy for staying sane. So he was committed to keeping them playful tonight, amusing her.

"Do you know, my love Milena, that Princip died there, in the fortress town? Gavrilo Princip, who murdered the Archduke Ferdinand."

"You offer me a history lesson? I thought you were going to tickle my back."

"I will. I am. But we can still talk."

"All right, then tell me. To begin with, what exactly is an archduke?"

"What is a duke, for that matter?"

Her cotton gown was thin as tissue paper but he lifted it anyway, so they each wore nothing at all. As yet, the Nazis had not forbidden them this.

"Start there," she said, approving of his hands on her shoulders. "And while you are at it, you can define for me a duke."

"Whatever it is, my darling girl, he kills one—Mister Princip does—and an arch one at that. Which starts the World War, and so naturally enough he goes to prison. And Terezin was that prison. That's where he died, in the very place where we too may die."

Whoops. So much for perpetuating foolish illusions! Unable to suppress his dark humor even for these few minutes, Karel had slipped from his resolution. She could not say he was morose, though. They were still having a good time and Mila was willing to let it pass.

"More likely," she said, "we will die from breathing the stink of Mrs. Drillich's sauerkraut. Which might come as a relief."

"I am consoled. Thank you, my love, for consoling me."

"Consoling you is my full-time job," she laughed, reaching back to remind his hands of their assignment and perhaps expand it, as after all her bottom needed tickling too.

"Another interesting fact about Princip," he said, while obliging her, "is that he also murdered the Archduke's wife that day. The Archduchess."

"Whatever an archduchess is."

"Just so. But the interesting part is that this didn't matter, did not signify a bit. Maybe it wasn't even against the law to kill a mere archduchess, because history is quite silent on the subject. The poor lady is a footnote."

"Unless God took the matter in hand," said Mila, rolling over onto her back. She was hardly the slip of a girl she had been, but no one would guess this body had borne three children. Her skin still fit perfectly. Karel shaped her breasts with his palms, tasted the sweet salt skin of her belly.

"In God's eyes," she continued, "Princip may have died in prison for killing Lady Ferdinand, not her husband. God may even have preferred the Archduchess."

"Who could blame Him," said Karel, "if she was half as fetching as you, my love."

"Shhh now," said Mila.

To Karel, she seemed happy, yet her eyes were damp and he could not tell if these were joyful tears for their love or tragic tears for all she pretended not to know. Tears for Benno and Helena and Lucie, whose breathing sounded around them like a quiet chorus in the stilly night. He did not tell Mila (who was asleep by then in any case) how certain he was that the Germans' great goal was to extinguish their sweet breathing and ship their small bones, along with perhaps a scattering of representative toys, to the high-minded Museum for Extinct People, as soon as the walls could be whitewashed and the floors freshly waxed.

1950

"So then why sell?" Carl is asking because the man, Sam Janney, has just finished telling him the business is a sure thing.

"I open my books to your wondering eyes," says Janney. "Nothing to hide. I have had enough of it, that's all. I'm sixty-one years old next month."

"You could starve at sixty-two if you didn't do a savings."

"I did enough. And my kid is a lawyer. He doesn't know it, but he could be buying his old man a few dinners. I fed them all, didn't I?"

Carl Barry has no problem believing the business is sound, or that it will double in the coming years. Ten years from now there will be twice the number of automobiles rolling past this spot and, at a minimum, twice the sales. Sell a better product at a better price, maybe four times the sales.

He has no trouble understanding why Sam Janney is done with it, either. It is a can't-miss enterprise, but so what? It's just the making of the money and Janney has enough money saved. Janney would rather go fishing.

"Where do you do it?" asks Carl.

"Oh no you don't. My books are an open book, but no one gets to know my secret fishing hole. When I disappear there, my friend, I disappear."

"Poof."

Carl has not fished even once since the months he passed in Borva. There he had a life of peace and natural beauty, but he is not interested in those things now. He is interested in action, and here in America the making of the money comes along with action, unless you are stupid. Some people are, though; in America they do crazy things. "They shoot yourself in the foot," he declared last week to John, when they drove out here together to look over the premises.

Really, John came along to add his endorsement, because although Carl was convinced the deal was sound, he was undecided about going ahead with it. He wanted—another of his newly acquired phrases—a second opinion.

"Why do you always hesitate?" said John. "And what's America got to do with it? Would you need a second opinion if this joint was in Brno or Pardubice?"

Carl shrugged. The question was unanswerable. If the shop had been in Brno, everything in life would be completely different, including Brno itself. Besides, the reason for his hesitation was not one he could explain to John, namely that it was pointless to own things simply because they might show a profit. The point was in *doing* things, making things happen.

John's Chicago wife Sylvia has been ill. This is not new, but recently it has grown worse. Syl may be dying and no one discusses the fact directly. It is how are you feeling, I'm feeling better; how is she doing, she's doing okay. But Syl looks bad and lately she stays home instead of meeting John at the Greenhorn Tavern. Ever since the children moved out, they have had a tradition of getting together for a drink around six o'clock, sometimes stay and eat. Now John has two drinks for himself and heads home to watch the evening news with her.

So one day John's buddy Paulie, at the bar, says "Johnny Johnny"—here Jan is not just John, he is Johnny, like a little kid—"I'm telling you this gal is thirty-two and gorgeous."

"I'm happy for her."

"You're no spring chicken," says Paulie, "you want to start shopping early."

John's friend is not the most delicate of souls; marriage to him is more an inconvenience than a bond. So John is supposed to "shop around" as if he is not 52 and long married. Paulie's gorgeous girl is 32 years old? John and Sylvia have a daughter nearly that age.

But John did it, he had a drink with the spring chicken, once, twice, three times—getting to know her, he says. And that's not all. "I met her sister and Carl, listen to me, she is younger and even prettier than Elsa. Honest to God. Nice girls too, from a lovely family. The mother is a doctor. The *mother.*"

"I'll remember this, next time I take sick."

Carl has no interest in John's beauty contestants. The beauties are fine with him and what John does is between him and Sylvia, none of Carl's business. You can't tell John certain things in any case. Just as you can't tell him that a thriving business can be boring, you can't tell him you have no interest in Elsa's little sister. Didn't he have the same conversation with Jaro, in Praha? Everybody has these sisters, but for Carl the beauty contest ended with Milena.

To which John would just say "You're crazy." This is something he says quite often to Carl and Carl can smile at it, because John may be right. They batted it back and forth that day last week, when Carl said he wanted to go to the ocean. "Long Island is an island, no? An island in the sea?"

"I thought you didn't care about pretty girls on the beach."

"Who said girls? I want to see the water, the waves coming. How far away can it be?"

"In through here? It's everywhere and nowhere, that's all I can tell you about the Island. I'll take you out to Coney some time, on the Brooklyn side."

"What about today?"

"Takes too long. I have to get back to town. But we'll go. You'll see, there'll be ten thousand girls in bathing suits and most of them will be ugly."

"I never said—"

"Not all, of course, but plenty of ugly girls, to satisfy your discerning eye."

Carl lets it go. Actually, he likes when his cousin makes fun of him because the jibes always feel like affection, not scorn. It's a familiar kind of ribbing. As for this new phrase, "discerning eye," he can check up on that later. No need to ask. If he can spell it, he can find it without help.

1943

So far, the money was safe inside the lining of his coat. The coat was safe because he never took it off.

Karel had withdrawn their cash in increments, anticipating a day when the confiscations and exclusions ratcheted down into "law." Though the account was still accessible the last time he went, he felt obliged to forestall curiosity by lying with sad eyes to the teller that they would "be needing this money for my wife's surgery."

The money would help, no matter how and no matter where. It would purchase a few privileges and fend off a few small disasters, as it already had when their names came up for transfer to Terezin. They were instructed to pack only two suitcases—two per family was the limit, as storage in their "new facility" would be restricted for the time being. Karel was cautious in mentioning the money and at pains to convey that 30 crowns was the all of it, every last crumb he could lay his hands on. Had he begun peeling bills off a roll, the rest would have been gone in a flash.

So they had more clothing than some—extra coats and shoes—plus a small satchel containing some of his books and her Aunt Monica's silver candlesticks. They rode the train in seats, in a passenger car, while many were packed like freight. And when they reached the fortress town, Mila and the children were granted a larger space, to be shared with just one other family. These mitigations did help.

Karel would not spend a solitary crown on himself. Any relative comfort he could negotiate was for Mila and the children. If not for them, he would sooner spit in Fritz' eye than grease his palm for petty favors. Who knew if the remaining money would help any of them later on, or how? It was simply prudent to squirrel it, to retain at least the possibility of possibility.

"Why are we moving?"

"Why is the sky blue?"

"No, Poppa, tell me. Why are we moving if we don't want to move?"

"Darling, you know when we say that you are not the boss, and that we decide? Well, we are not the boss of everything either. Sometimes other people decide."

"What people?"

"Government officials."

"Policemen?"

"Bigger, higher up than that. These are the people who tell the policemen where to stand."

"Like God, you mean?"

"More like Petr, at the office, who tells us all what job comes next, you know, and what the client wants us to do for him."

"Poppa, I'm hungry."

"Me too," said Karel, fearing that Benno understood the situation all too well. "Shall we open the chocolates now, or save them?"

Milena just smiled at them as the votes for chocolate came in.

"Thank you for being so good," she said, later.

"Good, was I?"

"Yes, Karel. You even called it home—our new home. Believe it or not, this helps them a great deal."

"We won't be able to fool them forever, you know."

"Fool them for now, then. Try."

"I am trying."

"I know. But keep trying. Don't make them unhappy."

"Me!"

"You are their happiness, you and I. Poppa and Momma. Be that above all, and be the citizen just a little."

"I *was* a citizen. That's the whole point."

"Okay, be the outraged citizen. The abused, the persecuted—I don't disagree. Just first of all, be the Poppa."

From the Southern Hill, they could see out past the ramparts, ditches, marsh, and meadow to the distant blue hills. They could see two dozen men cutting a bed for the new rail track through a level meadow decorated with what seemed one bright yellow dandelion for each blade of grass. Along the dusty road, they could see both horse-drawn carts and lorries, as though two different centuries were being illustrated for a lower form textbook.

Aromas rose up to them as sharply as the sights, from the dewy grass, the ripening grain, the horses' toil. Early windfall apples lay crushed and bruised, giving off a hint of something like cider. It was all so lovely that Karel felt like crying.

"Next week," said Karel, "I will be working out there. It's the best job to have here."

"I want to run," said Benno, neither noticing his father's emotion nor responding to his rationalization concerning the work. He pointed to the green field below. "Can we run?"

"Better in the Stadpark. We can kick there, with your pals. Maybe we can get a game."

It was clearer each week exactly what they were to be denied, how extremely they were to be deprived. For Karel, the most wrenching aspect was deceiving the children, scheming to put them off with palliatives and excuses. That had become next to impossible by now; soon the children would have to be told they were in jail.

Karel knew exactly what his son would say to such a preposterous suggestion. Possessed of a literal and logistical mind, Benno would say: "*But what did we do?*" Karel could see the boy getting exercised over the injustice and eager to prove them "wrong" by ticking off all the good behavior to his credit, all the forbidden fun he had dutifully resisted. Why would anyone punish him for being good?

1952

Out over Little Neck Bay, it seems the wind is *visible,* as sailboats tilt and right themselves, then tilt again. The sound of sails snapping carries across the water. A breeze flows warm and steady to the large, elaborate houses facing the Sound.

The day is made to order for this Shore Park fundraiser. As the host Harv Greenberg put it with a wink, "Conditions are conducive." Colorful mixed drinks glisten as the white-jacketed waiters bear their trays from one scrum to the next, this knot of women to that cluster of men. The lone sour chord struck is the news that Stevenson will not be coming in person—his person having been detained at an earlier event in Manhattan.

Carl Barry stands on the periphery of this scene, at a corner of the tent canopy, where he holds the metal tent-pole as though bracing it should bigger gusts push inland. His cousin John has brought him along to meet the candidate, but John knows people here, he fits in, and has left Carl to make his own way. His way, thus far, has been to observe the assembled guests.

There are 60 or 70 expensive Jews ("Rich," John had quickly corrected him, "not expensive. But don't say rich either.") who have come to write the candidate a check. Stevenson is fine by Carl, though Eisenhower is too. Stevenson is the thinker, Eisenhower the doer. Melded together, they might make a good leader.

Eisenhower was there to help end the War, that's his story. Where was Stevenson? What was he up to? No one talks about that. This is not about the politics, merely a question that interests Carl Barry as he stands holding up the tent and waiting for his chance to speak with Fleischman, the loan officer from Chase. For while he would have been happy to shake hands with Stevenson, Carl is here primarily to gain an audience ("In an informal, friendly way," John winked) with Fleischman.

The woman approaching him was a late arrival. He had noticed her coming through the gate, late but not hurrying. She accepted a glass from one of the white-jackets and went from there to greet the Greenbergs, likely to tell them what a lovely home they had. Already Carl had heard half a dozen people recite this line. Then she stood panning the lawn like a cameraman, as if selecting the most desirable cluster to join. Instead, for some reason, she started straight for Carl and as she advances on him now she is smiling like an old friend.

"I don't really know anyone here," she says, in a cheerful, confiding way.

"You don't know me, either," says Carl, presuming she has mistaken him for someone he resembles.

He is surprised by the way she has materialized already speaking. She in turn seems surprised by his accent—not bothered by it necessarily, possibly even amused—which she would not have anticipated. Here in America, no doubt, she expected to hear an American voice.

"Yes, but look, I could. You could say your name and I could say mine. You know, like at a party."

"Yes. I am Carl Barry. Pleased." He offers his hand, in the American manner.

"Clara Weiss," she says, with a comic half-curtsy. She is an oddball, for sure, and Carl is drawn to her oddness.

"I do know two people here," he says, "and will be meeting one other."

"Me!" she says, with a flourish. "So that's that, then."

"You and also Max Fleischman, the banker. You don't know him?"

"I told you, I don't know anyone. Many of these people my husband knew, that's why I was asked. So I came to see Stevenson and, you know, push myself forward. Get myself going."

"You stopped going?"

Smiling at his playful quip, Clara Weiss surprises him again: "Well, he died. So I stopped in some ways, yes."

This lady came right at you, first as a projectile and then with her painful information, as if boundaries, or proprieties, do not exist for her. A dead husband is private, or at least should be private when greeting a complete stranger. Yet there it is, and in the pause Carl is left to state the obvious: "In the War."

"No, actually. He was in the War. He was gone three years. Then he comes back and dies from cancer. Isn't that something?"

Carl nods in silent assent. For sure, it is something.

"It's enough to make you wonder. About God, for instance. What's *He* up to, for God's sake? What's the plan here? Because first the War and then a good man—only thirty-nine years of age, with two children and a wife—dies of *cancer*? Please."

Carl starts to speak, then realizes he has no words in mind yet, has formulated no response. But it seems that none is required, since Mrs. Weiss is still going.

"I was the wife, you know, as in two kids and a wife? So I go to Temple and I am still waiting for someone to explain why we are keeping the faith there. Because everyone hates us? Because everyone persecutes us? Is that the argument for being so Jewish you believe in this cockamamie God who takes away a thirty-nine-year-old man who also happens to be a wonderful thirty-nine-year-old man?"

One man? If only He stopped at one—or at one million. For some reason, though, this lady's babbling does not trouble Carl.

He is charmed, really, by the way she unwraps her thoughts and lays them out for a man who has done nothing but nod twice and loosen his tie a little. All around him he has watched people who agree discussing their agreement agreeably. This one is different. Apart from the rest. Like him in that way.

"So you're a Stevenson," she says. She leaves a gap of two or three seconds for Carl to take up the thread of conversation, before taking it forward on her own. "I like him fine, I just don't know if he can win, you know? I mean Eisenhower's nothing much but he's a hero, he's Army, and because he's nothing much he doesn't say much, which leaves nothing much to use against him. You know what I mean? He's bland, Eisenhower. Plus he's the Republican."

Behind Mrs. Weiss, Carl can see Max Fleischman moving away from a pod and strolling solo toward the buffet table. Camping out by the sliced meats. Carl does not wish to give offense to his talkative new friend—on the contrary, he would gladly hear more of her monologue—but above all he needs to secure the loan.

"I will tell you something about Eisenhower," he says, by way of excusing himself, "if you are here still, little bit later."

He approaches the buffet casually. Outwardly, he should appear to arrive there at random. Inwardly, there is a churning intensity of purpose, the pressure to expedite groundbreaking on 59th Street, but he can't help being distracted by the smiling suntanned faces of all these jolly Jews. Is it that they have forgotten, or that they have so much less to remember? How many were there, in uniform? Most of them, surely. Yet they behave as though it all evaporated in the breezy American sunshine. John says it and others have said it as well: America is a country with no memory.

Seven years ago, Hitler was alive. Not a century ago, not even a decade. The War is not a subject for the academy to pick away at and pull apart. It's what just happened to us. Seven years is not even time enough to go gray or get fat. Certainly not to *forget*.

Eisenhower was Army, a hero. This much the American person knows. But how many connect him to the horrors he witnessed firsthand, the sights and smells he must carry in his head? They wonder what is his position on the tariff, and Korea, and the Communists, not what did he witness over there, what did he learn. He will win the election, regardless of how much money the jolly Jews donate to his opponent, because he is a hero who also happens to look friendly, reliable. He looks like the greengrocer touting you onto his freshest lettuces, or like good old Klima with his precious cuts of meat. The War? No one here is talking about the War. It never happened here.

Even at this event, where the Americans happen also to be Jews, they eat and drink and chatter, the salt breeze ruffles the rhododendron, sunlight whites out the greenhouse windows—and the War never happened. Eisenhower is not the man who stared into the abyss at Buchenwald, he is the man who will serve as America's greengrocer for the next eight years.

And his noisy new friend Clara Weiss, also Jewish, pushes the simple fact aside. Yes my husband was in the War, but it was cancer that took him. If Carl talked to this person for an hour, or for a week, would she ever wonder why no wife stood with him, or what it was that took *her*?

Clara Weiss calls herself a widow. The word, or the idea behind it, comes as a revelation. Ten years after Milena was murdered, the term *widower*, in any language, had never crossed his mind until this very moment. It never occurred to Carl that widower is his category.

Perhaps the circumstances serve to explain this. When millions are killed, when an entire race of widows and widowers is created—such a time might call for a brand new category, and a new word to define those few who were *not* killed.

Not that Carl has concerned himself with any of this, with creating the correct category or finding the right word. Really, he has never said any words at all about what happened in Europe. What is there to say? He has not forgotten a single detail; he could not forget if he tried. But he says nothing. None of Mr. Greenberg's virtuous Jews say anything about it, either. They click their champagne glasses and dance the *hora* as though life began one hour ago over roast beef and potato salad on a sun-buttered Long Island lawn.

"Mr. Fleischman," he says, clearing his head, extending his hand. "Carl Barry. Pleased."

"Barry, yes. John Barry—your cousin?—mentioned you were here. We should talk sometime."

"We did—on the telephone, a little."

"I mean talk turkey," says the banker, a bit cryptically. It is not an expression Carl knows.

"Yes," he says, nodding affirmatively with regard to the turkeys. He is always mindful of John's advice for getting past sticky linguistic instances: say yes and nod.

"You heard he's not coming? Stevenson? Can't say I'm surprised. To tell you a dark secret"—leaning closer, simulating a whisper—"I'm not so down on Ike as some are. Don't shoot me now!"

"No, no more shooting please. I feel the same." Carl hopes this is not a test he is failing. What if Fleischman is just trying to flush him out? If so, it is too late now. "He was a good man, in the War. Eisenhower."

"He was a good general and he'll be good for business. Worse things could happen."

"Settled, then. We are for Stevenson, but we like Ike."

"You're a bit of a comedian, aren't you, Barry? It's Carl Barry, right? Just keep your voice down with this crowd."

"Agreed. And we will talk sometime, with regard to the loan?"

"Sometime soon," says Fleischman, with reassuring emphasis. "Why don't you come in Monday morning so we can cross all the t's."

This sounds affirmative and at the same time dismissive. Carl offers another handshake, though it feels a bit foolish coming just two minutes after the first one. Fleischman's grip is sincere, nonetheless, and Carl decides it was the right thing. When Fleischman involves his other hand, gripping Carl's shoulder with that one, it begins to seem possible that their salutations will take up more time than had their conversation.

Peering back across the platters of cubed fruit and sliced meat, he notices that Mrs. Weiss is watching him, smiling at him, as though they are sharing a joke. Even with his hand and his shoulder still in the banker's grasp, he can't quite help smiling back.

1943

"You went there? And the Germans were inside our flat?"

Both things were true. He had walked past the building where they had lived for three years and found the place crawling with Nazi brass. This was more of a shock than a surprise—after all, what did he expect to see? The only surprise was that he and Josef, the other trusty on this trip, had actually been trusted. That Gerhard, the stout Kraut who was always at pains to show what a fine fellow he was, had granted them half an hour's leave before the return trip to Terezin. So while the Germans took their meal at Café Phoenix, Karel and Josef were privileged to divide a stick of bread and eat it as they walked the streets.

"Not just Germans, S.S. Officers. They are occupying the flat, Milena, coming and going as they please."

"You spoke with them?"

"What exactly would you have me say? Run along now, fellows, and take your machine guns with you when you go?"

"Those people have *guns* in our house, Poppa?"

Benno, who was not intended to hear a word of this conversation, had come up stealthily and was positioned in the doorway before Karel saw him.

"They have guns everywhere they go, Benno. They take their guns with them to the toilet, guns when they go to bed at night."

"Are they afraid?"

"It's a good question. But here is a good question for you: should we go outside for a little while, maybe until dark?"

"It's dark now."

"It only looks dark from here. Come on, keep me company, before they blow the whistle on us."

No need to walk all the way to the hill or the park, with a game tilting back and forth across the square. A wild game, with no set teams, just men and boys running to the ball, surrounding it, ridging it free, then running again as it bounced away. Even a stray dog was participating, draping his thin torso over the rolling sphere whenever he could manage it.

This was too chaotic for someone Benno's size, so Karel hoisted him to the saddle of his shoulders and they stood aside watching and listening. Shouts and manic laughter alternated with intense silences punctuated by scuffling and snorting. During a brief lull, Mrs. Harkova's piano became audible, two measures of Mozart spilling from the windows of L514. Then the arpeggio gave way to the resumed din of the game and a moment later to the siren assaulting the streets like a swarm of angry birds. Beams of overbright light swept the sidewalls and doorways, shimmering on the curtainless windows.

The children, including Benno, hustled home to their barracks, while half a dozen of the men drifted to the café on Neugasse, where they would huddle at the curb until the guards came to roust them. They knew there would be a bit of time yet.

Tonight the talk was again of Poland. According to the Poland rumor, there were labor camps—just over the border, not far—where Jews were being starved to death. And some said they were the lucky ones. The unlucky ones were being shot, hung, or gassed inside vans.

"Who provides these facts, that's what I'd like to know," said Franta Wollner.

"Yes, who?" said Josef, his brother. Rumors were rumors, after all, and these days you heard some wild ones. "Has someone returned from Poland to file this report?"

"As a matter of fact, yes," said Pavel Paral. "It's that Nazi pig Klaus, who chases after my sister. Believe it or not, he tells her these things to impress her!"

"Well, isn't that reason enough to doubt the bastard? He wants to frighten her, so she will rely on his good offices for protection. It's just a sick game being played."

"Believe what you like. But he's not the worst of them by a long shot, this guy—he hasn't forced her—and he says he was there and saw it all. He helped take five hundred Jews off a train and he saw the ones who had been there a while, a race of skeletons."

"Why would he tell anyone about this?"

"Like I said, this guy is half human. Says he doesn't like the rough stuff."

"What he likes is Mariana, that's what. He's after your sister."

"Well at least he is being polite about it."

"Sure, until she tells him to get lost. Then he'll put the knife to her neck."

"Believe what you like."

"I won't believe this starvation camp nonsense. If that's their goal, why wouldn't they starve us right here?"

"He's right," said Ivo Priess. "These are Germans, don't forget. Why would they waste valuable petrol transporting Jews, simply to starve them somewhere in Poland? It's the height of inefficiency."

"Besides which," said Wollner, "here we are, smoking out in the open air, speaking quite freely. Terezin is a terrible place, a terrible fate while we remain here, but it is a far cry short of hanging and gassing."

"You don't see it, do you?" said Karel. "Why we are still here, why we are still alive. Yet it is so obvious."

"He's saying it's a put-up job, all for show. Aren't you, Karel?"

"You think that we are all acting in a Nazi theatrical?"

This was hardly an original position. All the men who had worked here in A1 and A2 knew the Nazi scheme. Doll it up nice, was the running joke, before the photographers arrive.

"Of course we are," said Karel. "And soon will come a day when we are not smoking in the open air, as you put it. Or speaking freely. Or breathing. Wait and see."

"Suppose you are right, Karel. What do you propose we do about it—run from Terezin? Start out at night and pray it stays dark for six months?"

"Yes, run. Why not, if the alternative is death? Get outside the gates, to begin with, and then from there see where the road leads. The Nazis can't be everyplace, after all. They are not like the air."

"The day they put it to me as a choice, then certainly. When they say run and we'll shoot you versus stand still and we'll shoot you? Then you will see me running."

"Too late," said Karel with a shrug. "*Then*, Wollner, we will see you falling down dead. Which, by the way, is the opposite of running."

"Maybe so, but at this very moment I think I am going to the hall to eat my soup and bread. Which is the opposite of starving."

"He makes a point. If the choice is between eating supper and dying, I have to admit I'm with Franta."

"You call it eating?" said Priess, to lighten the tone. "Even in the army, they never served us crap like that."

"It's twilight, Karel. If you are going to run for the hills, you had better get started before the roundup."

"Yes, Karel, go—and who gives a shit that they will line the rest of us up and shoot us in celebration of your freedom."

"Relax, he isn't going," said Priess. "He is hungry too—aren't you, Bondy?"

Clearly, the craving for freedom of speech had given way to hunger, and the informal meeting was already adjourning when the guards appeared. In truth, the mood of the group was more one of camaraderie than despair tonight. No one was too grim around the mouth, after football and before supper. Even Karel could concede that Mila had carrots, potatoes, and a box of crackers under her bunk. And he remembered that the two liters of beer he and Josef had snagged during their privileged assignment that morning awaited them now, back in the Hannover barracks. There was no denying that things could be worse. The trouble was, Karel was certain they would be.

1953

"Madeleine will only come if you promise Joy will be there," says Clara Weiss to her sister Alene. The cousins, her daughter Maddie and Alene's daughter Joy, are the same age. "That's her line in the sand."

"Joy lives here," says Alene. "She will definitely wake up here. But that's my best offer, toots. These days, she's a moving target."

"And Philip refuses to come no matter what."

Alene was tempted to make her sister swear to that one, as her nephew Philip was hardly an anticipated pleasure. Instead, she asks, solicitously, "What will he do if he stays home?"

"He's thirteen going on fourteen, A., he can amuse himself. It's not as if he'll burn down the house."

Over the telephone, of course, Clara cannot see her sister's mischievous smile, or read her mind—that Philip Weiss does seem likely to burn down someone's house, sooner or later. He likes playing with matches, just as he likes playing with his pet snake, and maybe for the same reason, that making people uncomfortable seems to please him.

"He never has," says Clara, "if that's any added reassurance. There are no scorch marks on the wallpaper here. Anyway, I don't want to push him. Maybe you've noticed Philip is not the best company when you bring him against his will. Really, he takes after Carl that way."

"Carl! That's a good one."

Though Alene is about to meet Carl Barry for the first time, she knows he bears no genetic responsibility for Philip Weiss. He was in Czechoslovakia most of his life, apparently, so whatever else he turns out to be, the man is innocent of all charges with regard to Philip.

"I don't mean it that way," says Clara, "I'm not talking about eugenics."

"Genetics," corrects Alene, who would be loath to blame anyone's genes for Phil's eccentricities. As her husband Kenny once remarked, quoting something, Phil might have sprung full-blown from the head of Satan.

"Eugenics, genetics, whatever you say. I mean that by chance they share this trait in common. My Carl can be a real boulder in the road when he's not interested in a topic, you'll see. He takes no interest in children, for example, so don't expect that from him."

"I'll warn the kids that an ogre is coming to eat lunch. Or I'll warn Lewis. Joy isn't exactly a child anymore. Just Lew."

"And he is a lovely boy. I'm just telling you not to expect. To you, on the other hand, I can guarantee he will be very nice."

"He takes an interest in adults?"

"In you, interested. Because you are the one sister and he has been pushing to meet you. He likes you in photographs, by the way. He likes the way you look."

"I'm flattered."

"That he won't do. Flatter. But I guarantee he will be very nice to you."

Carl Barry is nice to Alene, even affectionate. *Familial*, is the word that occurs to her, as though she is already his sister-in-law. Given the way Clara referred to him as "my Carl," it seems that could soon be the case. But his leitmotif from the outset is that Alene has the task of vetting him. "Approve, disapprove," he says, mimicking the scales of judgment with his upturned palms. "Maybe you will nix me."

"What makes you think my sister listens to anything I say?"

"I think she wants you to approve or disapprove."

"Nix or not nix?" Alene smiles.

"Yes exactly," says Barry, with a spark of delight in Alene's easy manner.

While Clara was right about Carl's interest in her, it appears Clara was wrong about his lack of interest in children. This would not have been the first boat her sister had missed. Still, it was an understandable mistake if Madeleine—a full-fledged teenager, a different animal—and Philip the Strange, as Joy called him, were Clara's only barometric readings.

Maybe Carl has seen photographs of Lewis too and "approved" in advance. Whatever the reason, he connects with Lewis from the first, when he shakes Lew's hand with exaggerated formality, then draws back in mock surprise.

"What's this?" he says, reaching behind Lewis' ear. "We have here a golden boy, with gold growing from his ears!"

Carl is brandishing a gold coin, something foreign or possibly a specially minted commemorative, which he then presents to Lewis. "Do you produce such treasure at will," he asks, "or only upon greeting the new guest?"

"*You* did it," the boy exclaims.

"I did? How can I do this, when I am just getting here?"

"Where? What do you mean?"

"I mean Connecticut. I never was here before, in Connecticut, how can I know where they keep the gold?"

"You're funny," says Lewis.

"And this is bad? To be funny?"

"I never said it was bad."

"I am asking. Is it good?"

"You're still being funny."

"Okay, I'll stop." And Carl Barry turns himself into a statue, his face frozen in a mime's mask of sadness.

"Stop it," says Lewis, clearly worried by this latest turn.

"He did, Lew," says Clara. "That's his point, that he stopped."

"Stop stopping, then."

Moving only his mouth, and that just slightly, Carl Barry says "I should start starting?"

"Yes," Lewis laughs. "I want you to stop stopping and start starting."

Later, the two of them in the kitchen, Clara presses Alene for an opinion: "Tell me already what you think of him, A. You know I can't stand suspense."

What Alene has thought thus far is that the whole business is surprising. She had not pictured a second husband for Clara, of any sort, anytime soon. That much she admitted to herself. Approve or disapprove, this man came out of nowhere. Or from far outside their circle, which was in truth a small closed circle, from decades back, in Brooklyn. Ben Weiss had grown up around the corner from them. They all knew each other from the age of zero.

"For starters," she says, "I think you are wrong about him."

"I'm wrong? You don't like him? I want the absolute truth from you, Alene."

"Not that, sweets. He seems perfectly approvable, for all the forty minutes I've known him. But you're wrong about him and children. He might keep up his vaudeville routine all day if we don't get busy and feed him."

"So you do like him?"

"Sure I do. As I say, for the short time I have seen him. And you yourself know him how long? Three months?"

"Much more than that. At least six months. Three since he started coming to the house and talking seriously."

"I can't believe I haven't seen you in that long. It was winter, I suppose, and we had the big snowstorms early on."

Sliding a platter of cold cuts, bread, and pickles into the pass-through window, Alene watches for a moment as her son and her sister's fiancé hobnob easily. Clara's European suitor not only enjoys children, he has a knack for them. It's a riot to observe them, this grown man in a suit and her six-year-old in his dungarees, yakking like magpies about who-knows-what.

1943

Crazy, the way one adjusted. Karel was constantly astonished by this and at the same time disgusted—with himself as much as the others. He had been adjusting too.

If they take away your home, you make a new home, and so what if it's an airless attic, lodgings only a mouse would choose.

Not so many stars to recommend the Hotel Terezin, yet all too soon you are glad of these dark warrens where even the mice have lice. At least you can close your eyes at night and sleep.

Helena was miffed when the streets were assigned names, in particular when L Street became Rose Street. She was not yet reading, but she had all her letters and numerals. That the Nazis had taken over her nation meant less to her than that she could proudly declare the number above her dormitory door. Already, though, she had adjusted.

The grandparents took heart from the fact that the shop at L4 still opened up each morning, with Mrs. Neumann safely installed behind the wicket—and so what if she had practically nothing to sell. Who had any money left with which to buy?

Meanwhile, the Nazis kept chipping away at their lives, shrinking their world by increments. They might as well have been dismantling each Jewish body limb by limb, or one organ at a time. Today, they announce, we will be conscripting your left arm—"for the war effort," of course—and you adjust. After all, you are right-handed. When they take the right one too, you fall back on the fact you still can walk.

It was still possible to smuggle food inside, even possible to slip outside the walls of the fortress for a time, maybe not return. You might not even be missed right away. Someone young and on his own might make it clear, leave the country at a remote spot along the northern border.

But then where would he be? That nearby northern border took you into Nazi Germany. And every able-bodied Jew, everyone physically capable of flight, had to ask himself the question: why would I leave behind everyone I know and love in order to wander penniless through a world with no friends and a million enemies who would as soon murder me as eat a piece of pastry? A world where even the cowardly ones would sic the Gestapo on you in exchange for a packet of cigarettes and where every border you crossed now led to "Germany." Most of Europe was now under Hitler's thumb.

And as Wollner pointed out, it was difficult getting past the small matter of who they would kill in your wake, as a cautionary tale to those who remained. While you were sleeping in a hollow log somewhere out in the countryside, the gendarmes would be putting your mother up against the wall and shooting her to death.

Regardless, Karel was hardly on his own. He had Milena and the children, and though he sometimes urged the notion of flight, he knew that she would refuse the penniless, friendless prospect and he knew, once he stopped lying to himself and *adjusted*, that they had no chance of slipping outside as a family of five.

He never adjusted so thoroughly that he could lie to himself. The filthy bunks did not constitute bedrooms, the rag shops were farcical, and any small freedom the Judenrat insisted they should be glad of ended ten paces shy of the gates. Those enticing green hills one glimpsed beyond the ramparts might as well have been a continent away, since any Jew seen walking there would be gunned down like small game.

Yet now Karel found himself outside the ramparts every day, in the valley bounded by those green hills. He and his buddy Pavel Kantor had been placed on the Bohusovice rail detail, the same crew that he and Benno had watched from their Mt. Pisgah, as it were, from the Southern Hill, shortly after they were brought to Terezin.

The day he was selected for the Bohusovice crew reminded Karel of the day he applied for and got his job at Pikorny-Kovy—cause for celebration. It truly was the best one could hope for here, even better than working in the bakery, because apart from the extra rations they received, this job kept him fit while so many were wasting away. And Pavel, with only the one brother here, often added to Karel's portion so he could further supplement Mila's larder.

He adjusted so well to being a slave laborer for the Reich that he almost enjoyed it. The truth was he liked to work. Certainly he preferred it to doing nothing, but he enjoyed the physicality of labor, even knowing that the fruits of his labor would be a sleeker, faster means of propelling the Praha Jews to their doom. Karel would sing, admittedly in an ironic vein, and Pavel would join him in song.

"I been workin' on the railroad," they would belt out, *"all the liff lawn day."*

The words were in English, taken from someone's recording of the American spirituals and chants that supposedly had inspired Dvorak's obsession with the Negro race. The two Czechs spoke little English and knew only snatches of the song—butchered every syllable in fact and produced skewed and varying versions of the tune. Still, it made them smile to belt it out.

"Do you mind performing a different number today?" said a man named Oskar one morning. Their singing did not make Oskar smile. "Or if you prefer, maybe shut up altogether?"

"So we can listen instead to the beautiful music of our sledges and shovels?"

"Shovels would be fine. That much, at least, we have no choice about."

"But Oskar, isn't this the whole point? To sing something we do have choice about?"

"Just so, Bondy, we can choose *not* to sing. Or, please God, to sing a different tune just one day out of the week."

"What do you say to this music critic, Pavel? You decide the matter."

"Well, on the one hand, I say that slaves ought to be happy and sing in their chains. This is a well-known fact. On the other hand, we should be democratic. So perhaps in fairness to Oskar we should stop working on the railroad for a day or two. An intermission."

"Pavel has spoken. But there is another one I can almost remember. *Nobody knows the treble I see?* We will see if I have the melody right."

"Why don't you keep workin' on the railroad," allowed Oskar, with a grin, "just so long as you don't sing about it."

"Let us all hope we keep workin' on the railroad," said Pavel. "I for one am not eager to know where we will be going next."

1955

Clara and Alene sit opposite one another at the small banquette drinking coffee as they monitor the backyard action. These built-in benches are the one thing in Clara's house that her husband approves, albeit with a qualifying footnote on the counter-intuitive proportions. The kitchen is large yet here, Carl points out, is this dollhouse arrangement, two cramped seats at a table the size of a tea-tray.

Still, it's where he always sits. Carl loves his half hour there, with two cups of coffee and two newspapers, the *Times* and the *Post*, each morning before driving in to the city. He never goes in the dining room, which because it is landlocked—with rooms on every side and therefore no windows, no natural light—he likens to a prison cell.

"Who would design such a room?" he complains, as part of his campaign to move. While Clara makes no case for windowless rooms, she does remain attached to the house where she and Ben raised their children.

"Philip and Madeleine are both at camp?" Alene asks.

"Different camps this year, but yes," says Clara. "And this time around I hope he stays a little longer. Or if he refuses to stay, he calls and tells me instead of just taking off into space."

"He's still unhappy?"

"Unhappy? You could call it that."

"What about with Carl? Are they getting along any better?"

"Truthfully? The answer is no. But no isn't even the answer. They don't get along or not get along. It's more like they aren't even living in the same house."

"I'm surprised. I mean, with the way he is around Lewis. It's true that Lew is so much younger, but look at them."

"I'm looking. And I am even seeing Carl's mouth move, which is some kind of miracle, really it is. Normally when I see his mouth move these days it's because he is chewing his food."

“Clara, come on, you make it sound like a problem. He loves you, he adores you. I can see that if you can’t. And you know how important this project is to him. He’s absorbed.”

“He is very sweet to me. He comes home with flowers. He provides.”

“What? You’re not saying he gets nasty, ever?”

“Of course I’m not. He is a gentleman, A. He’s a European.”

“Is that what you think?” Alene laughs. She is the younger by three years and has always been much younger at heart. Privately, their mother (who never saw the film about the Seven Dwarfs) called them Happy and Grumpy. “That all Americans are brutes and all Europeans are gentlemen? You could think this after living fifteen years with Ben Weiss, the nicest husband anyone ever dreamed, not to mention the most perfect gentleman?”

“Rest his soul. Carl is a nice man too. He is not much of a talker, that’s all I’m saying to you.”

“He must have talked when he was courting you.”

“More. But you know me. Maybe I didn’t notice him not talking because I was talking so much myself. Or so I’m told. Haven’t you been telling me this since the day you were born?”

“You married him.”

“Stop it. I’m glad I married him. I’m happy with him. He makes a lovely husband.”

“You didn’t have to marry him. You chose to.”

“I said, I’m glad. Though who else was asking for my hand, you know? I’m not like you, A. They never busted down the door for me that way. When Ben died, I figured my luck ran out. Thirty-eight years old, with a couple of kids?”

“Jerry Helfer,” is Alene’s rejoinder. Recalling Jerry and their glory days at Erasmus Hall makes her smile, reminds her almost subliminally that they are two sisters who grew up in a cold-water tenement in Flatbush and who are now sitting in a fancy modern kitchen, out here on the Island.

“Jerry Helfer was a nut. Everyone knew he was nutty as a fruitcake.”

“Still, kiddo, it was you he went nutty over, not me.”

"Call it the exception that proves the rule. The rest of my life was a one-way window."

"Ben loved you very much, and so does Carl. It's obvious you under-rate yourself, with your one-way windows."

"Honestly, I thought we had things in common, Carl and I. I figured we lined up pretty well. Plus, for whatever reasons, he finds me attractive. So it turns out what we had in common was I lost a husband and he lost a wife, and neither of us preferred being alone so much. There are worse marriages, I'm sure."

"Better, worse. What I said is that he loves you."

"Look at them laughing," says Clara, watching her husband and Alene's son almost in disbelief. "Even when they're running they laugh. Who knows what gives with those two."

"As hard as Carl works, he might find it relaxing to run around like a kid on a Sunday. And you know how Lewis is, the little question man. He makes you talk, because he never lets up with the questions."

"What could he ask Carl?"

"I know the game of soccer is one. Carl calls it football and according to him this kind of football is the biggest sport in the world—by far, no less. To Lewis this is impossible because whatever you call it, it's never on television. To him the biggest sport is baseball but he doesn't like to contradict his nice new uncle, so he checks in with me about all this."

"As if you know from footballs and baseballs."

"Let's just say I know the world extends beyond New York City. You never hear about a baseball player from France or Italy and they must be selling tickets to something over there."

"In France, the big sport is eat, drink, and be merry. Oh, and they ride bicycles."

"Lew ponders things. He asks a question, then he ponders the answer. So okay, they never play soccer in his school; now he is pondering if they play it in a French school."

"Architecture. That's Carl's one topic with Philip. He points out everything that's wrong with everybody's house, starting with our own. What's wrong with the Temple, what's wrong with the schoolhouse. What they should have done instead, what *he* would have done. This Phil listens to. He must be interested, because he asks a question here and there. For all I know, he could be pondering too."

"Carl is different, don't forget, with a different angle on life. Some people are put off by a foreigner, where Lewis is only made more curious."

"What's so foreign about architecture? We don't have architecture in this country?"

Alene shrugs and lights a cigarette, one of her ten allotted Luckies for the day. Her son is curious about everything, really. Right now he is kneeling with his new foreign-born uncle to examine a head of lettuce. Carl is indicating certain facets of the lettuce, or so it appears, just as it appears that Lewis is following his words attentively. But lettuce? It occurs to Alene that her son may be a bit peculiar. He takes a different angle on life too.

"He's faking it, A., he has to be. Lewis is a well-brought-up child, acting polite to his elders. He's what, seven, eight? How can an eight-year-old be interested in a vegetable?"

"They like each other. Maybe it's that simple, kiddo."

Clara shrugs and accepts a cigarette from Alene. "Yeah, and like I say, maybe he's faking. But who knows, maybe your Lewis has a vocation to become the next what's-his-name, the guy who invented vegetables. Lex Luthor?"

"My sister the scholar. The man's name is Luther Burbank."

"That's him. He invented the potato, if I recall correctly."

1943

Everything changed when the transports began. What had seemed so terrible, the dislocation and all the deprivations, suddenly seemed almost like the normal strophes of a life one treasures. Certainly Milena felt that way.

"If we are not taken," she had said, "then we will manage this. We are managing it, Karel. You can see that."

He could in fact see it. Much as it had in the "normal" life they had lost, hard work filled his days. Ironically, his value to the Nazi cause had kept the children healthy. This was a crude reflection of how any society worked: success, by whatever definition, was rewarded materially. There had been moments when he could lose track of the obvious, could forget that the terms of their lives in the fortress town—the work he did, the places they slept, the food allotted them—were brutal conditions imposed by vicious criminals, even if one was a pitcher of fresh milk more fortunate than some others.

"If we are not taken—" This was the way Mila began a lot of her sentences now. She was still a dreamer and would not admit how bleak the parameters of her dreams had become, right down to the day when, inevitably, they *were* taken.

Were told once again to pack, made once again to stand in a herd passively waiting to board a train, bound this time for "the east," as the future of every Praha Jew was now known. Some believed this east to be a safe haven while others, perhaps more realistic, anticipated a life of forced labor. Not a few feared it simply meant death.

But Mila said, "We will manage this too."

"How will we manage the unmanageable?" Karel asked, as mildly as he could. Solicitously, as though she might have the answer. He admired her courage so much and had vowed never again to undermine it.

"How will we not? We don't know how, Karel, we only know we have no choice."

The train car was airless, the ride endless. The young cried steadily and the old ones moaned. Another "almost half-human" Nazi guard confided to Mr. Weinberger, whose wife could not be consoled, "Tell your missus this is the luxury trip. We will stop for toilet, there will be water. You are the privileged ones. God is watching over your people."

One toilet stop notwithstanding, the air was close and foul. No one was remotely comfortable for a single minute. The children became so frightened they stopped crying. Blithe Benno, rarely bothered by anything, stared blankly into space for hours. And of course it only got worse as the monotony, the fear, and the filth compounded.

"Travel is never easy," said the talkative Nazi, shortly before his shift ended and he repaired to a commodious dining car, or so Karel imagined. No question "travel" was easier for him and his cohorts.

"The longer we ride, the more we are becoming older sicker people," said Pavel Kantor. "All of us. Like those people who are so old and so sick that they prefer to die."

"So it's a suicide train? Where we will all wish to die before journey's end?"

"I have seen it, Karel—old folks in such misery they just want out. What if this damned train keeps going forty days and forty nights? Do you think anyone could stand it?"

"Don't worry," said Karel, nodding in Mila's direction. "We will manage."

"Manage? Maybe we will manage to kill ourselves," said Ivan Pollak, taking a verbal position halfway between his two friends. This was a lifelong pattern for the three of them, the three musketeers as they once called themselves. They had grown up together, come to Praha together at 18. They played on the same football club there, just as they had in the lower school at home, and now were together in captivity. As close, Pavel always joked, as sardines in a tin.

"Kill ourselves? And do the Nazis work for them?" Karel responded, just as Ivan expected he would.

A month later, two months, they were still privileged, or so the kapos kept telling them. And though one could only say it with a warped smile, there was one respect in which their lives in Auschwitz were easier. At Terezin, one had to plot every get-together. Occasions were easily enough arranged and rarely interfered with, but officially every one of these meetings was forbidden. Here in the so-called family camp at Auschwitz, where their home was more a sheepfold than a room, they were able to stay together. Even their parents, Milan and Jitka, Vaclav and Helena, lodged in barracks barely a hundred meters away, were together.

And once more the musketeers drew prized assignments. Karel and Pavel had earned a reputation, best of the best at level-bedding the ties, so here too they found themselves workin' on the railroad. Apparently a Jew, however venal, foul-smelling, and immoral, could be defined as useful. So they were slaves and the conditions were barbaric, but to go off to work each morning and come "home" at night to the family camp—to the family—gave them the semblance of a life.

This point was reinforced emphatically as they began learning the truth about "the east" and what was happening here. Happening, that is, to everyone except the Terezin Jews. The east was Greek for killing fields and death camps located across the Polish border. Day after day there were hundreds, thousands, being poisoned in Birkenau. An endless stream of trucks took them there and did not even bring their bodies back. The bodies, incinerated in immense factory furnaces, explained the smoke that stung their eyes and the stench that filled their nostrils.

Ivan Pollak was their source. Ivan's plum assignment, the most sought after of all, was the Canada detail. Each new wave of victims was divested of every valuable, a category which did not stop at money or jewelry or leather shoes. Even hair and teeth had value to "the war effort" so the hair and teeth also were confiscated. If toenails were proven useful in any way, Ivan assured them, toenails would be harvested every bit as systematically.

The men on the so-called Canada crews could pocket some of what they sorted and stacked, so they could also count on pocketing token bribes. Beyond that, they saw everything, they knew the whole operation. What was going on here? Ivan's reports were as raw as could be: what was going on was ruthless plunder and relentless murder, on a scale unimaginable.

The Praha Jews were oppressed. They too had been stripped of any worthwhile possessions. Yet here they were, intact in the family camp. This was a status, Ivan reminded them nightly, only they enjoyed. "Maybe," he speculated, "somebody's beloved ancestor was secretly a Praha Jew. Goebbels' grandma or Himmler's auntie."

They had food (enough to live, not enough to thrive) and they had each other, which, as the weeks of relative security accumulated, inevitably calmed them. It was a harsh unsanitary life, in which privacy and any sense of purpose beyond survival were all but forgotten, yet some of the fear had subsided. For whatever reason, the Terezin Jews were not being murdered and remaining alive could seem purpose enough.

Even Karel found his rage damped down. Not for one second did he trust the situation—not without an explanation as to why they had been accorded this status. Nonetheless he found himself lulled. He could tell his outrage now was often more a matter of lip service, of mere words. Emotionally, he found himself increasingly compliant.

"You see," said Mila one night, as they watched a three-quarter moon rise through the tiny window above their garret bed of planks and straw. So great was their good fortune that their section was not yet infested with bedbugs or fleas. "We are managing. We will be all right."

"My love," said Karel, more weary than he could recall ever having felt and seeing in Mila's face a concomitant strain, the sharpened facial bones coming into focus slowly, like a photograph in an acid bath, "my love, you are a wonder."

When life changed again, Karel was in the hospital. Up until this very week, such medical attention was to be expected. In spite of the constant threats—slack off for one minute and you will be shot where you stand—the stronger workers were maintained in good health. But Karel's deepening weariness turned out to be something more than overwork.

When he was first admitted—when he was still sufficiently clear-headed to be capable of protest—Karel was sure they had poisoned him. "But then why would they bring you here to cure you?" asked Pavel. It was a reasonable question and Karel had no answer to it. One day later he had no answer for anything, having descended into a fog of ache and sleep. His temperature hovered around 39.5, a result Pavel had no intention of sharing with Milena.

It was during these strange days that dramatic changes came. Suddenly the water pails were being tended haphazardly and the bits of cabbage and potato were absent from the soup. Movement and communication became so difficult that no one doubted they were simply incarcerated. Mila no longer knew what was going on with her parents or with Karel's.

Even Ivan Pollak could not say how anyone's particular situation stood, some poor soul in 21 Block or someone's cousin in 22. He did know full well, however, that some of the Terezin Jews were now—in Sturmbannfuhrer Lindauer's phrase for it—"being processed." There was a reason why no one was bothering with the water pails.

Fear seeped back into the camp quickly. Once again, no one could sleep, even those with nothing else to do. Most were so tired they could not remember what it felt like to be rested. Many were rendered stupid by the fear and fatigue; they hunched their shoulders and stayed close to walls as if this made them invisible and therefore safer.

Just as he had concealed the extent of Karel's fevers from Mila, Pavel now kept Karel in the dark about the new danger to Mila. Then abruptly his daily visits to the hospital ceased, with no explanation to Karel, who had recovered enough strength to press for information. He could walk the halls, he was gaining back weight, but no trusty was willing to chat anymore. All Karel got were shrugs and silences.

With no idea how much time had passed, Karel could only picture them as they were, sleeping in the sheepfold, the children huddled like lambkins with their momma. He presumed Milena was still praying for her miracles—the Russians would arrive in time or, failing that, the Golem would show up. He remembered how her little students loved the day she would dress up as the Golem, in a big filthy costume that was harder each term to fold and put away.

She would refuse to lose hope, not with every sort of rumor to choose from in support. Whether gleaned from the echo of a distant reality or from pure hallucination, the Russian Army rumor surfaced hourly. People believe what they want to believe. Still, no one in the family camp was sleeping.

Karel, in hospital with a pitcher of cool water at his bedside, drifted off easily, sleeping at least ten hours a day.

1956

Carl always enjoys the ride up to Connecticut. He likes driving on the Merritt Parkway, a road fashioned by men who cared about more than speed and cost. A road can respect the landscape, just as a good building can, and clearly the Parkway designers understood this.

This state of Connecticut feels peaceful. Something about it reminds Carl of childhood, or of the blissful ignorance of innocence. It cannot be true, it makes no sense, yet it feels as if bad things never happened here and never would. Even he cannot imagine armies of organized killers vaulting over the tidy stone walls or smashing through the doors of the clean white clapboard houses.

The approach to Alene's clean white clapboard house is a gravel driveway cleaving two rows of pine trees, each of which looks like a steep green isosceles triangle, a Christmas tree. For some reason, Carl experiences a rising in his chest, an uplifting, upon making this brief final passage from the mailbox to the turnaround where they park.

Alene's home is in no way extraordinary, but the wild roses, the long runs of rhododendron, and the grape arbor all excite his instinct to cultivate and to prune. Alene's husband Kenny was never around and now he never will be; he has become her ex-husband. But the grounds are not poorly maintained, it's more that Carl feels so at home here, ready to pitch in. He has felt this way from the first time he visited. He is *relaxed* here and relaxation is a state Carl Barry rarely achieves.

He is a good deal less relaxed on occasions when they bring Philip, though this would be true anywhere. Clara's son often behaves inappropriately. This is the word they have decided on to describe it. He seems to enjoy frightening children, and can be cruel to animals. It can be as petty as putting a turtle on its back or as nasty as kicking a dog without provocation.

More worrisome are his impulses toward Alene's daughter Joy. Phil always wants to "play" in her room, as they did when all the children were much younger. Joy wants no such thing, so a tug of words, where direct truths cannot quite be spoken, usually takes place. Philip is 16 now, Joy 15.

Neither Clara nor Alene seem particularly concerned about Philip going upstairs. While regretting her daughter's displeasure, Alene expects it will be minor and brief. Carl, on the other hand, does worry about what might transpire and can't help listening for sounds of distress. At the same time, he feels guilty, because he is glad to have Philip disappear for a while, so the sisters can do their gossiping while he and young Lewis spend an hour outdoors.

Carl loves the boy's unblinking directness. In the not too distant future, he wagers, Lewis will be saying out loud what everyone else suppresses: keep that creep away from my sister. So many Americans hide behind a social mask, making what they say seem phony to Carl; they don't say what they mean. Not so with this kid. Maybe he is simply too young, or maybe he takes after his Aunt Clara. After all, it was this trait that had drawn Carl to her, perhaps above any other. From the moment they met, Clara Weiss came unfiltered.

How had they come to be man and wife? This much he knew: they would never have done so if not for her extraordinary directness. Here was a woman a little noisy and maybe a little crazy (and with the much crazier son as added freight) but with a good heart. She had lost her first husband and for some reason concluded Carl Barry should become her second. This at a time when Carl had never for one moment considered who, if anyone, should become his second wife.

For years it had been Carl's lot to dwell upon, even obsess over, the story of the Gentile women in Berlin. These were women,

2,000 of them, who had married Jews and later on, when their Jewish husbands were rounded up by the Nazis, did not say Heil Mister Hitler and begin praying uselessly for the return of the husbands. Instead they screamed *Give them back to us.* They assembled 2000 strong outside the holding pens on Rosenstrasse and refused to stop wailing and shrieking, refused to leave or to do anything else they were ordered to do—even at bayonet and gunpoint—until the Jewish husbands were set free. And, *mirabile dictu*, the Nazis freed them.

Carl has carried this incident close, carried it everywhere; the tableau keeps coming back to nag at him. Had we been half as smart as Jews are reputed to be, or half as unyielding as those Gentile women, imagine the outcome. If 2000 could accomplish this much, what could millions have accomplished? Six million angry Jews standing shoulder to shoulder, speaking in one loud voice? We might have ripped the gold from little Hitler's own teeth and given the sick bastard a dose of his own lovely gas. We might have turned the tables. Instead, we let him tell us what to do, where to go—even what to bring along on the trip!

Now whenever this waking dream comes to plague him, Carl can smile at the knowledge that this could never have happened to six million Clara Weisses. Pack for the journey to Hell? No chance. This American wife of his would have been one of those unappeasable, steadfast women who refused to move a muscle until they got what they came for.

"You are forgetting one thing, my friend," Jaro said, the first time Karel revealed his preoccupation with the Rosenstrasse women. "You forget those Harpies were all Gentile. Otherwise"—and here Jaro made a pistol of his hand and opened fire with his index finger.

"You're thinking," says Clara, as they coast down the Merritt Parkway exit. "I always know when you're lost in thought because I can smell the wood burning. What's up?"

Laughing, Carl waves away her surmise as though it is an amusing remark rather than a question to be answered. Not surprisingly—after all, her persistence is precisely what he was thinking about—Clara persists until he does provide an answer of sorts.

"It's a nice road, in a pretty state. This is what I was thinking. That I like very much where your sister is living. Who knows, maybe we would move out to here, some future day."

"That's not what you were thinking, Carl Barry. I can also smell a rat, you know."

"But it was," he says, laughing again. His 'was' still sounds as 'vuz,' but Clara has stopped wondering when his heavy Czech accent will relent. "It was what I was thinking."

"And a rat is what I am smelling," she says.

"What is Phil thinking in the back seat? This is the real question," says Carl, as if Clara can't guess he is simply changing the subject. "Philip is the quiet one today."

"Leave me alone," says Philip, from the back seat.

"Why bother him?" says Clara.

"Yeah," says Philip, smirking, triumphant. "Why bother him?"

Carl knows better than to say another word. The best policy now is act as if the car has only a front seat, carrying himself and his wife to Alene's house, now a few minutes away. Soon they will cleave the avenue of isosceles trees, eat a nice lunch, maybe drive down to the beach for a walk along the strand. He might try again to interest Lewis in the natural world, or in the specifics of it.

The boy loves to be outdoors, he just doesn't care about the specifics. Every other subject, he demands to know the ins and outs. If there was a gun, what *kind* of gun? Only with the natural world is he content with generalities. To him, a flower is a flower, this color or that, and a tree is either a pine or it's not a pine. The grass is smooth and green, and a ball will roll over it nicely. To Lewis, this is the outdoors.

1943

He never saw her again.

The Russians did not arrive. Instead came the days when streams of Terezin Jews were marched from the morning lineup to be processed before the noon whistle, at which point the Nazis stopped to eat their lunch before processing countless more in the afternoon. The favored ones, the inexplicably privileged Praha Jews had seen their privileges inexplicably revoked.

After three days of this, only a handful of the most able-bodied workers remained. Foul exhaust kept piling out of the smokestacks at Birkenau and fueling this acrid smoke were the corpses of Karel's loved ones. His wife reduced to ash, his children disposed of as leaves are, or litter. His parents, his cousins, his friends.

And Karel did not know.

Then he did. And despite the years of cynical efforts to brace himself for the worst, reality fell on him like a building too large to crawl out from under. It seemed to crush his chest, literally. For days he could barely breathe, could barely recall the breathing reflex; air kept collecting in his chest like giant clots.

To his two remaining friends, Karel was unrecognizable. Surely he was in hibernation mode, Pavel and Ivan agreed, like a turtle gone under the mud. They could not imagine him so defeated. *Incapacitated,* as though all his muscles had been disconnected.

Of course they understood he was in shock. According to Dr. Maisel, they were all in shock, everyone who had yet to be gassed. Whatever it was—hibernation, paralysis, or shock—it was what kept him alive. Because from the instant he learned what had happened to his beloveds and understood that he had failed to save them, Karel had no desire to save himself. Had he not gone under the mud, he would have been killed instantly in some futile act of rage.

Then there was Pavel. Like smelling salts, Pavel's crisis brought Karel back around; it became the next thing that kept him alive.

Because inevitably Pavel got the fever too. Was it typhus? They had never said definitively when Karel was in hospital and now no one was being sent there, much less being diagnosed. Pollak had passed the word—if you could not work, you were smoke. So for Karel, there was the need to improve his friend's condition, and, perhaps more daunting, the need to conceal it.

The confusion helped there. So many were gone so suddenly and so many new ones had arrived that not even the Germans with their checklists could avoid some confusion about who was standing and who was smoke. The rabbis advised them to mill around, keep changing places, and speak softly. When the kapos began complaining, the rabbis advised that they be more subtle, not move so much, just dance a little.

In an attempt at shoring up solidarity, the rabbis declared a day of mourning, a tiny out of season Yom Kippur. This seemed perfectly crazy to Karel. That the Jews should undertake a day of atonement? They should refuse the paltry crusts and the scullery water—fast and go around chanting the Kol Nidre in Aramaic? There was gallows humor here, but Karel's stilted, mocking, mute response to Rabbi Berg only looked like a smile.

He had never been a good Jew, or better, had long assumed that to be a good man was the definition of what it took to be a good Jew. If not, so be it. Here in the death camp there was no longer any way to be a Jew *or* a man, so he would have to leave. It was that simple now. The very notion of faith was such an absurdity, such a bitter pill, that all it shored up was Karel's need to act. He would have to leave both the Nazis and the rabbis behind. There was nothing, not even the likelihood of sudden death, to stop him anymore.

As soon as Pavel was strong enough, they would take Ivan up on his scheme. Would it give them a real chance? Probably not, so with Mila alive, and the children, he had not given it serious consideration. Now the odds against success were irrelevant. If they were shot or hung for trying, so be it.

When first faced with his losses, Karel was drained of will, viscerally devastated. A week later he was feeling charged by outrage, bursting with the unvented burn of it. He had never harmed another soul in his life, not even in a fistfight, but given the chance now he would kill a hundred Nazis without the slightest hesitation. He felt this so keenly he could forget it was far more likely a hundred Nazis would kill him—and without even noticing, as one kills a bug.

Meanwhile there had been no sign that Pavel was rallying. More and more of the time he was incoherent, his fever unrelenting. Instead of coming through it—as Karel had, as Karel therefore assumed he would—Pavel seemed to grow weaker by the hour. Try as he would to will his friend back to health, Karel was beginning to see a corpse, not a man, lying there. They all had learned to recognize the tipping point.

This complicated the situation both practically and emotionally. The train would arrive tomorrow. If it departed the following morning without them, with it would go their one opportunity. After this shipment, they were shifting Ivan to the factory site—or so he had been informed. It might be a lie, of course, he might be going up the chimney. Either way, whoever took his place on the platform would have no interest in helping Karel and Pavel.

Karel struggled to think his way past this problem, refusing to concede it might be insoluble. In the end, in his mind—which he did understand might be working imperfectly—this further complication actually simplified the matter. They had no choice but to go as planned. If they got outside the camp alive, and managed to exit the train still alive, he would carry Pavel across Europe.

His mind was working imperfectly enough to hope for a miracle—and yes, why not take Mila's part for her?—namely that Pavel might rally overnight. They still had twelve hours. Terrifying fevers broke and passed all the time. In Dr. Maisel's opinion Pavel was no worse off than a dozen others. To Karel that night, this passed for optimism.

He could hardly miss the aimless drift in Pavel's eyes, yet who was to say that he, Karel Bondy, did not look exactly the same way? How long had it been since he glimpsed his own face? The Fuhrer had neglected to supply their dressing rooms with bulb-lit cut-glass mirrors.

It rained that night, which made it possible for him to spill cup after cup of water past Pavel's chapped lips and to press cool wet rags against a face he realized he had known through all its changes since childhood. Rainwater was always a boon. Maybe this rain was an elixir, because Pavel, who had uttered nothing coherent all day, suddenly reached for Karel's hand and spoke with absolute clarity: "My friend, it tastes better than beer."

"Have more!" said Karel, jolted by the sudden strength in Pavel's grip and the authority in his voice. "Here."

"Please, let it run through me like a river. I can feel it. But listen to me, Karel, I feel death running through me too. I really am dying."

"How would you know such a thing? I felt the same way, you know, and here I am."

"No, listen, it turns out that death is real. It has a certain weight—"

"You'll drink, and rest, and tomorrow we will move on from this place."

Karel's words were not mere palliatives, not when Pavel was so familiarly loquacious. Not when even his negativity was tenacious.

"Dead weight cannot move," said Pavel, still loquacious, still tenacious, also still wedded to doom.

"If you are feeling lazy, I'll carry you."

"Is that so?" Pavel coughed, in a burst of what had started as laughter. "How far?"

While Pavel's ironic jibe was perfectly typical of him, there was something new and alarming in it. The timbre of his voice was almost, Karel had to admit, otherworldly. Coming from the other side. Then again, maybe a celestial being would make for a lighter impost!

He knew his vow to carry Pavel could prove a hollow promise. He was a great deal stronger than his friend, but Karel was far from strong. On the rough unyielding planks, his bones no longer shielded by sufficient flesh or muscle, he felt sore all over every night. And who could say what would be demanded of them tomorrow, in the way of strength and speed? Plenty was a fair guess, unless of course they were gunned down before the train left the platform.

"Did I tell you yesterday," said Pavel, who had in fact not spoken a single word yesterday, "how I was craving a cigar? I wanted to smoke one last cigar before I died. Is that logical? To entertain such a useless craving?"

"It's perfectly logical. A logical proof against death, to have a craving for life. Just close your eyes for now. You need to get some sleep."

But Pavel's eyes were closed. He was already sleeping. An hour after he had made such sense, his mind as animated as in its prime, Pavel was dangerously becalmed. His forehead felt strangely cold. Surely it was good that he slept, but now as his sleep deepened, each breath was tailing off in a long dry wheeze. Bile began collecting at the corners of his mouth.

Karel drifted and, succumbing after the days of relentless intensity, slept a little himself. It was daybreak when he woke to find a new roof leak dripping on them. Pavel's brow was ice cold now and in the dim light his face was paste. Steam was rising from his body as it cooled.

1957

Carl Barry has a talent for keeping his own counsel, but it is not easy sidestepping the questions young Lewis throws at him, one after another like little punches. Because of the boy's relentlessness, and because it feels stingy to thwart a trusting child's drive to understand the world, Lewis will always get a *version* of the truth from his uncle.

No one, not one soul in all Carl's years in America, had spoken a word to him about the numerals tattooed in blue on his forearm until Lewis asked if he could touch it. Then he asked why Carl was branded. What he received was a version of the truth.

"It's what they give you when you check into the Hotel Auschwitz."

When Carl was pressed to amplify the matter, Auschwitz became first a "camp" and then a prison camp, located in Poland, where Carl had spent some time.

"As a prisoner?"

"Yes, a prisoner. When criminals run a country, they don't put in jail the criminals, they put the good people."

"But that's crazy," was Lewis' conclusion.

"There is no fooling you!" was Carl's.

Today Lewis is pursuing the subject again, with a resolve that places him in league with the Rosenstrasse women—he will keep asking until he gets a straight answer. He felt cheated the first time and he won't be cheated again. So sitting on a screened-in porch in the tame, safe state of Connecticut, Lewis extracts a more troubling version of his uncle's tattoo. He hears, glancingly at first, of the many innocent people who were sent to prison, their jackets branded in yellow, their arms then branded in blue. This is insufficient, though, so he also hears that it was the innocent *Jewish* people of Europe who were herded, branded, tortured—and murdered.

"Who murdered them?"

"The Germans," Carl shrugs. Surely this much requires no explanation. Who else but the Germans?

"Don't tell him that, Carl. It's the Nazis that did all those terrible things."

"Germans, Nazis, they looked like the same people to me. Polish, Ukrainian, Lithuanian, there were plenty to help them out, believe me. But the Germans thought it up."

"This was a long time ago," Clara is quick to reassure her nephew. "What happened to the Jews and to your uncle over there. It was terrible, but it was back in history, okay?"

"History schmistory," says Carl.

"How far back?" says Lewis, who has at his fingertips a

thousand facts never learned or long since forgotten by the adults at the table. Although the vast majority of those facts concern the world of baseball, Lewis can also supply such data as the complete succession of U.S. Presidents, the state capitals, the major rivers, the dates bracketing every modern war. He can recite the Gettysburg Address and half of Hamlet's soliloquy. The boy "has a mind on him," according to his grandmother.

"Your Aunt Clara places it back before the Greeks and Romans, but this is the War we are talking about. Which happened day before yesterday."

"It's not the ancient Greeks," says Alene, taking up the role of mediator, "but it's not yesterday either, thank God. The War was over years before you were born, Lewis."

"Before Jackie Robinson, then," says Lewis, for whom world history is defined not by B.C. and A.D. but by Before Jackie and After Jackie.

Later, when the two of them are in the yard, Lewis takes his inquiry one step further. "If they murdered all the Jews, why didn't they murder you, Uncle Carl?"

"I didn't let them. Do you think I should have let them?"

"Course not. Did they torture you?"

"They froze my toes."

"In a freezer?"

"In the forest. But this is a long story..."

What Lewis gets is a short version of the long story. And to shield the boy from bad dreams, the short version Carl supplies is a tale of adventure, in which danger is almost fun and escape is like a Technicolor movie with only the frozen toes rendered in black and white. There are no monsters; certainly no mention is made of Sturmbannfuhrer Lindauer.

"Do your toes really still hurt? I mean, you can run and stuff."

"They hurt *except* when I run. That's when they forget to hurt."

The boy is a natural athlete and already as fast as his uncle, but Carl is calm with the ball, measured in his movements. Lewis kicks it quickly, Carl controls it. He lets it bounce off his knees and chest and belly, sends it foot to foot and then to his head for three deft caroms, and he does all this while weaving his way across the lawn. Lewis gives chase until Carl allows him to steal the ball. They both laugh at Lewis' eager attempts to mimic the intricate tricks he has witnessed. "It takes practice," Carl tells him. "Three hours a day for maybe ten years."

Clara is leaning through the open screen door, calling to them: "Not in that suit, for God's sake, Carl. You'll rip the trousers."

"Trousers!" Carl roars, spinning away from his tireless young pursuer.

"Yes trousers. As in twenty-five dollars."

Clara withdraws to the kitchen shaking her head and Alene takes over. There is a pitcher of cold fresh lemonade and a tray of brownies on the table, she tells them, in case anyone is interested. Lewis, she well knows, will be interested.

"No rips!" declares Carl, rotating 360 degrees to demonstrate that his trousers are intact, then rubbing his wife's head affectionately.

"There's a smear," she says. "Look at it. You got a grass stain, which won't come out, you know—a grass stain."

"I have a trick for that," says Alene, still mediating.

"Mom, did you see Uncle Carl's big kick?" says Lewis, between bites of brownie. "He kicked it way over the stone wall. Twenty meters, at least."

"I hope you didn't break a window at the neighbors," says Clara.

"Meters, is it!" says Alene, grinning.

"I can convert meters into yards, Mom. And kilometers into miles."

"He can," says Carl.

"I'll bet he can," says Alene.

"He can do anything, this guy," says Carl, now rubbing Lewis' head. Carl is a chronic head-massager. He understands that for Lewis to speak in terms of meters is an act of respect. He appreciates this respect and he enjoys the boy's eagerness for knowledge as much as he enjoys the feel of his American nephew's thick brown hair.

"Where is Philip?" Clara says suddenly, as though she has just remembered her son came with them. "Lewis, do you think you can find your cousin for me? Your Uncle Carl assures me you can do anything, so maybe you can do that."

"Sure, Aunt Clara. But I'm pretty sure he's just upstairs."

"I'll go with you, Lew," says Alene. "We'll make it a treasure hunt."

"Phil is a treasure, Mom?"

"Don't start," says Alene.

"Can I take a brownie with me?"

"Not upstairs. You know better."

Carl winks and keeps his own counsel as he watches the boy slide an illicit brownie into his shirt pocket for safekeeping.

1943

Everything was perfect, insofar as it went. Pollak had it all like clockwork. He had brought Karel his outfit in the morning before going to the platform. The rest was easy, so easy Karel was sure at each successive second it must fail. He sifted in with the crew, disappeared into the alcove when Ivan gave the sign, buried himself in the last cart as Ivan wheeled it by, and listened for the sound of the doors sliding shut. Right then, Ivan assured him, was when they would be counting heads. When the heads added up correctly, they would wave the train into motion.

But if it was this easy, why did it not happen more often? Karel tried going at the question backwards: if it did happen more often, it would not be easy. But no such ratiocination could keep him from trembling involuntarily, or from expecting every second to be probed and poked by a rifle. Then it would be like the old joke, shooting a fish in a barrel.

Every sound from outside the car was amplified. Every sound and every voice seemed to be getting closer. It was if an entire army of men in iron boots was marching inside his skull. On one level, Karel could not quite believe in his own death. At the same time, more realistically, he could not believe he would still be alive two minutes from now. The deepening cramps in his legs as he crouched were almost a welcome distraction, so long as he could keep from shouting each time they tightened their grip.

Then the train began to move. Cars clanking into position, wheels grinding and then pounding, with increasing speed and regularity. A minute passed, two minutes, and he began to believe he was still alive. He knew he was, from the stench. Long estranged from proper bathing and swimming now in nervous perspiration, Karel reeked so badly he could smell it on himself. Never before had he smelled his own fear.

Five minutes, ten. They must be beyond the gates and out into open country. Such a desperate fling of the dice, yet maybe it had worked. Maybe, one way and another, he would not even be missed for a while. When he fought through the leg cramps and dared to stand, he discovered that the tension and compression of an hour in the cart had made his entire body feel like one big cramp. He was alone, though, in a rollicking car packed with large burlap sacks, wooden crates, and canvas carts like the one he had just climbed out of.

Tin facing on the boxcar walls kept him from assessing the passing landscape. All he could see were strands of daylight, a filament here, a flicker there. He had counted on listening for clues, the rush of a river or the movement of bridges, but the irregular clangor of the steel wheels drowned out everything else. Karel had no sense of who he was hiding from at this point, who might be watching and from where. He was literally in the dark.

He understood that his first critical decision would be how far to go. The longer he rode this train, the likelier he would be found out; the sooner he left it, the closer he would be to the camp. Time was a sense he had lost, distances were pure guesswork, the local geography a mystery. Twice Karel had traveled to Kracow for work; he had never set foot in this part of Poland.

He knew from maps that the River Sola, which skirted the camps, would converge with the River Vistula near the rail line and that the Vistula might represent opportunity. But was that confluence one hour away or four? Any scrap of information from inside the camp was unreliable—ask five people, get five different answers.

Part of what made time so tricky was Karel's impatience. Forced to be patient for so long by now, he felt his old intolerance of hesitation come back in a rush, almost like transfused blood. Too soon or too late, shot or not shot, increasingly he was driven to get on with it. There was no sound basis for a decision anyway, no move that made greater sense than any other. Even if he managed to get the door open, hardly a given, he could be shot in mid-leap like a grouse on the wing. Alternatively, he could find himself broken in a hundred pieces on the ground.

In the end, the moment he chose was dictated by nothing more profound than his growing impatience compounded by an intense thirst. Somewhere outside this train car there would be water. He kept unraveling his limbs, rotating his neck and flexing his back, in an effort to make himself more limber. He touched his toes and touched the ceiling, three times each, before pushing through the traffic of baggage to the doors.

At once he saw they were chained on the outside, but the chain was just loose enough, the doors slid just far enough apart, to let a thin man squeeze through. At this point, Karel qualified. He wormed himself into the opening, took one quick confusing glance at the jittery over-bright landscape—and jumped.

The jolt was violent and the speed at which he rolled away shocking, but he had landed on a grassy embankment and rag-dolled down onto rougher gravel. Lying on the loose stones, he knew it was too soon to calibrate the extent of his injuries. Surely minor, though. He was scraped, not skinned; bruised, not shattered. Watched the train curve away, taking with it first the smoke and then the clamor, he was astounded at how fortunate an exit he had made. He was whole and the increasingly soft silent hum of the air was almost holy.

Even before he stood and began to verify that all his limbs were functional, he caught the musty reek of nearby water. Though this would not turn out to be the river, only a brook the width of a country lane, it solved the immediate problem of thirst. Beyond that, it could only help when the dogs came after him.

He drank his fill, breathed and drank again, then lay back on the grass and let his mind go blank for one blessed moment. Closed his eyes and opened them to the spectacle of a cello-shaped cloud trundling across a Delft blue sky. This benign miraculous sky actually saddened him briefly. That he could not share with Milena the unexpected gift of this moment—along with his confession that she had been right, some miracles were possible—pushed into his ribs like a blade. A moment later, it occurred to him some of those ribs might well be broken.

Soon enough his mind went blank again, this time on its own. With no clear sense of how exhausted the strain of events had left him, Karel fell sound asleep on the rumpled turf.

He woke with a start to a changed situation. A sky pearly gray and dimming, a misty rain falling. Exhaustion had made him careless; had cost him precious hours.

He was fortunate that no one had seen him, or at least no one had come after him yet, but the lost hours would work against him as surely as the rain and the shallow brook would help. He scrambled up a rocky outcropping, the highest point on a relatively flat landscape, and heard dogs barking at a distance, voices intermingled with their raucous volleys. It sounded like a conversation, the dogs and the humans debating back and forth. None of it sounded close by, though, and as he walked the stream for several miles, the squalls gave way to a night heron's wail from a nearby marsh. Darkness was blooming.

Karel groomed a spongy cushion of composting leaves and pine needles. It made for a damp bed, but a soft one. Tomorrow, his first full day out, could be critical, so he used enough of his larder to approximate a proper meal—bread, carrots, mushrooms—and resolved on getting some solid sleep.

Traveling with and at times directly in the brook, he had paid little attention to how much his feet hurt. Surely that was the least of it. He was far more focused on making good guesses, cognizant that this back-country waterway might travel to the Vistula and it might not; cognizant that he was lost and had no plan. How could he have guessed that his first serious problem would be an inability to remove his boots?

He had prepared for the initial flight from Auschwitz-Birkenau. In truth, he had prepared to be killed on the platform. When that didn't happen, he braced himself for a rough exit from the train and another excellent opportunity to be shot dead. If after all of that he found himself still breathing, he expected to rely on his wits, taking trouble as it came. But boots?

At first this was a triviality, a joke. The boots had never fit properly—had never been his own—and the thin cotton socks provided no better protection than newsprint. Now either the boots had cranked tighter or his feet had swollen. Either way it was becoming the farthest thing from a joke, as discomfort gave way to pain and pain to an agony so intense that before long Karel was ready to amputate the boots, feet and all.

Desperate as he was for sleep, he knew the pain would not allow it. A powerful drug—morphine?—might have extinguished the blaze in his nerves, but Karel had no morphine in his medicine cabinet. He had only the force of his will. This was becoming the worst physiological pain he had endured in his life and it owed entirely to tight shoes!

He recalled the football kick that shattered his nose, and the sharp deep stab of a kidney stone. He recalled the night in '41 when he was assaulted in the street outside Café Tichota. Four Nazis "detained" him (their word for it, just as "for no reason, Yid" was their explanation as to why) and beat him. They clubbed him to the pavement and kicked him with their sledgehammer boots until they became bored or perhaps were satisfied he was dead. They were finished with him in any case and strolled on in high spirits, as though such casual sadism was a required element in their exercise regimen and now it was on to a well-earned tavern supper.

As he lay bloodied and writhing on the cobblestones that night, dozens of passers-by crossed to the other side and kept walking. This was understood; this he expected. Sooner or later, some brave soul would help him. If not, he would eventually be able to help himself. Already the blood was drying on his face and in his scalp. His right eye had swollen closed. When he touched it, he felt a protrusion there like a raw chicken breast and could only hope that, somewhere inside, the eye itself was intact. The first time he tried getting to his feet, the pain came so sharply that he bellowed involuntarily.

Yet *this* pain, from the tight shoes, was worse. His toes screamed at him so loudly he wanted to scream back. He wondered if such toes could prove fatal, if the annals of medicine featured instances of men who had actually died from tight boots. After all he had borne, would his final moments be so radically absurd?

When the notion of "dying with his boots on" like an American cowboy occurred to him, when he heard himself laughing out loud at this, he feared he was already delirious.

Then, whether mercifully or fatally—who could say, at the time—the toes began to grow numb. It was almost as if they weren't even there and his mind began to relent in turn. By now, however, Karel could not trust the sleep he craved; he was fearful he might wake up dead, so to speak. It was another hour before he finally closed his eyes and drifted off to the sound of individual raindrops falling, striking this leaf and that, like musical scales.

He woke to a succession of fresh miracles, commencing with a clear, calm sunrise and a layer of quiet like a soft quilt spread over the land. He could hear the brook buffeted, hear the crisp responses of brush along its banks, but he heard no dogs, no shouts, no shots. The decision to stop and rest despite those lost hours had yet to cost him his life.

Could it be that the Nazis were finally jaded, that they were losing interest in death? Perhaps by now they would forego an instance, spare the odd Jew just to keep their hideous game interesting. It seemed plausible that death was no different to them than anything else they produced in factories, that at bottom it was repetitive and therefore boring. Of course it seemed even more plausible they would find him by noon.

The next miracle was almost a magic trick: off came the boots. They slipped off his feet so easily he might have dreamt the nightmare entirely. The feet appeared intact, the toes moved, the pain was bearable. Normal pain.

He set the boots on a small boulder to dry. Barefoot and shirtless, his smock drying on a limb, he paced back and forth the way he had in the camp, trying then to maintain a little strength, trying now to regain a little. Though to Karel his legs looked thin as kindling, they somehow managed to feel heavy as logs.

Suddenly he was famished, fiercely hungry, and by now it did not seem miraculous, almost expected, when he found three peach trees a short distance downstream. Announcing themselves with bright gold fanfare, the old trees were warped and leaning but they were loaded with fruit.

He tried to eat slowly, carefully, for the small sweet peaches had been tunneled by insects and were far from flawless. They were also delicious. He ate slowly, carefully, and gratefully. Grateful not to God, or the Golem; not *to* anyone. Grateful in the abstract.

Or better, he concluded as he filled his sack with peaches, to the natural world.

1960

"Why do you always say it's ugly."

"Because always it is ugly," Carl shrugs.

"But it's yours. I mean, you built it."

"I built it in America the Beautiful, bubula. Little did I know that in America the Beautiful, nothing can be beautiful. Maybe at one time the public library or the Gracie's Mansion, otherwise forget it. Beautiful they don't have time for here."

"It's different where you were?"

"It *was* different. Believe me, it got ugly there too, after Heydrich's face was in the paper every day."

"Whose face?"

"Doesn't matter. A nobody, a criminal. A puppet."

"What do you mean?"

"Not a *puppet* puppet. Listen, it's complicated."

"That's what you always say."

"It also always is true," says Carl. "But listen, the real Praha was never ugly. And I am not talking castle, or opera house, or national library. I am talking houses we lived, like little castles up and down each street."

"What happened to it?"

"To Praha? The Nazis happened. And the postwar. In the War and in the postwar, everything in Europe was made ugly. By law!"

"But you think America is ugly."

"The buildings, that's all. This is what I do, however. I make buildings."

"So why don't you make them beautiful?"

"You cannot do this. It cannot happen. Why? I'll tell you why. It's the saving of the money, the making of the money. You put boxes on top of boxes until you get to the sky. Then turn on the water and start collecting rent. This is the way it is done—by law!"

Lewis nods as if satisfied with this explanation. Rather than disagree with his uncle, he is willing to pretend the matter has been clarified. But isn't Uncle Carl the one who turns on the water and collects the rent? Isn't he the one who makes the money? Besides, the high-rises his uncle has built in mid-town Manhattan do not strike Lewis as "monstrosities" (Carl's word for them), just plain. Lewis would say the buildings seem plain, especially from the outside.

Inside is different. The one on 61st Street, where Carl keeps his office, has a little gymnasium and a swimming pool in the basement, plus a restaurant Carl "sort of owns" on the street level. One winter night when his uncle had desk work to do, Lewis went swimming. This was a freezing cold night in December and he had an entire warm blue pool to himself. Indoors, on a winter night! How could such a place be bad?

"If Uncle Carl is rich—"

"He is pretty rich, I think, but so what?"

"If he's rich, why can't he build things any way he wants to?"

"Such as what? What are you asking?" says Alene, stopping herself from pointing out he has just ended a sentence with a preposition. She tries not to punish Lewis for being the son of a grade school teacher.

"A beautiful house. Or a beautiful, I don't know, stadium. School."

"No one just builds a stadium, Lew. Or a school. The town hires you to do it and they tell you what it can cost. Say your uncle wants it to be nicer looking—with fancy doodads, is that the question?—then it costs more and maybe they hire somebody else."

"How does a school make money?"

"It doesn't."

"But the making of the money," he quotes.

"The saving of the money," she smiles. "He says that too. With a school, I guess it's the saving. With a business, the making."

"I guess I get it," he says, though something still isn't adding up, something is missing.

Alene can tell her son has stepped back, has learned to respect the limit beyond which his questions are no longer welcome. She can also tell his brain is still "churning." By the next time they see Carl, the brain will have churned up a whole new batch of angles and inquiries.

Well, good luck to him getting the dope from Clara's inscrutable second husband. Is Carl Barry a sweet-natured reserved man or a hard-headed withdrawn one? Are those dark eyes soft with feeling or are they shields walling off secrets? Inside Carl's attractive smile she has seen something troubling and hard to pin down. It can flash toward aggression, edge toward accusation, or shade toward sadness. But sadness lodged within the smile; sadness when outwardly he seems content.

"It's just the language," Clara always says. To Clara, "the language" explains everything inscrutable about Carl Barry. This has become her default position. "When he tells you a subject is complicated, he means complicated to put into English. So you can understand how it frustrates him a little."

To Alene, it is just one piece of a puzzle. She sees Carl Barry as an iceberg, largely submerged. At any given moment, he may be one-fourth present among them, three-fourths elsewhere—worrying about the price of concrete for all they know. The iceberg is a notion Clara does not embrace, if she even hears it. She is sticking with the language.

And maybe this is the reason it has become Carl's own default position, an escape hatch any time he is pressed to refine or clarify his mood or meaning. "Speak English, dear Clara," he will say, humorously turning the tables on her. "Speak to me plain English."

1943

Circumstances—if so bland a word could encompass all the hardships and atrocities perpetrated by the Germans and their collaborators— had so long conspired against him that Karel was astonished by the extent to which they were now conspiring in his favor.

He had followed the brook all morning, periodically stone-stepping barefoot through the water in his continued effort to neutralize the dogs' pursuit. At times he felt safely concealed inside the birch-and-fir thicket; at other times the same thicket seemed an endless maze from which he might never emerge. All day, though, he felt surprisingly strong, and had traveled roughly 30 kilometers.

He had decided to stop for the night when abruptly the sky widened out over a vast empire of fields sloping steadily down to the broad flat water of what could be the River Vistula. The meadows, demarcated by lines of windrow oaks, surrounded a farmhouse and a phalanx of barns, all of which lay between the trees and the river. There was a club of polite cows grazing nearby who took no notice of his presence.

He could see the main house with all its els and elbows, three barns of varying shapes and sizes, a henhouse, a woodshed open on two sides, and a privy with a crescent cut out of the door. If he could not hide here, find shelter and gather supplies in such a sprawling establishment, the fault would be his.

All day the world had yielded up such bounty. Cold fresh water, ripe fruit, plentiful mushrooms, and a sun strong enough to penetrate the thicket. Karel had stumbled into a fertile valley with no one to bother him and no one in close pursuit.

After dark, he advanced cautiously toward the carriage barn, which stood farthest from the main house. It had no door, just a wide portal through which, earlier, he had watched two men steer a hay wagon. Inside he found a stack of burlap sacks, shook out half a dozen, and carried them up a wooden ladder to a loft above two incurious horses. For one day, at least, even the equines and bovines were on his side, his very own collaborators.

The soundtrack of the farm tapered off in steady measures. Wagon wheels and wheelbarrows, doors swinging and gliding shut, snippets of talk, the sounds of animals settling. Chickens squawked as they jockeyed for their favored spots until finally there was just the wind in the grasses. As the mercury began to fall, Karel looked with just a speck of envy at the curlicues of wood-smoke drifting from the farmhouse chimney. He pictured the scene inside, a family supper with warm bread, hot soup, cold pilsner. Nonetheless, he was grateful for the bed he had fashioned of burlap and straw, and for the sleep into which he soon descended.

He slept soundly, dreamt nothing, and did not wake once until daybreak, when the rooster's rowdy shrieks reached him. Sunlight was already flooding in, sweetening the hay-flavored air.

Straightaway he saw that his good fortune had carried over in more ways than one. Though he never sensed a human presence in the barn, Karel found a basket of food hooked onto a rung of the ladder. Freshly baked rolls (still steaming), boiled eggs, and a jar of milk had been left for him. More benign collaborators, a *mitzvah* for sure, yet at the same time a serious comeuppance to someone convinced he was alert to all danger. The obvious truth was he might have slept through machine-gunfire that night.

His presence, so assiduously concealed, had been perfectly apparent to the farmer and only by unlikely chance had it resulted in charity instead of capture. Pure luck! His presence was not merely noted, it was *approved*—or at least tolerated—by a Pole who while perhaps unwilling to own up to his own decency had demonstrated it regardless, by means of this generous feast. All that was missing was a carafe of hot coffee.

Karel was stunned to feel warm tears tickling his cheeks. Despite himself, he could only acknowledge that here, in an invisible and anonymous farmer's largesse, lay some sort of affirmation. But feeling fortunate was too strange to last for long. As he made his desperation break from Auschwitz (Ivan's last words to him, "Go, my friend, like a ruptured duck in a hailstorm") Karel secretly believed he would make it. Always headstrong, he told himself there was no way those fuckers could kill him. Now as he was reminded of the ways in which life could be pleasant—dry bedding, fresh bread, faint seductive hints of freedom—he was also reminded how easily life could be ended. How easily he could have been killed in the night without even knowing it!

So while he ate the food with pleasure, he guarded against relaxing his vigilance. He kept death close by taking stock. Mila was dead, the children were dead, Jitka and Milan, Helena and Vaclav, Pavel...Ivan alone might still be alive—and Karel himself. Having been granted this slim chance of living a while longer (an hour? a day? a month?) he again faced the question of why he would wish to do so.

Or rather why he *did* wish to, since such was the case. Every Jew at Terezin, every Jew at Auschwitz-Birkenau, had answered this question minute by minute, simply by not charging the muzzle of a gun. There were always opportunities for small action, moments when a bit of damage could be inflicted before one's death sentence was carried out. A guard in an unguarded moment—such instances did present themselves. In this regard, Karel had been no different from the rest of them, the ones he and Pavel called The Sheep.

They were foolish enough to believe that by living on a while longer they might find a way to do greater damage; not just crash one fist against one Nazi nose but kill Nazis by the dozen, kill Hitler or Goebbels. *Kill Lindauer.* Karel had a recurring dream in which he steered a truck of explosives into one of their Berlin galas, where they were laughing and dancing and toasting their great successes with champagne.

He liked to believe it was not a question of courage. That he would have welcomed a fair fight—even an unfair fight, say one against four. But to assault a guard was to perish on the spot, to choose that specific instant for your death, and the impulse to suicide contradicts the most basic human instinct. It was always easier to choose going on instead, choose to die later. After all, every living creature died "later."

Nor were they so sure that to invite a summary execution even allowed the privilege of choosing one's moment to die. If one is thrown into a pit patrolled by hungry lions, would not the lions do the choosing? Or the men who put the lions there. All this might be, in Grandfather Bondy's favorite phrase, a distinction without a difference, but it was one he and Pavel tortured intellectually, as if such philosophical hair-splitting might be worthwhile.

Up in this hayloft, with sunlight lancing through the barn-board gaps like a hundred bright bayonets, Karel was more content than ever before with his decision to bypass the lions. A faceless Polish farmer—undoubtedly Gentile, most likely Catholic—had by providing breakfast to a fugitive Jew in rags radically transformed his prospects. Because of this man's decency, Karel's temporary reprieve might become a distinction *with* a difference. God knows he had burned to arrive at such a moment, for there were monstrous debts to collect and none of them were payable to a corpse.

As he began to move around, dust from the hay and shavings swirled up into the sun's rays. The pungent scent of the horses below mingled with the aroma of fermenting hay. Surely someone would come for the horses soon, to feed them and harness them, and Karel was at a loss for the proper greeting. Probably that part would see to itself.

Through a high unglazed window opening, just a rough rectangular cut-out in the siding, he could see how the pastureland sloped down to the silt-brown river. Two fields had been cut recently for hay, two others were planted with potatoes and corn. Karel pictured the work being done: horse, harness, and harrow; men shedding their blouses as the day warmed; the ritual of sharpening scythes; stopping at noon to unpack their bread and cheese and beer. Sated, they would fall back upon the earth they ministered to and present their faces to the bright blue sky. Much as he envied them their well-earned respite, Karel envied even more the fruitful labor by which they earned it.

1960

"Absolutely not, dear Clara. All could not be better."

How could anything be better, when here at one table are his American wife and her children, the lovely Alene and her children, their kindly brother Jules, and sweet old Sarah Wohl from next door, who has nowhere else to go. Here too is the traditional meal, even if it happens to be the U.S. version, which has come from Sol's Delicatessen.

Everything they say and sing sounds wrong to Carl's ears—the melodies hold small surprises, the words are of course foreign—but here, today, it truly could not be better. Hearts are in the right place.

"It's just you had your faraway look, that's all," Clara persists. "He did, didn't he, Jules? Did you see it, A.?"

Alene pats her sister on the arm. The faraway look is okay with her.

"Carl looks fine to me," says Jules, as he would, admittedly, even had Carl been blowing poison darts across the table at him.

Alene and Clara agree that their brother's one shortcoming is that he is "too nice."

"You examined him, did you?" says Clara, to her brother the doctor. "You took his temp and listened with your stethoscope to his heartbeat?"

Jules, who is impossible to offend, claps his hands once lightly and laughs. He admires the way Clara can fold her "inner yenta" into pointed humor. "You wanted my opinion," he shrugs.

Carl responds to their exchange with a smile. To his wife's inner yenta, he generally responds with forebearance. The battles she likes to fight rarely matter to him. Moreover, Carl rarely argues a point with anyone. He issues fiats. Often he begins a sentence with the phrase "The truth is—" and this wording tends to close discussion, not open it.

Except with Lewis; always the exception is Lewis. He alone can cause Carl to reconsider a verdict. Earlier in the day, Alene said she wasn't ready to trust young Kennedy as a candidate; she trusted Adlai Stevenson, who had hinted he might run for President a third time. "The truth is," Carl instructed her, "if he is a politician, he is a crook." There was a moment of silence before Lewis inquired, somewhat puckishly, after the nature of Stevenson's crime. Why wasn't Stevenson in jail?

What followed was not a concession, quite. Carl did not retract the charge, exactly. What he offered was a modification: "It's not a crime you prosecute, bubula. Different kind of crime."

"Like lying, you mean? Like a sin?"

Carl smiled at the concept of Sin, and allowed Jules to respond for him. "That's right, Lew, like being dishonest. Your Uncle Carl believes all politicians are dishonest."

"To *begin with* dishonest," clarified Carl.

"Do you think that too, Uncle Jules?"

"It's unfortunate, Lew, that so many of them are. Maybe most are, to a degree. It comes with the job. But I would say no, not all of them."

"Name one," said Carl.

"Who is honest?" said Jules.

"Yes, exactly. Name one. Please."

"Stevenson himself, possibly. I've never heard otherwise. Or how about Ben-Gurion?"

Carl waved Ben-Gurion away like a wisp of smoke. Lewis was loathe to admit not knowing about Ben Gurion. It was clear from the context that he should know, and he could tell you a great deal about Ben Franklin, or Ben Chapman, who behaved so badly toward Jackie Robinson. He has seen enough photographs of Benny Goodman to recognize him and link him with the clarinet. Ben Gurion, though apparently famous, is a blank slate.

Now, just as Alene is calling attention to the arrival of the main courses, Carl stands to excuse himself from the table. As if his faraway look wasn't enough, now this.

"For one small minute," he submits, index finger up to ward off Clara's protest. Carl Barry's sudden cravings for air are well established, along with his conviction there can be no genuine air indoors.

"Sit," says Alene, as Lewis starts up in hot pursuit of his uncle. "Leave him be."

"He doesn't want me to leave him be."

"*I* want you to," she says.

Again Jules intercedes, in his gentle way. "Lew, come on now, you have a reputation to uphold here. This is the brisket we're talking about. You better get started, if you are going to eat your twenty slices."

"Can't I be excused for just one minute?"

"*May* I be excused," says Alene. "And no, you may not."

"What if I had to go to the bathroom?"

"Then you could."

"What's the difference? If I can be excused for one reason, why can't I be excused for another?"

"Because you can't," says Alene, this time opting for governance by brute force. She is always relieved when a direct over-rule does the trick, ever leery of the day when Lewis simply ignores her ruling. He is a nice boy, but frighteningly logical.

Jules, the healer, smoothly papers over the breach with a story about one of his patients, a car salesman who can't sleep unless

Jules prescribes him a pill. Unknown to the salesman, the pill he gets is composed of cellulose and sugar.

"A pill that's not really a pill, you see. He takes it and he sleeps like a baby. A *good* baby," he adds with a quick grin, before Lewis can remind him how finicky babies can be.

In Brooklyn, where Jules still resides, the neighborhood is populated (or so it seems, from his stories) by a tribe of demanding, unappreciative lunatics and hypochondriacs, all of whom he holds in high regard and cares for with great devotion. Another of these oddballs, a schoolteacher who came in complaining of sweaty palms, is under discussion—Lewis is invited to suggest a protocol or prescription for her—when Carl finally returns to the table. He has been gone for the duration of two cigarettes, not one minute.

At first he stands directly behind Jules, placing both hands on his brother-in-law's shoulders to apply an affectionate ten-second massage. Then he is back in his own chair, cutting his meat. "So how is the brisket?" he asks, while the others pretend the meal is not half over.

1943

"I won't ask you, you won't tell me, I won't know," the farmer explained. "If anyone here has a problem, or if anyone from outside comes snooping—"

"I understand," said Karel, who understood and fully appreciated what the farmer was telling him. Not-knowing might afford the man a small measure of protection.

It also might not. This good man was taking a big chance, and so for both their sakes, Karel would play the game. He was still far from strong and they were, he learned, only 80 kilometers from the camp. It was risky for the farmer and risky for him, but he accepted the offer to stay on and work. To be a Gentile.

The work itself was a blessing. Difficult at first, easier each day. Four men were sent out to the fields; two were set about warming tar in a metal tub and patching the roofs with it; Karel was assigned to a team of three processing stove wood for the winter. The bolts of wood that slid down to him were ready to be split four ways and then stacked in head-high rows under a lean-to roof slanting off the main barn. Each day, sun-up to sun-down, this was his primary assignment.

His were mindless tasks, or so he thought, only to discover that keeping the pace and maintaining the simple progressions required more than just energy, it demanded his full attention. The rhythm of the work was so relentless—assess the grain of each log as it arrived, strike it several times just so, then nest each quartered bolt on the piles—it left no time for his mind to wander. Meanwhile his shoulders, so sore the first few nights, grew stronger than they had ever been. His hands grew harder, until splinters lost their ability to pierce him.

The food was plentiful and fresh: bread straight from the oven, chicken in the soup, fruit and custard puddings for dessert. A hog had been slaughtered and cured, though, and he soon faced the question of pork. Would he eat it? *Could* he eat it? Everyone he knew had a story— maybe every rabbi told the same story, to every Jewish child—about eating pork and becoming violently ill. And here, of course, it would also be a litmus test for *goyische*, a sort of yellow star of ingestion.

Never committed to keeping kosher, merely someone who went along with it, Karel tried to go along here. As a part of the bargain of not-telling, he did take a small helping of pork and it did make him ill. It gripped his intestines like a claw. Fortunately, he was able to sort the matter out in private, past midnight, when he sat doubled over for an hour in the privy. By morning, after a difficult twisting sleep, the pig relented and ceased clutching at his innards. By late morning, when the sun came around to his chopping station, he felt himself again.

That next night, his portion of pork went into a pocket on the sly, its destiny to nestle in the bushes behind the two-holer after dark. The bread, he commented while slicing himself a fourth slab, was especially delicious tonight.

Also as part of the not-telling, he steered clear of the bath-house. His family back in Bohemia, he explained, lived on a riverbank like this one and bathed in the stream, regardless of the season. It was a fast-moving river, spilling down from the Ore Mountains with such force it never froze over. "Could be freezing cold, you know, but never frozen. A tribe of masochists, we were."

It turned out Karel was freezing his arse for nothing. One day, Oskar, the fellow who sent logs down the chute to him, sat beside him on the plank bench, the two of them wrapped in blankets following their respective bath routines, and said: "You think we don't know it?" But Oskar was smiling, not threatening, as he spoke. "We know it. So next time, you might as well use the hot water—not that it's all that hot. But it won't shrink your balls into acorns."

He had been equally naive about the church. The building was lovely, a century-old jewel with stenciled decorations and millwork brackets. The invitation ("Aren't you coming?") was rendered pleasantly. Karel reported that he was a bit unwell and would make his peace with God next time around. A week later, it so happened he was unwell again.

They called it his Sunday morning sickness and took him, or so he presumed, for a blasphemer who feared to stand inside the house of God. The rest of them attended each week, without fail. Oskar would wink and remind him he was missing out on Mrs. Ryboska's apple cake and strong coffee after the service.

But Oskar's sly aside ("You think we don't know it?") informed Karel retroactively that no one could have been surprised at his failure to attend Mass. They knew, and they had tolerated him. After Oskar's revelation, and after the weeks of working and eating with the men, he almost trusted them. Most of them, certainly. But there was little conversation that did not concern the workings of the farm or the slipping away of seasons, the difficult shift from growing to storing to wintering over.

The weather, as inscrutable as it was germane to everything they did, was easily the foremost topic, hour to hour, morning and night.

Then came word that German tanks had rolled through the market in Scokzow. A sizable regiment pointed north. Advance patrols had been spotted in the Sneznik foothills, one company had billeted at the Rajecka farm. Though Karel could not parse this local geography, it was sufficient to know the Nazis were nearby, if not everywhere.

"It might be best you stay in the loft for a few days," Krakowski told him.

Karel was far from sure. Did he wish to risk being trapped in the hayloft while Nazi dogs paced and snarled below? Krakowski would not turn him in, but what about one-eyed Woijek, who stared at everyone during meals and rarely said a word? Was the man unreliable or merely odd? And what if the blade of a bayonet was laid against the throat of Magdelena or young Agnes, in the kitchen? The Nazis were ruthless. Simply by pointing to the barn, or silently inclining her head that way, Agnes could dodge the awful consequences of moral action.

"Or," said Krakowski, "you could try and get to the forest. I know a man—"

Karel had hidden in a cart full of rags, every piece either blood-stained or filthy, why couldn't he hide in a wagonload of potatoes? By the next morning, he decided he could. Life on the farm was fine, so far as it went, but staying out of harm's way was a temporary goal. Besides, Krakowski would not want him when winter came. Karel had been welcomed here; soon he would wear out his welcome.

Not quite yet, however. In a final flurry of generosity, Magdalena fed him a grand breakfast and handed him a sack containing more of the buns, boiled eggs, a block of cheese, and a woolen shirt. Krakowski gave him a week's wages in advance ("In advance of nothing?" said Karel, thanking him) and he was ready to go.

Go where, though? For the moment, "north" was the only answer. That was where the potato wagon was bound and supposedly (rumors, always rumors) it was also where Polish and

Russian partisans were camped in a forest west of Opole. And north was a far less menacing direction than "east" had once been.

Krakowski knew a man, and that man knew another man. Farmers, potato haulers, foresters—this was how it worked, this was the new world order. You never knew what to believe, never knew who to trust. Although the truest new world order, hinted at on that damp morning in the wagon and deepening steadily in the weeks to follow, was the coming of winter.

1961

The restaurant, called Allegro, occupies the sunnier corner of Uncle Carl's new building, at street level. The entire first floor is glass, or appears that way at a glance. There are columns of steel rising between the huge slabs of plate glass and Lewis remembers when that was all you saw—a skeleton of steel like a giant erector set. Now twelve storeys of brick appear to rest on a glass foundation, as if something clear as water might support a mountain of rock.

At Carl's chosen table, in the corner of the corner, they are practically sitting in the street, or in the middle of a busy Manhattan sidewalk. Elbows fly past the window like a sped-up movie; funhouse faces approach and recede; now and then someone spits on the pavement, where it glistens briefly. Carl notices none of this, Lewis registers every detail.

A blue vase filled with flowers is the centerpiece on each table. "Seasonal, fresh always," says Carl. They come from the flower shop one door down from Allegro, from Angelina, who is always characterized as Carl's favorite tenant. "It costs money, the flowers," Carl will state proudly, and having gleaned the precise monthly figure ($120) Lewis has of course multiplied to determine the annual outlay for flowers. It is a worthwhile expense, he is assured, a sound investment, which at the same time helps Angel out. "Because, you see," Carl adds, unnecessarily, "she sells the flowers."

Carl orders for both of them. While he is always certain he knows what Lewis wants to eat, Lewis has no idea how his uncle arrives at the choices, which do vary. He would be happy every time with the corned beef sandwich or the pastrami, but never would have chosen *tongue*, not after learning what it was. A slice of warm cherry pie with a scoop of vanilla ice cream makes the most sense and fortunately Carl never varies that part.

"Eat, eat," Carl keeps saying, as if his nephew has been doing anything else. Lewis is thin—his mother says skinny, his father says wiry—so Carl assumes the boy needs to eat more.

"*You* eat," says Lewis, who has begun to master the art of the counterpunch. As usual, his uncle has left untouched the medley of expensive food on his own plate. Eventually he will declare he is not hungry and have it all packed up in a cardboard box. Whether he eats any of it later, Lewis does not know, however many times Carl answers "What else would I do with it?" to the question.

"So, everything is good today?" says their waiter, in what sounds to Lewis like a Russian accent. It is very close, in any case, to the way the Russian pole-vaulter sounded on television.

Uncle Carl nods, a quick downward flick of the head which doubles his chin briefly and which the waiter takes for a resounding affirmation. Carl's nods do have gradations, they bespeak a nuanced language which clearly this fellow feels qualified to interpret. Lewis recalls kicking a soccer ball off the garage door, barely missing a glass panel. His mother exclaimed "Jesus, Mary, and Joseph" (as she often will, curiously enough, since Alene is Jewish) but Carl, while saying nothing, dropped a barely discernible nod into the discussion, a gesture Lewis understood perfectly to mean strong kick, *solid*, well done.

Then there is the slightly diagonal nod he grants to Nadia when she stops by their table, as she invariably will, "to make the small talk." Lewis cannot imagine why Nadia is always so nice to him, why she should care so much how his school is going, or in today's case, his summer, but she is so pretty and pleasant he manages not to care why.

Nadia too has an interesting accent—"From Bucharest," Carl had told him. Then, months after he looked up Romania in the

Encyclopedia Britannica and pictured Nadia living there, Carl insisted she was raised in Budapest, not Bucharest. In Hungary, not Romania.

"Why would I say different?" said Carl, by way of dismissing the Romanian claim. "Hungary, no question, Lewis. I have been there."

I have been to Vermont, thought Lewis, which doesn't mean I am from there, or even know anyone who is from there. He will not introduce such contrarian logic into the conversation, nor will he state the obvious, that they could ask Nadia directly. What was okay to ask, here at Allegro, since different venues impose different boundaries, was when exactly Carl had gone to Hungary. Had it been before 1956, when, according to *The Weekly Reader*, the Russian tanks rolled in?

"Bubula, it was before the German tanks rolled in. What do you think about that?"

"So what was it like there?"

"Finish your dessert," says Carl, fingers drumming on his cardboard take-home box. "We have work to do, you and I."

"I'm finished," says Lewis with a shrug. He is left hanging on the particulars of Budapest circa 1930-something as Carl waves for the check to be brought. As always, Nadia waves back, dismissing with a shake of her pretty brown curls the very notion of payment.

And as always, Uncle Carl lays a twenty-dollar bill on the table, irons it smooth with the edge of his palm, and pins it beneath the blue vase.

1943

They had come far and each leg was slower going; for the past hour the forest seemed to be closing its doors around them. And while Wazda remained outwardly confident about finding the Russkies, he would mutter periodically how often they moved their encampment, how nothing could be certain.

"Nightfall is certain," said Karel, mindful of how Wazda's confidence on the first day of the journey had left him unprepared for two nights on the damp ground. The wayside hut Wazda postulated was no more than a sales agent's inducement to travel; it never materialized.

"We are getting close," said Wazda. "And with just light enough to make it there. Trust."

Trust was not an option for Karel, and certainly not trust of a mercenary like Wazda, who had told him straight up, "There have been Jews I was paid for and Jews lost in transit. No one can tell you the forest is a safe place."

There were moments Karel believed the man might actually know what he was doing and other moments he feared they were shooting in the dark. The so-called pathway kept disappearing on them, or crossing other pathways that created frequent pauses for study. "Yes," Wazda would say each time he made his choice, "we are right on target."

Questions of trust and of moving targets notwithstanding, there was nothing for it but to keep going. Darkness was infilling the forest, twilight lingering in the clearings, when they saw the orange licks of fire behind a curtain of fir trees. This could be anything, Karel cautioned himself, or anyone. It could be the squadron of Polish partisans known for killing as many Jews as Germans. But Wazda's step was distinctly lighter, his voice restored to glory: "This is it."

The flames rose from a cone-shaped arrangement of logs, set inside a neatly laid circle of stones. Above the fire, depending from a rod, hung two cast-iron pots. One contained water, the other bubbled with something that smelled enticing. It was strange that no one challenged them as they moved toward the fire and that they saw no further signs of life until a lanky sharp-shouldered man came walking out of the earth toward them.

Or so it seemed. From 15 paces away, it even seemed he had been fashioned from earth, his jacket smeared with mud and his face with soot. In fact, he had emerged from a sort of cave carved out of an earthen hillock and further camouflaged beneath a thatch of grass and brush. This surreal portal was shaped like an enormous eye-lid, as though the underground itself was peering out, safeguarding the encampment.

The tall silent soul continued to ignore them, as though casual visitors came and went all day. Wazda smiled and waited as the fellow tended the fire and stirred the potion in the pot. Meanwhile Karel noticed a second shelter, nearly invisible though it was a sizable military tent of green duck. Set back among thick laurel bushes, it blended into the foliage enclosing it. But the man who came through the door-flap of this green canvas mansion had little care for camouflage—or understatement. He was in full regalia, Red Army issue complete with epaulets on both shoulders, and he addressed them in a booming voice that resonated like stagecraft. Perhaps the acoustics were unusually good in this natural amphitheater.

"I have told you," he said to the Polish guide. "No more."

"Regrets, General," said Wazda, "I misunderstood. I thought you said just *one* more."

"Like hell you did, you sly Polock. How much did he pay you?"

"I was hoping you would pay, if only a little. This man says he is ready to fight."

"Good. But he will not fight here. Take him back with you."

While Karel's Russian was quite sufficient to follow this exchange—including Wazda's outrageous lie, for Karel had given him 20 zlotys—he restrained himself from joining the debate. Best, he thought, to let it play out between these two. But soon it became clear that as far as the chieftain was concerned, it already had: there was nothing more to be said. So when he started back toward the tent Karel was forced to intercept him.

The chieftain mimed surprise at such presumption, his gesture every bit as dramatic as his speaking voice. Then he made allowance: "Forgive me. Naturally, you have not understood."

"I think you have not understood," said Karel, in perfectly grammatical Russian. "I am here to join the fight."

"I wish you luck in your endeavor," said the Russian, with only a hint of secondary surprise. "But you are not welcome in my unit."

"Fuck yourself, Boris."

At this, the Russian brayed like a donkey. The impudent fellow not only spoke Russian, he went as far as the idiomatic! "Allow me to rephrase," he said in a softer tone. "You are not welcome in my unit, *please*, my good man."

"Fuck yourself twice. You think I can't fight? Try me right now." Karel was relying on the larger man's restraint. He was bluffing, really, just trying to prolong the discussion.

"Do you even know where you are, my friend?"

"I know where I am not."

"Meaning you were in a camp."

"Camp, is it? Yes. We sang songs and played games and wrote letters to our parents in the idle hours."

"And yet you left such an agreeable place!" Though he tried to maintain a supercilious tone, the Russian was clearly entertained by their jousting.

"What is the problem, Boris? Do you imagine I am a spy for the Nazis?"

"I imagine you are a Jew."

"And you are a Jew-hater? You fight the Germans but hate the Jews?"

"There are many who fit that description precisely, but no, I don't. There are complexities, quite simply. You would be better off joining one of the Jewish bands."

"I'm afraid I misplaced the keys to my limousine. So here I am."

"I see that, but let me be clear. We have had some bad blood here—there are some who like to make trouble for the Jews. One who killed a Jew."

"So you do have Jews."

"A very few," conceded the chieftain, philosophically.

"Well now you have one more. Recruit enough more Jews and your troublemaker will quickly become a friend to all mankind. A good Communist. No, Boris?"

"My name is Socrates, not Boris."

"Yes? And mine is Plato."

"You are a tall talker for someone who stands so short."

"As I said, Boris: try me."

"And as I said, they call me Socrates. But do you know what, Mr. Plato? Right now, I think I will feed you a nice supper. Would that meet with your approval? I may even introduce you to your countryman, a Czech partisan who is not a Jew. His problem is that he can't speak."

"A mute?"

"A Czech, who can't speak Russian. He and I converse through one of the Polocks, you will see how. First we will whip up something kosher for you, with a split of kosher champagne to rinse it down. Come have a look at the menu."

"Sounds to me like a bowl of gruel and a shot of cheap vodka."

"It will look like that too. Though we could just kill you, if you prefer?"

By now, both of them were smiling.

Jaroslav Heyduk was neither a Jew nor a Jew-hater, merely a Czech patriot. None of his family members had been robbed or displaced, much less murdered. Nonetheless, shortly after the occupation, he and his brother left Praha to join the fight. While his own people might be "safe," the fact remained that his nation had been invaded.

Hearing the Czech language was a welcome balm and this Heyduk was a large, likable soul with a ready sense of humor, an instant pal. Throughout his life Karel had many friendships with Catholics. In Praha, in the past, even the bad ones, the ones who muttered Christ-killer behind your back, lacked the courage or perhaps the license to take their ignorance any further than that. Most Czechs accorded Jews the status of human beings.

The two of them were comparing notes—football leagues, neighborhoods, taverns—when Socrates reappeared, decked out this time in a black woolen greatcoat. The smoke from his cigar curled up into a hat that looked like a scattering of pelts on top of his head.

"Tell me, monsieur, was your soup satisfactory? Have you adequate blankets for the night?"

"For the night?"

"For your provisional stay with us—during which, please be sure to watch your back."

"Isn't that your job, Boris? You're in charge here. Don't you keep your men in line?"

"He is still a smartass, even after I feed him! Listen, my new Jew, I am tired of being outgunned by your mouth. I command you to shut up."

Karel was happy to comply, albeit with a sarcastic salute and a mock-ceremonious clicking of his heels. He had maintained his mouthy aggressive act only because something of the sort felt necessary. While this crude campsite in no way resembled paradise—he presumed it would soon enough become a hell of its own—he was at this moment closer to cheerful than he had imagined ever being again.

"If you are half as hard on the fucking Germans as you are on me," said Socrates, "this may come round right."

1961

Mr. Barry has some idiosyncratic quarrel with the hardhat, refuses to wear one on site. This is why Bingo Furillo, his steel contractor, gave him the nickname Hardhead. The workmen, all of whom expected Mr. Barry to bristle at this liberty, were surprised to see him dismiss it with a swipe of his hand. Furillo's sunny nature, which was apt to bypass the standard social cautions, apparently defrayed offense as well.

Most days Mr. Barry wears what he—jokingly!—calls his "softhat," a fedora halfway between natty and kitschy, in a busy plaid that cries out for the finishing feather. To Furillo, the hat conjures up the image of a railbird at the racetrack—not that he can picture Barry out at Belmont, cheering his nag to the wire. But Bingo's habit of mind is to see parallels everywhere. Balanced on a girder in his blowing overcoat, Barry had reminded him of a headwaiter surveying his tables. Crouching to eyeball a line, Barry in his compactness and energy suggested a prizefighter, a tough welterweight in his corner. Given all of Mr. Barry's quirks and silences, Bingo has made a game of filling in the blanks.

They all talk about the boss man (his malapropisms, in particular, provide fodder at coffee breaks) but no one on the crew addresses him directly. Only Bingo Furillo—handsome, outgoing, and somewhat authoritative himself—can get away with the occasional joke. No one else will even venture into routine pleasantries; something of an invisible wall in front of Barry and something formidable behind that wall.

Not that anyone can pinpoint what it is. But there is an implied threat, not so much in spite of his small stature as because of it, somehow. A concise, coiled threat.

While he rarely steps outside the hard shell they see each day, Mr. Barry has taken a liking to Ken Attles, one of the hod carriers. He will pop Attles with a friendly fist to the shoulder and kiddingly call him Atlas. Once he struck a body-builder's pose, flexing as he growled the name, "Atlas." They assumed he meant Charles Atlas, the guy who sells muscles on the back cover of comic books, even though Mr. Barry did elaborate the mythic reference: "Carries the world on his shoulders."

"Why Attles?" complained Richie Simpson, the other hod man on the job.

"Why not me?" said Attles, who enjoys the attention, even if it is purely a function of his name. Attles, Atlas.

"Maybe," said Joey Santini, "it's because Attles works twice as hard as you do."

"Yeah and maybe he can't spell and thinks Attles' name really is Atlas."

"And you are the great speller, Rich?"

"Anything you can spell, I can spell better."

"Yeah? Spell this," said Santini, giving him the bent-arm fungoo.

"I'm serious, asshole. Don't mess with me in a spelling bee."

"I'll keep that in mind next time I enroll," said Santini, taking the pencil from behind his ear and jotting down an imaginary note to himself just as Bingo Furillo came strolling over to intercede, clapping sharply to signal the end of break. Bingo's skill set tilted toward volume: no one could clap, whistle, or snap his fingers half as loud.

The next day, when Mr. Barry made his appearance, Richie Simpson paused at the drafting station and flexed for him, shooting him the big grin. Barry waved him away like a mosquito that had floated into his line of sight. No sale, wrong guy. It was Attles he liked.

There is always relief when Mr. Barry concludes his daily visit to the site. Not that he ever cracks the whip or, apart from the way he went after Fred Knuble, calls anyone out. Never disciplines a slacker directly. There is just something oppressive that goes beyond his status as the big boss, a challenge in his stance. He has a way of staring at the form-work taking shape as though the intensity of his gaze can get it knocked together in half the time.

Then there is his unflappability. One day he was standing on the utility platform when a number six rivet, straight from the hopper and glowing hot, fell right at his feet. Barry's attention was fixed on a girt spinning on the crane hook and it never wavered from that piece as it was being positioned, aligned, and secured. Or never wavered apart from the millisecond he took to kick the red hot rivet ("Soccer style," Santini pointed out later, "with the instep") off the plywood decking and down onto the concrete slab below.

And there was the business with Knuble. As exceptional in its way as Mr. Barry's liking for Ken Attles, his dislike of Fred Knuble went a ways toward explaining the crew's discomfort. They had been on the job two weeks, feeling safely anonymous, when Mr. Barry singled Freddie out and instructed Bingo to fire him.

Bingo laughed in his good-natured way. "For what?" he said, spreading his arms.

"I didn't say for what. I said tell him. He is gone."

Later there would be speculation this was a standard trick in Barry's kit bag—fire one guy irrationally on every job just to put the fear of God into everyone else. His M.O., so to speak. But that was a theory that got batted around after the fact. On the day he axed Knuble, no one even ventured a guess.

"Mr. Barry, you gotta give me a reason," said Furillo. "I mean Freddie's a good man. Good worker."

"Tell him then peremptory challenge."

Furillo drew back in genuine astonishment. This was a rich one. Beyond the sheer eccentricity of the concept itself—a subtlety of American jurisprudence that you would only know from the movies, or maybe if you caught jury duty—there was the fact that Barry had the phrase at his fingertips. The little gent could definitely surprise you.

"Boss, you are a funny one."

"No joke," said Carl Barry, drawing an imaginary blade across his throat to reiterate Freddie Knuble's job status. Furillo was forced to move his man to smaller jobs uptown for the duration.

It was all of a piece, in a way, as Bingo came to see that night, when he recounted the incident to his wife. Mr. Barry liked Ken Attles and he disliked Fred Knuble, in each case for no reason. Or no reason anyone could discern.

"In that case," concluded Essie Furillo, "I guess it's a good thing he likes you."

1944

They had a fresh source in the capital, with access to the Praha-Wroclaw timetable. The source had no name, of course, and the information no known provenance. Procedure was to view it as a baited trap.

So they bided their time, twice allowing the train to run unmolested. Only then did they lay plans to strike the "Christmas delivery," as Socrates called it, though by then it was January. So much patience had gone into what seemed a pittance: blow up a section of track, disable a few cars if they were lucky, wreak a bit of havoc. If their luck was really running, they might hijack food supplies, clothing, and weapons.

To Karel the war felt so big and their actions so small. Nor was he the only one desperate to slay bigger dragons. But this was what they could do, Socrates counseled. It was *all* they could do, if indeed they could do it. That the Nazis were sending units after them in the forest should provide corroboration that such pittances were worth the effort.

Occasionally there was heartening news from Moscow. At Novogrudek, in Belarus, hundreds of men and women had come through a tunnel; many had survived and reached the Russian lines. Needless to add, many had not. Socrates insisted that each man freed was equivalent to three men—the one set free was also one more not murdered and one more soldier in the battle. He was keeping score, as though they were engaged in a football match. "Everything is relative" was his watchword.

Karel could concede that such drops in the bucket gained significance by comparison with a dry bucket. The news from Novogrudek was "good" news. Relatively speaking, it was wonderful news. It was just that he had yet to experience the emotion which Ladislaw described as a burst of childlike joy which came whenever one of their ventures met with success. The Wroclaw train would be Karel's first field assignment.

To date, he had served as a wood-gatherer and a watchman. Biding time and abiding cold nights had constituted the brigade's whole program. His tasks were presented as positives, almost as achievements, but Karel had difficulty seeing it that way and whenever he aimed at striking a positive note, an unintended negative inevitably escaped him. Nothing new there.

To guard against this happening before the raid, he had taken one of his vows of silence. He was silent that morning as they toasted "the nations represented" over beech-nut coffee and silent that night when they toasted with hard cider the prospect of a derailment.

The night, which began mild and stilly, changed dramatically while they slept. The wind rose, the mercury fell, and they woke to ankle-deep snow. The Wroclaw train might well be cancelled or it might run simply because the Germans hated to change a plan. If it ran, said Socrates, "We should not expect it to come off like Swiss clockwork."

"It is pretty," Ladislaw pointed out, a comment that might be expected from the self-appointed poet-in-residence. He had introduced himself to Karel that way: poet-in-residence and freedom-fighter extraordinaire. "It's a fairy tale snow."

"Fairy tales?" said Karel, whose toes were cold and whose self-imposed silence was slipping a bit with the prospect of a delay. "Sometimes, in those stories, the ogre eats the child."

"Your momma should never have read you that one. We read only the stories that are bathed in soft sunshine and end in joyful reunion."

"Like The Novogrudek Two Hundred," said Jaroslav Heyduk.

"Jaro, I cannot believe the way your mind works. Or fails to work."

"We know how yours works," said Big Boris, passing by their circle. "Socrates" had become Big Boris to the Czechs ever since a second Russian "officer" had arrived in camp. The new man, Kharlamov, immediately became Little Boris.

"The Novogrudek Two Hundred?" said Karel. "What about the Novogrudek Ten Thousand? And what about the ones who died in the tunnel? Of course, we know from Boris the Big—excuse me, from Socrates—that all things are relative."

"All relative," nodded the general as he drifted out of earshot.

"Still, Karel, it's true," said the poet-in-residence. "Look at us. We are what, the Budzow Twenty-eight? You take what you have and you make from it what you can."

"And what we have is next to nothing."

"To me it's something," said Jaroslav.

"To me," said Ladislaw, "it seems the only thing."

"Something, nothing," said Karel, at a loss how to keep the unintended negative notes from flowering into full-blown chords.

"In the end it will be the same thing. Of the two hundred, there will be maybe ten standing this time next year. Of the twenty-eight, maybe three of us."

"But that's ten. And that's three. It's different from nothing—especially if you happen to be one of the three."

"You win, Jaro. I'm sure your calculations are more precise. It's just a Hobson's Choice, that's all I am saying. It's a Hobson's Universe now."

"Hobson Who?" said Smolinski, who had been a baker in Opole.

"No choice at all, is what he means," said Ladislaw. "But then he is Bondy, Prince of Darkness. I say there is real choice, every minute. I say every breath we draw is both a privilege and an opportunity."

"I agree with you," said Karel, "so long as it counts as a privilege to freeze in the woods and an opportunity to attempt the murder of strangers. Because this is what the Nazis have left us for choices. Everyone in the world is out hoping to murder a few strangers, when they should be drinking beer, holding their wives, playing with their children."

"It is good to see you so cheerful, oh Prince. Let us pray for good news from the front more often."

"He doesn't mean it," said Jaroslav, clamping Karel's shoulder.

"No? Just playing the devil's advocate?"

They all turned and saw that the speaker was Little Boris, who had a way of lurking on the shrouded fringes of the camp, then throwing cold water on the conversation. Jaro walked Karel away from the fire. With a twig he had brushed through the flames, he lit one of his precious few cigarettes and granted Karel first draw.

"We'll have a nice smoke together and remain patient a few hours longer. Then, if luck is with us, we will go murder a few strangers on the Wroclaw train. Maybe take some guns from them into the bargain. Some decent blankets and a crate of apples, yes?"

"God willing!" replied Karel, with that saturnine twist of a smile.

As they devoured the cigarette, they looked back at the clearing: at the "roof" of pine boughs and mildewed canvas, the walls of packed snow, the ragged men sprawled around a damped-down fire. No one was talking anymore. Big Boris, coat collar drawn tight to his thick neck, ice chips flecking his beard, had fallen asleep standing up in the swirl of snow.

1961

His is a greatly reduced Judaism, an adulterated product. He does not read Hebrew to any useful extent. Today, at his Bar-Mitzvah, Lewis will merely give voice to syllabic transliterations, scratched onto his pages as interlinear gibberish. In his case, Reform Judaism is really Ersatz Judaism and the same is true for most of the boys who have been preparing for this day with Schmuel Katz. They are doing it for their parents.

Not that Lewis' parents are terribly observant, themselves. Basically, they were habituated to the synagogue and never examine their motives for continuing to attend. To them, it is simply the correct thing to do. To their son, who has never accepted the notion of God, the hours spent reciting ancient irrelevant texts have been a waste of precious Saturday mornings.

Once it ceases to impose upon him—from this day forward, in fact—Lewis will have no quarrel with Judaism. At least as practiced here in Connecticut, by successful, educated Reform Jews, it consists largely of well-intentioned like-minded people gathering socially and helping to fund a number of worthy charities. Why quarrel with that? At the same time, he will see no point in going to Temple.

His uncle is the one who likes to quarrel, so persistently and vociferously that Lewis did not expect to see him in the congregation. He was sure Carl would skip the service, steer clear of the synagogue, and then show up at the house in the afternoon. Yet there he is in the front row, glowing like the one live coal in a bed of black char, and Lewis' surprise is not entirely pleasant. It is almost embarrassing to be (or worse, pretend to be) observant in Uncle Carl's presence.

"You never went?"

"Of course I went."

"When you were a kid."

"And after."

"You stopped because you became Agnostic?"

"Who says that?"

"I'm just asking, Uncle Carl, no one said it. Is that your religion now?"

"No, I am still a Jew. Jewish religion."

"My father says he's an Agnostic."

"Not me."

"Dad says it's the smart thing to be. Agnostic. Because it means you're smart enough to know what you don't know."

"Kenny is a very smart man, Lewis. But this is not the smartest thing he ever said."

"What do you mean?"

"I mean that sometimes you can know a thing. Sometimes you must know it."

"But how can you know—I mean really know—that there isn't God?"

"I will tell you how!"

Up on the stage with six other boys (*men*, allegedly, an hour from now), five heads of dark hair alongside Danny the K's pinkish-orange Brillo pad, Lewis recalls that conversation word for word and recalls grasping that Carl's emphatic "I will tell you how" (pronounced, of course, I *vill* tell you) was always code for I will *not* tell you. His way of saying the matter at hand was too obvious to require any telling.

"So you are Agnostic, like your father?"

"Not necessarily."

"Listen. If you know God, you are a religious. If you don't know God, an atheist. And if you don't know what you don't know, then an Agnostic. This is how it lines up."

"But I honestly don't know, Uncle Carl."

"Okay, relax, don't worry. You don't want to be called Agnostic, I won't call you one."

Lewis feels as if he has spent two solid hours doing nothing but thanking people for coming. Part of the deal, simple good manners, especially as they have all come bearing gifts. That has been his other activity, pocketing dozens of generous checks. A lot of soft handshakes with checks tucked inside, many of them from relatives he barely recognizes and who understandably summon only the short stock phrases of congratulation. Uncle Carl is a different case with his envelope of cash and some real conversation.

"I wondered if you'd come."

"Lewis, be serious. How could you wonder this?"

"This morning, I mean. I thought you never went to Temple. Never went near a Temple. Since the War. That's what you said."

"Since before that, in fact. But I am not here for God, bubula, I am here for you. You can make this distinction, no?"

"I can, Uncle Carl," says Lewis, and as they embrace, he is fairly sure they are each recalling a specific conversation. Someone on television had gone to Heaven, a character in a show, and Carl inquired whether his nephew believed in this Afterlife of which they all spoke so assuredly.

"Or are you still Agnostic?"

"Not about Heaven. I don't think it's possible there's a Heaven or a Hell."

"Hard enough believing in life, forget Afterlife? Unless Afterlife is what I have been living all these years!"

Lewis was confused, briefly, not getting what must be a joke. Then he was afraid he did get it and it might not be a joke exactly.

"You see it? That I am alive so long after my life was ended. But you know, Lewis, that at the bottom this is a distinction without a difference."

The phrase tickled Lewis. He loved the way Carl could mangle an expression like "at the bottom" and follow it up with an almost scholarly usage. It was a mystery why his mother and his aunt found Carl's English lacking. His English seemed vivid, concise, and *flexible*—he could dress it up or dress it down to suit an occasion. He had overheard Carl telling a city official to "take a flying fuck at a rolling doughnut" and in the next breath tell his secretary Rose he would be "delayed indefinitely" as the two of them headed out to lunch. For a man who spoke Czech, Russian, Polish—plus German he would only reluctantly admit to—that seemed a fair range of English to command.

"So tell me," says Carl. "It feels good, being a man?"

"Actually, it feels completely weird. I hope everyone goes home soon, so I can stop smiling."

"No, bubula, you keep smiling. I will send them home."

1944

The entire universe had frozen overnight. Even the fire froze. Doused with fresh snow just before dawn, it now showed a delicate nest of white ice crystals, through which shadowed the black coals. Karel's toes felt like stubs of ice attached to his feet.

Though everyone woke chilled and miserable, they were soon energized by the prospect of action. General Kharlamov, alias Little Boris, had been scouting the village of Dobrice for weeks and they huddled to absorb the particulars of his report. A small regiment of two dozen soldiers were posted there. They took supper together at 5, drank at the inn until 10, and by 11 were chambered in four adjoining houses along the main street. Each night, the same two sentinels were positioned at opposite ends of the town. One of them, guided by the tolling of the church bells, would slip into the inn hourly and spend two minutes getting warm. His counterpart could have been a statue, apart from one brief excursion into the alleyway between church and vestry to urinate. That alley dead-ended at a small stone building where supplies were stored.

The plan was simple. The instant Hans the First stepped indoors to warm himself, Little Boris himself would take Hans the Second by surprise, drop him with his much-touted club to the mouth method, and drag him into the alleyway. The three Czechs would do as much for Hans I when he emerged from the inn. Ladislaw and Imre, the Gypsy, each toting sizable canvas bags, would already be moving toward the storage shed to procure whatever was loose and useful. "Not because I am skilled as thief," the Gypsy had clarified upon receiving his assignment, "because I am quickest."

It would just be the six of them on this mission, so they wanted no part of an engagement. Little Boris stressed over and over that no shots be fired. Reminded everyone five times that "speed and silence are our friends." One rifle report from either side would compromise the operation, not to mention get them killed. "Let us insure the Germans get their beauty rest. We can make more noise at a later date."

But he knew there might be shots. Lack of discipline, necessity, stupidity, panic: there were always the vagaries. And silence after midnight was always a relative matter, especially where certain dogs were known to be light sleepers.

Little Boris finished the briefing with one final mention of their good friends speed and silence, then slipped inside the tent where Big Boris was studying the map and smoking. They had the only tent, a pot of coals going inside to keep it warm, and they had the lion's share of cigarettes.

"It's a hierarchy," said Karel, when Imre started grumbling about the injustice. "We are a society of sorts, so naturally there must be a hierarchy. With Borises at the top."

"A pecking order," said Vilem, the third Czech and a Moravian chicken farmer by trade. The lighthearted remark, presumably in honor of his beloved chickens, was a departure from his incessant humorless cries for violent action.

"A smoking order," countered Jaroslav. "Haves and have-nots. Do you think we should protest and begin fighting amongst ourselves? That would make us a truer society."

"But a less successful army."

"All I am saying," Imre persisted, "is that the great Russian idea is a pile of shit. All this equality and brotherhood is just propaganda with a Russian accent."

"Besides all that, how hard would it be to hand us each a few cigarettes?" This was Smolinski, weighing in. Smolinski, who did not care a fig for politics, would happily kill for a packet of cigarettes.

"Maybe after the raid. Maybe there will be cases of good Turkish cigarettes in Dobrice."

"If so," said Ladislaw, "we will for once be glad the Nazi war effort is well funded."

"We fund it, Lado," said Karel. "From our banks and our pockets, but also with our hair and our teeth. Not just the Jews, my friend, you Poles as well."

"We are both kind and generous peoples," said Lado, his irony more delicately seasoned than Karel's boilerplate sarcasm.

"I say we stage a trial run right now," said Smolinski. "A raid on the Borises, as practice for the operation."

"But if we knock both Borises over the head, who will lead us into battle? No, Smolo, better you should stay and make us a nice soup. We will bring you back some smokes."

Simple though it might have been, the plan broke down early on when Hans I abandoned precedent and remained outside hour after hour. Was this just the vagaries, or had the Nazis been forewarned?

Forced to reconsider the entire action, Little Boris also had to consider his fighters' state of mind. They were fed up with preparation, and with waiting. Vilem had for weeks been pushing to engage the Nazis at once, and to hell with Boris' "opportune moments." Why should he have to skulk around freezing his ass while the Nazis slept under warm Afghans they had taken, he kept insisting, from his sister's shop?

An outlier not so long ago, the chicken farmer was by now merely the most virulent spokesman for a silent momentum flowing through the entire brigade and Little Boris respected this momentum. Though it might make more sense to retrench, he chose to go forward with a freshly devised plan.

So it was that around four in the morning Ladislaw emerged quite openly on the road and strolled casually toward the inn. When the sentry raised his rifle and issued the predictable command to halt, Lado complied cheerfully, stumbling a bit for show and giggling as if drunk. Altogether unthreatening in his peasant rags, he acted the harmless fool, just a soused Pole on a Polish roadway.

As both sentries moved in on him, Lado even laced his hands behind his back as though to simplify their binding him. Here was helpless, harmless, Good Citizen Lado. The security firm of Hans and Hans prodded him with rifles and pressed him to the ground with great amusement.

"But why this, my good friends?" Lado slurred in peasant Polish, feigning bafflement as they prodded him with their feet. He took his head between his palms as though stricken. As they bent over him, laughing, the sentries were swarmed and smashed in the mouth with clubs. Little Boris swore by this strategy for promoting his beloved silence and with good reason, as it turned out. Unconscious, gagged, the hapless guards were quickly dragged behind the church and deposited by the graveyard gate.

Little Boris dared to be pleased—so far so good—before he saw lanterns flaring in half a dozen windows and knew the Nazis were already alerted and mobilizing. Moving past the windows, they looked harmless at first, like cartoon ghosts in their baggy gray woolens. All too soon, though, the ferocious animal clamor of their shouts was spilling into the narrow street and the partisans were already in retreat as reams of gunfire from windows and rooftops tore the air to shreds.

The operation was not a wholesale failure. Imre was not merely quick, he was damned efficient. Working solo for all of two minutes, he managed to come away with sacks of bread and cheese, cartons of cigarettes, boxes of invaluable wooden matches. The Czechs had relieved each sentry of a Luger PO-8 pistol, old but serviceable, and a Walther rifle with full magazine. And despite the deafening clatter and dense veils of smoke they produced, the groggy Germans had not managed to hit anyone scrambling out of the dark village.

On the other side of the ledger, the fighters had lost any hope of staying on at this well-established base. They would have to move deeper into the forest, immediately, and their tracks would make an easy map to follow in the soft new snow.

Or so they feared until it began snowing again as they started the bivouac. It would snow steadily for the next six hours, which made a cold hell of traveling through the trees yet at the same time spackled over their tracks almost step by step.

"We should never have fled, we should have stayed and fought them," Vilem kept muttering as they marched. "We should have prevailed or died, just as God wills."

"Don't worry," Karel assured him, mildly amused three hours into their journey to think of the relief death would bring to his toes. "It will come to that, Vilem. We will do that—fight and die. Your God will grant this wish of yours soon enough."

1963

The developer had barely acknowledged their arrival with that quick flag of a hand. Presumably it was a hello, though they agreed it felt more like a get lost. Now Harry Ballantyne and Arnold Spiller await what Spiller calls their weekly "audience" with the man. Given that they will be renting 10,000 square feet of the building on a ten year lease, Spiller thinks they rate more than the five minutes their weekly meeting rarely exceeds. Ballantyne is quick to point out there is never much to discuss. If Carl Barry is not wasting his own time, he is not wasting theirs either.

At the moment, Barry is listening closely to his tall, affable general contractor—Barilla, is it?—and Barilla's voice, floating above the background noise of street and site, is all they can hear. From this distance, the contractor's presentation looks rather dramatic. He towers over Barry, his voice cuts through the din, his gestures are broad and emphatic. But their attention goes to the smaller man. Virtually motionless, always so sparing with his words, Barry is somehow the more compelling sight. Of course he will be their landlord long after Barilla and his workmen are gone.

"What is it about the guy?" says Ballantyne. "What makes him tick?"

"Tick? Like a time bomb, you mean?"

"I didn't mean that, no."

"But doesn't he look that way? As if you say the wrong thing and he might just explode? He looks that way to me. *Dangerous.*"

"Competent is the word that comes to me, Arnie. The guy gets it done. The way it looks right now, we'll be in there a month early. Any other developer down here and you know occupancy would come in six months behind. I call that somewhere between competent and downright magical."

"Competent as a fringe benefit of dangerous, maybe. Not lightly would you get in the way of that guy's permit process."

"You really think he might explode in some zoning inspector's office? I don't see it, Arnold, I really don't. Barry strikes me more as a Mighty Mouse—small but on the ball. He can be a little gruff, I'll grant you, but no one says he's mobbed up."

"I'm not saying he is. Just this: have you ever once seen him laugh?"

"That could be the language. They say that humor is the hardest part of getting a new language down. But what the hell, we're not looking for comedy from him, are we?"

Carl Barry is walking their way now, his gait faintly yet persistently irregular, a bit of a roll to it, which Spiller likened last time to a gunslinger's approach, six-shooter on his hip. Ballantyne just shook his head and speculated, a good deal less colorfully, that perhaps Barry had sprained an ankle.

More intriguing to him is that Barry's face is so hard to read. Opaque, or perhaps *expressionless*, would be his word for what Spiller sees as threatening. There are times, Harry Ballantyne concedes, when the absence of overt good will can look like ill will. Face it, in a world where backslapping and phony bonhomie constitute the coin of the realm, the absence of those elements can make a relationship less cozy. But Barry's poker face piques his interest. Spiller, by contrast, always feels he is about to be asked to make a concession—and worse, always feels he is about to oblige.

"Gentlemen," says Barry, bowing slightly. The gesture, rendered in tight harmony with the salutation, comprises Barry's entire vocabulary of backslapping.

"Carl. Good to see you," says Ballantyne.

"Yes," says Spiller. "Things still looking good?"

"Very good."

"Well that's good to hear," says Spiller, inarticulately, almost helplessly. Good, good, everything good. He can't shake the sense that he owes this man something, some debt that is escaping his recall, and though at first he takes this for a nervous response to Barry's tricky personality, it does come back to him that a check is due. A check Arnold Spiller was hoping to hold back for a week or so, yet which he finds himself writing here in the lot, using his raised leg for a table, fighting the windblown dust.

Maybe he can ask Barry to hang on to it a while, not deposit it straightaway. Without a few days grace, Spiller will be scrambling to cover the check. But Barry has already taken it and without a word of acknowledgement—without even a glance at the check—folded it and slipped it into his jacket pocket. The exchange is already history, the subject is closed. Spiller will have to scramble.

The three of them turn toward the structure, caged on all sides by staging, as masons apply the brick cladding. Right now the high-rise appears half-dressed, as though wearing a long brick skirt, hemmed at the glassed-in ground level.

"Takes them more time to stage it than mason it up," says Barry, just possibly smiling as he renders a remark which for him is downright garrulous. Ballantyne regards the man (jacket now slung over his arm, the sleeves of his blue shirt rolled up) and sees in his quick resolute movements more of a laborer than a businessman. He entertains a flashing image of Barry springing up onto the scaffold, impatiently elbowing the masons aside, and beginning to slather and set bricks. *Competently.*

"Take no prisoners," says Spiller, as moments later they watch Barry ducking into his car, a white Lincoln convertible with a black top, parked just inside the chain link gate.

"You still on that kick?"

"They say he was in the War."

"I'm sure he was. Who wasn't in the War? I was. You were."

"I mean from over there, in Europe."

"You don't mean to imply he was a Nazi?"

"No, no, not that at all. Just that maybe it went hard on him."

"Well let's hope he frightened the Germans as much as he does you! All five-foot-five of him."

"You think he's that tall, Harry?"

"Something like that. Whatever Napoleon was."

1944

The games they played to distract themselves often took on a grim cast, even the card games. Canasta was played for points: high man got to live another day, low man got the gas.

Grimmest by far was the story-swapping game of Evil. Each of them would relate the most unspeakable horror he had witnessed or heard. The "winning" entry would be that tale which crystallized evil most vividly. This was nothing less than a new art form, a *genre*, according to poet-in-residence Ladislaw Rozek, its creator.

According to Karel Bondy, it was a new form of masochism and he refused to participate. Which is not to say he could avoid hearing Gildenman's Tale.

Isaac Gildenman, with his long face and a façade of frozen snot constant in his auburn moustache, had not a sliver of imagination, so while others might embellish in order to "win" the game, they knew Gildenman would be telling the literal truth.

"The child was perhaps two. Old enough, you must understand, to speak and think. And these Nazis were not even drunk. Not even that much to excuse them."

"*Einsatzgruppen*?" said Smolinski. "They were drunk on blood."

"In broad daylight, without shame, one of them takes the child in his arms—he dares to embrace the child, cradle her in his arms, before tossing her into the air. Whereupon the other one shoots her to death in mid-air like a game bird."

"Good God."

Karel started at the phrase, coming on the heels of the account they have just heard. Good God? How could such a phrase escape anyone's lips, least of all at such a moment? "Have you finished?" he said.

"I will never forgive myself for seeing this," said Gildenman. "The look of pride on the fat one's face as he turns to the mother—the mother of a tiny child he has just murdered—and assures her his pal was provincial champion, shooting skeet. 'Three years running, was it, Klaus?'"

"And no doubt Klaus blows smoke off his rifle like a true hero."

"What, Bondy, you don't believe me? You think this never happened?"

"I think this game is over and you are the winner. Congratulations."

"Hold on," said Ladislaw. "Without doubt, this is a strong entry, but what about Liowicki? I say it merits a vote."

Liowicki's Tale had begun with a woman regaining consciousness in a pit piled high with corpses, surprised to discover she is not a corpse herself. After all, she was gassed in a van with the others and the last thing she recalled was the sensation of her brain shutting down. Nauseous from the gas in her lungs and bloodstream, she crawls over bodies, over arms and legs and heads, until she finds herself crawling over her husband. His eyes were fixed like the eyes on a doll, she said, and his teeth were bared like those of a poisoned rat.

"He made up too much of it," said Henryk. "How the hell could he know what she thought or said? He admits he had the story secondhand."

"Exactly," said Smolinksi. "A little too much embroidery was performed."

"The doll's eyes and the rat's teeth? In my business," said Ladislaw, "this is called evocative description. Do we doubt the story is true?"

Who could doubt it, when everyone knew such scenes were commonplace. In a way, it was impossible to exaggerate. Ivan Pollak had told Karel of the trusty who was ordered to remove the gold from his own wife's teeth and who, when he pleaded for a bullet instead, was tortured until he returned to work.

"Let's simply agree we have two winners," said Karel. "Co-champions. So we can stop and go to sleep. Can we do that, Lado?"

"We don't have to listen to the Jew," said Henryk.

"No, it's okay," said Ladislaw. "It's enough. Tomorrow we can play my other game, the game of Good, and Karel can return to his normal cheerful demeanor. You see? Good and Evil."

"We are all very cheerful, Lado. After all, God is good."

"God is neutral. To quote, 'Did He who made the lamb make thee?'"

"I know a bit of Blake, Lado, and I am quite sure his meaning was otherwise. Not that God is neutral, but that clearly there can be no God."

"Quite sure, are you, Karel? Is there ever a time when you are not quite sure?"

Karel could not prevent his lips from hinting at a smile. Score one for the Laureate.

Sleep was even more difficult than usual and Karel was "quite sure" he had been awake every minute of the night. The grotesque stories went round and round in his head, the freezing wind kept snapping limbs, and the pain in his toes was so acute it seemed to be seated inside his skull, not at the ends of his feet. But he must have slept at some point, for he had dreamed...

They were on the mossy skid at the old dam site, quite specifically on the Saturday following his general examination. Those were real events, the exam and the celebration, and Karel's state of mind was likewise true to life—he had yet to see his results but felt confident he had qualified. In his opinion, he had been better informed than the faculty members he faced.

Helena kept straying close to the drop-off, whether oblivious to the danger or mischievously attracted to it. Or maybe she craved their undivided attention, as Mila concluded a month earlier when Helena fell in and nearly disappeared under the water. She *had* disappeared, except that Karel got there quickly enough to trail her pale sinking ghost to the bottom. Carried back and deposited on the grass, Helena coughed and then began wailing. Happily, she did not seem to understand what could have happened.

Or unhappily. For here she was right back at it, skimming the rim of the miniature palisade like a wire-walker, still oblivious to the risks. Karel was watching—he would never fail to watch, not even in a dream, apparently—yet somehow he was simultaneously watching Mila and stroking her taut slick belly. From beneath that round surface Lucie was stretching her mother's skin to the same silken texture it had achieved twice before. "You must always be pregnant, my love," said Karel, "and have this perfect skin forever."

Mila smiled and in her shy way told him that after October he would be putting up with imperfect skin forever. She had wished for two children, Karel for four. Before he could argue against the familiar compromise, a mere three children, they were swimming, just the two of them. Dreamwork had caused the children to vanish.

Mila swam away face down—bottoms up!—her hair spread wide over the surface. She glided away effortlessly, without kicking or stroking, as though propelled by a secret motor. Soon Karel gave up trying to catch her and began to laugh, laughing so richly he could feel his entire body shaking...

The next thing he knew, Jaroslav was shaking him awake. "Quiet down, man. You are shouting."

"Shouting? I haven't so much as sneezed the whole damn night."

"You have been rolling back and forth and shouting. Some sort of wild dream—"

"Shit," said Karel, raising up on his elbows. "It's snowing again."

"That's no dream, man. That's real."

Snow had been a regular occurrence, if not an inevitability, this whole month. Karel was surprised by the bristling snowflakes hitting his face only because part of him was still swimming in the dreamed river, in a sunny free Czechoslovakia.

"Fucking snow," he said. "Fucking wind. Fucking beech-nut coffee."

"Now that's the Bondy I know! Jolly as ever. I take it this was a bad dream?"

"It was a beautiful dream, Jaro. Reality is the bad dream."

"Come on, none of that. Let's stay jolly for a while."

Karel could not stay jolly. Awake, he knew he had not saved Helena. He had not saved any of them. Rendered every bit as helpless as the poor soul in Liowicki's grotesque story, he had lost them all. In the bad dream of life, monsters had murdered them. Who takes pride in murdering a beautiful child? Only a monster, or a beast.

And who could worship a God who made the lamb but made the Nazis too?

The geniuses had it wrong. It was not the case that we understand ourselves better when we wring some sort of logic or sense from our dreams. The dream is what does make sense; the dream knows more. It is reality that refuses to be logical.

1965

"So what do you think?" says Bingo Furillo, with his usual air of assuredness. It is less a question than an invitation to celebrate their progress. And why not, when the project looks clean and tight coming down the home stretch?

"I think we have done it," says Carl Barry, cheerfully. "Another monstrosity."

Even after years of working closely with the man, Furillo cannot help assuming at such moments that Barry must be pulling his leg. And maybe he is, in a way. Maybe it's some brand of European humor that gets delivered with a straight face.

"She's a nice piece of perfect, up and down," says Furillo, marking off the storeys with his hand as though polishing each façade with the pass of a magic wand. "What the hell is wrong with it?"

"Besides almost everything?"

Furillo can only laugh, whether Barry is kidding or not. From groundbreak to now, nothing has gone south on them. Hitting the benchmark dates, staying on budget, keeping all the guys going; even the weather Gods have been friendly, assigning any rain to the Sundays. This is the fourth high-rise they have done together, all between 59th and 63rd, and they have yet to catch a single callback. "Done is done and watch 'em run," Bingo likes to say.

Each time out Mr. Barry has been assured of full occupancy months ahead of completion. Christ, he must be getting rich on the strength of these "monstrosities." In any event, Bingo Furillo is doing well for himself. Let the boss complain if he feels a need to complain; that's his prerogative.

Except that Carl Barry has no complaints to make. The plans called for a monstrosity to be built and they have succeeded in building a monstrosity. Such is the formula for success in the United States of America: build cheap, rent expensive. Shops on the street, offices and residential above, services on the roof, money in the bank.

Not that Europe is any different. Construction now is all about efficiency, and efficiency is code for cost control. Even before the War, back when steel replaced stone, the trend was toward velocity. If you wanted beauty, you had better redefine it. As far as Carl was concerned, a world that did not wish for beauty did not deserve it, anyway.

"Listen, Bingo-Bango, it's a good job. It's nice work, up and down."

"The monstrosity is nice? The ugly pile, with everything wrong?"

"Almost everything, is what I said. But yes, exactly, why not?"

Yes exactly why not. Bingo shakes his head yet again at this headstrong developer, this one-of-a-kind guy he has given up attempting to fathom. He likes Mr. Barry without knowing how this is even possible. Who has a clue what goes on in the man's head? No point inquiring, that much is for sure. No way in. He has never asked where Mr. Barry lived before New York, nor asked about his accent. Never asked where exactly he lives now, for that matter, much less ask about the blue numbers tattooed on Barry's forearm. Barry never lets it be personal.

My regards to your wife, Mr. Barry will say, without a shred of evidence there is a wife, unless he knows a wedding ring when he sees one. Barry has never taken the trouble to ask Essie's name, or their children's names. Without exception, everyone he worked with in the past wondered about the nickname—why "Bingo?" Not Mr. Barry. "My regards to your wife" is as personal as he gets.

Once Bingo came close to replying, *Which one*? Trump up a Mormon joke, where he had seven or eight wives at home. Not that Barry necessarily knows from Mormons. So maybe say, *The wife is doing much better thanks, they give her a ten percent chance of making it.* See if he even notices.

Barry does have a wife. Bingo has never seen her, never even heard her voice on the telephone, but Barry will refer to her. My vife likes to shop here. Vife with a 'v.' He has never seen Mr. Barry with the vife, never seen him meet a friend for lunch or drinks, never seen him arrive or depart in anyone's company. The Lone Ranger rides again.

Except for the kid. Now and then, the kid shows up, a nephew of some sort.

"He sails his ship alone," Furillo tells Essie that night at the dinner table.

"Does he seem lonely to you?"

"Lonely? Not really. No."

"Angry?" she says. "Crazy?"

Essie, who has never met the foreign developer, has been listening to Bingo's field reports on him for years. It would be interesting to meet the man personally, but apparently that is out of the question. Invite him over for a meal? Her husband had burst out laughing at the perfectly ordinary suggestion.

"Not exactly angry. More like, I don't know, *fixated*. Dialed in on every detail. He is just way out ahead on all of it—permits, street parking, disposal, orders, shipments. All the stuff we handle together, he's got it so under control I barely have to think about it."

As he is telling her this, it occurs to Furillo he worked harder when he was just the steel sub-contractor than he does now as the general. Mr. Barry takes on so much of the planning and supervision that Bingo sometimes feels redundant, unnecessary, even a little guilty depositing the big checks.

"So that's good. You make good partners."

"You and me, Essie, we're good partners. Me and Mr. Barry are something else. Co-conspirators, maybe. We always hit our marks, we get it done, but it's almost like we're committing a crime."

"Except that crime doesn't pay," she points out, with a sly smile.

"Oh yeah? Says who?"

1944

Morning sun had been extracting clouds of ground fog from the soft snow. The sun was strong enough that the water jugs contained, of all things, water. Even the snot in Gildenman's moustache had thawed.

Meanwhile, arranged on the flat back of a shovel, chunks of squirrel meat were sizzling over the fire. Cheered by these morsels of brightness, energized by a breakfast with morsels of meat, they were roped into playing Ladislaw's other "game," the one he was calling Good. No more of evil: in this contest, only happy endings were permissible. The rare escapes, battles won, Nazi blunders, successful forays from the forest. Before Lado had settled all the rules of the game, however, Vilem Rovensky was demanding the floor for a late entry into the previous night's game of Evil.

"The floor, no less!" exclaimed Lado. "A floor would be lovely indeed."

"Please. It's only one more."

"There is always one more, dear fellow. There are always fifty more."

"Yes, but only one of them is this one."

"No doubt. But I am afraid our moral compass Karel Bondy has declared an end to Evil. Co-champions have been proclaimed, no?"

"Please. Allow me to speak."

Big Boris spat his disgust with these shenanigans, with these bloody foreign *civilians* and their great debates, directly into the fire. He strode to the tent and lifted the flap; like an audience they all watched his arse disappear. When their heads swung back, they turned in unison toward Karel for a ruling, as though this were a court of law—and Bondy the judge!—instead of a mindless way to pass the time. As though it *mattered* what he said, or what they did. Still, his shrug of disgust was taken as a grudging benediction.

Vilem began with his usual disclaimer: "We were not even Jews. You must understand this. Maybe a Jewish-sounding name, Rovensky, but we were none of us Jews!"

Jews or not, they were arrested and Vilem's cousin, also named Vilem, was enlisted by the Nazis as a barber in Majdanek. He could cut hair or be shot where he stood, those were his choices, so Cousin Vilem agreed to cut hair. But this was not Nazi hair, it was Jewish hair. He would be cutting off the hair of women on their way to the gas.

"They needed the hair, after all," said Ladislaw, hoping a little irony might soften the blow he saw coming. "To use for production, of blankets perhaps."

"Doesn't matter for what. He cut the hair. And he knows that every woman whose head he touches will be dead in ten minutes."

"Enough," said Karel.

He was desperate not to picture Milena in a barber's closet, desperate not to fail her yet again. But this time, the men revolted. Even Jaro ("Let him finish") and Ladislaw, who could see that Rovensky was weeping as he waited to proceed. "We should hear him out, Bondy."

Karel leaned over the fire to light a cigarette stub he had been smoking in small installments. He took one deep draught into his lungs and held it there, before extinguishing the stub and placing it back inside his pocket. Then he headed for the boulders at the edge of the encampment, trailed by Rovensky's words: "These women are naked, you understand. Exposed, humiliated, terrified—"

The rest, baffled by the boulders and a warm wind loosening ice on the pine boughs, Karel did not hear.

"*There he is, my cousin, a very sweet young man, and into this room, this terrible trap, now walks his baby sister Daniela. My cousin Dani. None of us even Jews!*"

Perhaps with a dash of the perverse, Big Boris paired them, Vilem and Karel, on the overnight watch. They were issued Italian rifles and five rounds of ammunition each, along with the usual caution against firing a single shot unless assured of complete success. "No misses, no witnesses. And no shooting at each other."

Over the course of four hours, no opportunity to hit or miss presented itself. Both pathways lay undisturbed, no Nazi patrols interrupted the night quiet. Boris' parting caution about "Waffen insomniacs out for a stroll" was just his way of keeping the lookouts from napping on the job.

As they started back to camp, Karel felt a strange state coming over him, an alertness to the sky he had been missing for years. The moon was going down, a three-quarter moon that rode momentarily on a float of rose-tinted clouds. Then the clouds enclosed the moon, draping it briefly in a fabric that soon began to fray and dissipate, leaving behind a child's version, pale white on a pale blue sky.

Vilem was edgy, eager to get back to his bedroll, but Karel stopped them a second time and stood listening to the staggered wail of wolves resounding through the hills.

The sky, the hills, the wolves. It struck him that none of the elements of the unpeopled world could remotely comprehend that the peopled world—the one they hovered over, surrounded, hunted—had gone mad. For the wolves, for every animal on every farm, the world presented exactly as it had ten years ago. The hills had not changed in a thousand years and would not change for a thousand years to come.

They were close to base, with absolute silence no longer required of them, when Vilem stepped into Karel's path and took him by the shoulders. The words he spoke were the first uttered by either of them in the four hours they had just passed together.

"Bondy, forgive me. I don't know why. I felt a need to tell it."

"And so you told it. But did you expect telling would take it off your back?"

"I thought it might."

"Did it work? Did it do the trick?"

"Please don't laugh at me. Of course it didn't work. But—"

"*But*!"

Karel proclaimed the word as if it represented a truth, the only truth, and in a way it did, even when severed from any shred of context. It was a word that would fit into every sentence spoken for the rest of time.

And Vilem Rovensky nodded his assent to the force of this simple conjunction, his understanding of its overarching meaningless impact. "Yes *but*."

Karel threw an armlock around Vilem's neck, in an absolution he knew he had no authority to bestow. Then, for the final 50 meters back to the now-stirring campsite, they resumed their silence.

1970

As demonstrative as Lewis' father has been all day, his uncle Carl Barry seems every bit as pleased and proud. "Believe me, this graduation business is only the beginning," he states grandly, implying that Lewis is destined for greatness.

It is Uncle Carl who organizes the family photograph, in which he stands side by side with his nephew, arms around one another's waists. Lewis is smiling and Carl (though reminded twice to smile and convinced he has done so) is merely wearing his least severe frown. When the three college roommates pose, Carl assigns them positions, like stage players their marks ("little bit this way, yah?") and even assigns them new names: Denny Mosher becomes Kosher, Nikolai Rostov becomes (the presumably generic) Boris.

Kenneth and Alene, though long divorced—their second spouses are also on hand for the occasion—announce that they have thrown in together on Lewis' graduation gift, a round trip ticket to London. He accepts this lavish outlay sheepishly: "I thought you'd be glad to finally *stop* paying."

"You're right. *Now* we stop," says Kenneth, hugging his son. "I'm throwing away my checkbook tomorrow."

Lewis detects a faint sneer on Uncle Carl's face, possibly just his instinctive recoil from the notion of checkbooks. Though he has seen Carl settle many a bill, including substantial sums on construction sites, he has never witnessed him writing a check. Can he really have paid out ten or twenty thousand dollars in cash? Lewis recalls watching one of those transactions with great trepidation, on a wide-open windswept lot; recalls staying poised and ready to round up any million-dollar-bills that threatened to blow away.

So it comes as no surprise when Carl produces the inevitable white envelope. "This is for you," says Carl, stating the obvious. He tries stuffing it into Lewis' jacket pocket and for a moment they struggle comically to make the envelope fit. Ever fearful of his uncle's careless generosity, Lewis knows from the thickness of the packet that the gift is excessive.

"I hope you didn't tell Aunt Clara you just gave away her new kitchen."

"Don't worry," says Carl, pronouncing it vurry. "She will get her kitchen." Pronouncing it vill.

"I don't have to tell you it's ridiculously too much."

"That's correct, you do not. Also you do not have to say thank you."

"Thank you, of course. I'll accept it if you let me buy lunch next time I come to New York."

"You will accept it, period. Buy round trip tickets anywhere. Buy ten tickets, take Kosher and Boris along for a ride. Buy *them* lunch—in Paris, France."

There were 2,000 people milling around as a squadron of blazer-clad undergraduates folded and stacked the chairs. Now, half an hour later, only a few dozen stragglers remain, the slow leavers. Depopulated, the campus landscape reveals itself: manicured grounds that have survived another graduation, a dozen venerable buildings (two of gray granite block, the rest of red brick faded to salmon in the afternoon sun) which define the quadrangle, and the tree-lined footpaths that score the quad in rough diagonals.

"This is a nice place you went," says Carl.

"Nothing but the best for this boy," says Kenneth.

Lewis wishes everyone would stop trying to say the right things and just leave. Let him be with his friends, and with Catherine. At the same time, he does want them to enjoy the day, even glory in the moment if they must. His parents, and his aunt—Uncle Carl too, for that matter—are all college graduates. In fact, he realizes, they all went beyond that to higher degrees. So did Uncle Jules, sadly missing today, dead a year ago at 46. But for some reason, they are acting as if this is one of those classic deals where he is the first in the family to go. As if he is a paragon, jumping up a social class or two, for *them* somehow.

"You are taller than your father!" says Alene, as the father-son photograph is posed. Though this can hardly be a revelation, she has not seen them standing together in years. "When did that happen?"

"Today! When he graduated," says Kenneth good-naturedly, though it happened years earlier. Lewis can't remember exactly when. After all, it was expected, it played out according to formula long established: you outgrow your dad.

He did remember outgrowing his uncle. Carl was a short man, more certain to be surpassed, but there is no convention with regard to uncles, some of whom are not even blood relations. Nor could you measure this particular uncle with a conventional yardstick. There is a novel called *Little Big Man*, which Lewis keeps meaning to read, mainly because it comes so highly recommended by friends. From the first time he heard the title, though, it summoned an image of Uncle Carl. *Little Big Man* might sound better, but *big little man* was a shade more accurate.

Finally alone with Catherine in a booth at Toomey House, Lewis shuffles the stack of bills. There are 25 of them—25 "portraits of Franklin," Uncle Carl's denomination of choice. "It's almost enough money to live on for a year," says Catherine.

"To hell with graduate school!" says Lewis.

Though she knows he is not being serious, Catherine does clarify: "He wants you to use it for travel. In the summer. Before you start school."

"He wants you to travel with me."

"The way I heard it, he wants you to have lunch with Denny and Nik, in Paris, France."

"Not Paris, Texas?"

"No, he was very clear on that. But it's your money now."

"Our money. You're graduating too."

"Not until next week. And I'll only have two measly parents, not six."

"Poor dear. You're practically an orphan."

"I know. And my present will probably be some high quality

pots and pans. Maybe a big fat cookbook to go with them."

"It won't be that bad. They know who you are."

"I'm joking. But it won't be money. We don't do that. Which is fine."

"It would have been fine with me too," says Lewis.

1944

Though they were inclined to believe him, they were still holding the farmer who had brought the information. That he had traveled far, that they had since confirmed the existence of the freshly limed pit, proved nothing. The pit might be meant for them.

Little Boris went with him the first time. A day later, ten of them set up a rude base about a kilometer from the excavation and a sniper's nest on the densely forested hillside directly above it. There they waited, anxious to learn what would unfold, unsure what they could do to impact it.

The only knowledge gained in the last hour was that Big Boris had gas. This was hardly news and each time he unleashed one of his spectacular farts they struggled to suppress their laughter. Each time, in turn, Boris would chop the air violently to cut short the commotion. In between the volleys of bad air, they fell so quiet that the wind drowned out their breathing.

The change that came began as a murmur, like the hum of a beehive, punctuated now and then by the unmistakable stabbing commands, *Los Schell! Los Schell!* The hum began to sort itself into voices, the murmurs gave way to moans and a few piercing arias, before the women, paraded side by side in pairs, emerged into the clearing. Forced to walk naked in the raw morning, they were bent over, clutching themselves in a futile attempt at modesty, warmth, or safety. The gingerly steps they took, on the cold bare bones of their feet, shot pain to their faces.

Their heads had been shaved, emphasizing the ghostly pallor of their skin. Only the minimal vestiges of femininity—the dark thatch of pubic hair, the wine-colored nipples—interrupted the dead white of each woman's body. Despite everything he had witnessed at Auschwitz-Birkenau, Karel was sickened by this demonic manifestation of cruelty and maddened at having to countenance it. In minutes, these women might all be slaughtered, yet Boris kept chopping the air, restraining them. *Not yet.*

Then suddenly, bombastically, he broke wind again, an intolerable absurdity at the precise moment when all hell broke loose below. One of the women had lunged at a soldier, shoving his gun aside and raking his face with her fingers. Whoever shot her shot the soldier as well, accidentally. His face registered surprise, whether at his own death or the fact she was swiping at him one last time as they fell. His mouth spouted blood. Her wounds appeared as an outbreak of red berries on her back.

As if a sluice gate had lifted, the women came swarming forward, headlong into a fusillade. They fell in clusters, as gunshots reverberated around the small glen. Another shooter was hit by friendly fire, his hand flying to his neck in horror as he spun to the ground.

Now, motioned Boris at last, and for a time they enjoyed a luxury, a rare military advantage, with the steady blasting of Nazi guns giving cover to their own salvos from the hilltop. All ten of them were firing away and half a dozen Germans were hit before anyone grasped they were under attack. The scene unfolding was surreal, for here was wholesale slaughter, so many human lives ending suddenly, and the resulting tangle of bodies did not discriminate between the naked Jewish women and Germans so heavily clothed they might have been polar explorers. It was obscene the way they fell together, intertwined and overlapping.

Once the Nazis cottoned on to the fact they were being targeted they charged straight up the hill, shrieking like hyenas and strafing the trees with wild machine-gunfire. Again they looked almost comical, a troupe of circus clowns slipping and stumbling as they tried to advance, except there was nothing comical about the bullet that caught Jaroslav in the shoulder, or the flurry ripping through the water jug. In the confusion, Karel thought he saw Smolinski go down.

It was too late to retreat so the fighters stayed low, holding their ground and returning fire. Karel doubted he could have run in any case as a new pain, like a cold steel needle pushing into a nerve, shot through his ankle. He was sure he too had been hit, even surer they were finally going to die, all of them.

But then, in another pantomime, another bizarre dance turn that might have been amusing absent their hellish intentions, the Germans stopped in their tracks. They had seen women rising from the pile, seen the undead and the partly dead separating themselves from the truly dead, and some of these women were fleeing into the trees. As if collectively recalling the order of the day, the assignment with which they had been entrusted, to kill these women, the Germans began scuttling back down the hill.

They made lovely targets and Big Boris, no doubt delighted with the score he would be keeping, yelled empty all guns. To breathe a sigh of relief and then hold fast on the hill taking potshots was a stroke of luck for the partisans, yet even as they stood and fired, Karel felt it was also shameful. The entire German company was crowding into the forest in pursuit of the women. If they did not in turn pursue the Germans, there was little doubt the pit would be filled with corpses by nightfall.

He was not the only one who considered disregarding the order to draw back—looks were exchanged—but no one acted. They had taken casualties. Smolo and Liowicki were dead, Jaro was wounded, and Karel was convinced his own injury would make any such mutiny futile.

Then he stood again and found the pain was gone. It may have been nothing more than a cramp or a pinched nerve, something silly, albeit serious enough to compound his shame. When he had no trouble keeping up with the others as they retreated, he accused himself of imagining a wound out of fear or confusion. Weakness.

No one spoke. They cleaned the guns, inventoried ammunition, washed up, boiled the soup. They dug two shallow graves. Drained by terror and by anger, traumatized by what they had witnessed and by the losses they had absorbed, they would nonetheless need to muster for another hard push before dawn. They had left a trail of blood no dog could miss and a trail of sweat that was not the sweet by-product of healthy athletic endeavor. As Little Boris put it, it was time to go shopping for new real estate.

They drank the last of the brandy and listened for the dogs. If they came, they came. Right now they were too shocked to think clearly; possibly they were so far beyond shock that clear thought no longer existed for them. Some were struck dumb by inescapable images of the terrified women, those whose deaths they had witnessed and those whose deaths they tried not to imagine. Images of wives and mothers and daughters dressed only in their own blood.

Some were hit harder by the deaths of their mates and by having to leave them behind, so far from home. Jerzy Koszyk, who had come with Smolo from Wroclaw, threw his cigarettes in with the body, in tribute.

They fed the fire incautiously, let it burn brightly. They might be inviting fate, but at the moment they were more concerned with recovering their souls.

Come morning, Jaroslav was disappointed with his wound. For him, at least, there had been a bullet, but the wound itched more than it hurt. The bullet had caught no more flesh than a rusty nail you brushed past in a barn. He was intact.

Karel was also intact and as he listened to Big Boris' victory address ("You see how a few clear shots can outdo a hundred wild ones") he felt shame about his phantom wound and searing guilt that two of those "wild" shots had killed Smolo and Liowicki.

They could only hope a few of the women were intact. It would take a mountain of luck for them to reach partisan lines on their own, or to find a nearby family who would shelter a Jewish woman in flight from the authorities. Karel knew such people existed, the Krakowskis of the world, but to find them at random was like finding a gold watch in a hollow log.

What he truly knew was that most of those women were far from intact. He shivered at the knowledge of who those women were. Innocent women, each of whom had spent a lifetime growing whole, accumulating knowledge, only to be dumped into a pit like fill. Meanwhile, a handful of Nazis would be flown back to Berlin for 21-gun salutes and Panzer parades. Ribbons proclaiming their heroism would be sewn on to the shirts in which they were interred.

It was absurd, it was surreal. Above all, it was evil. Perhaps Lado would accept it as a late entry in his ugly game. It was true a price had been exacted. However inappropriately honored or fraudulently decorated they might be, that handful of Germans would murder no more Jews. To Karel at that moment, this seemed less a grain of solace than a statistic for Boris' scorecard.

While it was far too soon for humor, Jaro would both enhance that solace and inflate the statistic upon recounting the incident a fortnight later. And he would do so far more dramatically years later, spinning it as a bar-room tale. In his final version, polished to perfection long after the war had ended, angry villagers joined the battle, and dozens of Nazis were rolled into their own mass grave. Salami, cigarettes and gum, warm coats and woolen blankets, all were appropriated in great quantities. Two partisans were wounded, none died. Most of the women were saved.

All that came much later. The tale that went around within the brigade (and beyond, as they merged first with the Pszcyn brigade and later with the Red Army) was the one about the dogs, who never came after them. Was this because all their noses froze? Was it because, far from freezing, their noses remained so acutely tuned that they turned back in horror when they hit a wall of Boris' deadly farts?

Or was Lado correct in postulating the Nazis had been hoist on their own petard? They were so quick to spit out the phrase—"Jewish dogs!"—that perhaps they were on to something. Perhaps, the Laureate speculated, the dogs were indeed of Jewish extraction and for that reason were prepared to take the partisan side.

1974

"Who else is coming?"

"If you're asking whether Madeleine is coming, the answer is no. Just Carl and Clara."

"I like Maddy," says Catherine. "I know she means well. It's just that the noise factor can get to me. You know, when she and her mother both get going at full speed?"

"Words do fill the air."

"Your mom is so great at handling them. She's brilliant at it, really. I never know how to even enter the conversation."

"I suspect my mom will be totally absorbed with Rachel this trip."

Rachel is three months old, a plump baby with a wide gummy smile. Alene came to Maine for the birth, came back six weeks later, and has been threatening to come again if they refused to bring her grand-daughter down to Connecticut. Not that they would refuse or have any reluctance, now that Lewis' teaching year is over and the beach is there as an added inducement. So they are coming.

And coming up from Long Island to meet the 16-pound guest of honor are Uncle Carl and Aunt Clara. They arrived early, though, and have been waiting there all morning. Typical of Carl to declare "Saturday means Saturday" instead of calculating the hours it would take Lewis and Catherine to drive down from Maine. As they turn in, Carl is posted in the driveway, impatience showing on him as distinctly as would a red-and-yellow clown suit.

Fred is with him, Carl and Fred standing side by side. A lifelong bachelor at 50 when he and Alene met, Fred is only marginally a family member, or in a special category. He was introduced once as Lewis' stepfather, but never again. Accurately or not, Lewis told his mother that you do not call someone your stepfather when you still have a perfectly viable father—especially if the man in question materializes as you are packing for college.

Though Carl and Fred are the same age, they provide a stark contrast in appearance. Carl's hair is still dark and full, Fred has just the white fringes above his ears. Carl's eyesight is still keen, Fred wears wire-rimmed granny glasses with lenses so thick they appear opaque. Noticing these details as both men come strolling toward them, Catherine whispers, "Doesn't Fred look twenty years older than your uncle?"

"To me," Lewis whispers back, "Fred just looks hungry. We may have delayed his lunch."

Carl, who seems never to be hungry, looks restless. He *bristles* with energy, Catherine has said in the past, with regard to the electrical charge almost visible around him. He can sit for an hour drinking coffee with the sisters and listening to their talk. Then he will jump up and grab a rake or a shovel, or possibly suggest to Lewis that they "go for a drive."

"I will handle this bundle," says Carl, leaning in to pry the baby from her car seat.

"Don't drop her," says Catherine, mostly, though not entirely, in jest.

"Whoopsy poopsy," says Carl. "I dropped her."

"Your uncle the comedian," Catherine prods Lewis.

"Uncle Carl won't drop her unless you remind him not to."

"He's like you, you mean? Can't tell him anything?"

"Look at this Thanksgiving turkey," says Carl. "Good enough to eat."

"First you want to drop her, now you want to eat her," says Catherine.

"Sure," says Carl, "why not? She looks to me delicious."

After lunch, the conversation on the screened porch is mostly rote. Rachel is adorable, Rachel is a good sleeper, Rachel is obviously so smart. Then comes the roundtable of who-does-she-look-like, with predictable results—everyone has a different idea. Fred sees Alene's eyes, Alene sees a carbon copy of Catherine, Clara sees her late mother's chin. Uncle Carl has the best line, though, and it's a real show-stopper: "She looks like me."

They laugh on cue—Carl is not a blood relation, there can be no genetic resemblance—until they see he is serious. His clarification ("like my side of the family") is not an extension of the gag, it's the result of fiercely concentrated visual study.

"Just by chance, you mean," says Lewis, providing Carl with an exit strategy.

"Not chance. What chance? I am telling you this, she looks like a Bondy."

Whatever a Bondy looks like. But Lewis is always interested, if under informed regarding Carl's European relations and sees an opening here: the Bondys and the Bondy family traits. Before he can begin the inquisition, though, Carl is on the move. Rising, clapping his hands, he announces he needs to get back to the city.

"No ocean for us today. No beach. That's it."

"But you said you wanted to swim."

"I wanted, yes. Five hours ago. Also to walk on the sand. So I lose out."

Clara tries to reason with him—why rush back, it's a Saturday—until a few paragraphs later even she sees Carl cannot be budged. She and Alene roll their eyes in unison, a gesture which often marks their sisterhood. *Men*!

Carl has come to meet the baby, have a little lunch, and now deliver the inevitable envelope: "That's it."

This time there are two envelopes. Carl hands one ("for you") to Lewis and the other ("for the baby") to Catherine.

"You have a savings for her?" he says, frowning his suspicion that Lewis may have overlooked this provision.

"A bank account? She's three months old, Uncle Carl."

"I know how old she is, but now she has money. She will need a savings."

They are in their room, Lewis' childhood bedroom, past midnight. The baby is asleep in her playpen and the television set upstairs is droning on—Alene and Fred often fall asleep while watching—when Catherine remembers the two envelopes.

Lewis does the honors, though he has no idea which envelope is which. Plain white envelopes, unaddressed, not even gummed shut. One contains three bills, the other six—all hundreds, of course.

"First time he's ever handed one of those to me," says Catherine, with a grin.

"He's unstoppable."

"Be glad. We can use the money."

"We don't need it."

"Neither does your uncle."

"Why can't he just give something reasonable, though?"

"He likes to do it, Lew. It pleases him. Why fight it so?"

Partly because he has nothing commensurate for Carl, no way to balance the books, so to speak, and partly because he wishes there was no book-keeping involved, no money changing hands. A hundred dollars might feel all right, nine hundred did not.

"I guess it's not the worst problem in the world," he says, trying to let go of it.

An hour later, they are both still wakeful. Knowing her husband and guessing that the money is still nagging at him, Catherine slides closer and takes his hand under the covers. "Maybe," she smiles into the dark, "he would have exercised more fiscal restraint if Rachel hadn't so powerfully resembled the Bondys."

1945

In the forest, the snow-pack had shrunk to fragile crusts and all their trails were beaten down to slush. In clearings where the sun shone uninterrupted, dormant grasses were already greening.

Increasingly released from the need for concealment, the brigade had crossed many of these pastures and had sometimes taken boldly to the main roads in their haste to reach the front lines and join up with the Russian army proper. "A million Borises!" said Karel, envisioning it. Astonishingly, after all that had happened, the war was nearly over, essentially won.

"My son was conceived in a field like this one," said Karel, out of the blue as they paused to sip some water. He had dared to remember, or been unable to avoid remembering, as they stood in this ripening meadow. But to hear him speak of such a thing? Even the voluble Jaroslav was struck dumb.

Conceived in Eden and died in Hades; this addendum Karel kept to himself. Watching the crows dip and rise, he also remembered Krakowski's farm and wondered what they would be up to right now, what jobs he might be assigned. From there his mind traveled back to carefree days when he trailed after harrow, rake, and cart at his grandfather's farm in Pribram. He dared to remember a world green and growing.

"It's good to see the flowering of your romantic side," said Jaro. "Meanwhile, all this sunlight may be enough to melt the snow but my arse is still freezing."

"My toes agree with your arse. And my son is still dead."

"I have two cousins and a brother, maybe both brothers, also dead, and do you know what? I sometimes forget these terrible facts when my arse is freezing."

"Good for you."

"When we were eating half a potato for supper and washing it down with melted snow instead of pilsner? When those planes flew so low that they rattled the ice cakes on the Borises' tarpaulin? I sometimes forgot everything except my own survival."

"And mine, I am sure," Karel smiled. "I never forget, Jaro. When those planes strafed us, it reminded me all the more, because it's all the same thing, you know? The ones they killed and the ones they happened to miss. Bombs, bullets, gas. It's all the same damned thing."

"I agree with everything you say, which by the way makes me wonder why you say it a thousand times a day. The fact remains, I wish to live."

"So did they, my friend."

"Which changes nothing for us, here and now. We can only do what is right in front of us to do. And try to survive."

"Survive for what reason, though? To what end? The animal wants to live. He will attack or he will run, whatever he thinks will work best. But does he know why?"

"First off, you have just proven it doesn't matter why. Secondly, the animal does know he likes to eat. He likes to lie in the sun. On one level, he may even fathom that this meadow can be quite pleasant in the summertime, especially with a female animal close by."

"Whose romantic side are we seeing now! Seriously, Jaro, do you believe we can start over? Would you—would anyone—conceive another son, into this world?"

"One problem at a time, my friend. First survive. Get out of the forest alive, out of these rags, maybe get out of Europe altogether. In Jerusalem, they grow oranges and swim in the green sea. I know, I know, it could all be a tall story, a brochure with a sales pitch. But maybe in a place like that, life could start over for you."

"For a Jew, you mean?"

"Sure. For a thousand Jews, or ten thousand."

"Even if a thousand survive, we are a very great distance from any orange groves."

"Geographically, yes we are. But we have come through winter. A year ago, even two months ago, who would guess we would be alive to witness the bare earth emerging again? So maybe for you Jerusalem is the next leap of faith, that's all."

"For you, it's geographical. For me, philosophical."

"Oh la la!" said Jaroslav, poking Karel with his walking stick.

"You refuse to be serious."

"And you refuse to be frivolous. My aim is to be exactly as serious and philosophical as a rabbit or a fox. Survive, eat, lie in the sun—alongside a female animal, whenever possible."

Karel's gaze panned the pale downtrodden grass. A fringe of snow persisted, marking the cast of the forest shadow, but soon there would be rye and rapeseed sprouting. Maybe those grains would come to be harvested. In an area this remote, the harvest might take place whether peace came quickly or not.

Those prospects—a harvest, a peace—did little to mitigate the hollowness lodged inside him. Like a rich man's bullion stacked to the sky, survival would serve mainly to reveal a future stripped of purpose and a ruined world where all the orange groves were hung with bitter fruit. Karel put his arm around Jaro and pulled him closer.

"Do you want half of my apple?" he said.

"No," said Jaro, "I want all of it. But perhaps I should settle for half."

1982

The hospital where Lewis' mother is dying sits in the shadow of the Throgs Neck Bridge. Alene came here six weeks ago to place herself in the care of an oncologist with a unique new treatment (offered as a "last resort, yet highly promising") in mind for her cancer. Because the disease "took a turn," the miracle cure, never specified, also never materialized. The sequence drew a predictably cynical response from Carl Barry: "I have seen this miracle before, with a dollar sign on it."

Some days Alene has been lucid and has drawn her son close to convey sensible final wishes. Apart from keeping an eye out for his sister Joy and her children, he must try to tolerate Fred, or at least keep in touch with Fred, and perhaps consider adopting their cat, who will starve if left in Fred's care.

Other days Alene will speak of the need to get her classroom ready for the new school term, which starts in September. She is delighted that Bill Rasmussen, the principal, has promised they will finally have a new mimeograph machine. Is his mother attempting to comfort Lewis with white lies or does she actually believe what she is saying? Or is it just the morphine promoting useful delusions, making Alene feel better in ways a medical staff does not trouble itself to measure?

Feeling his way, Lewis goes with each momentary flow, alternately assuring Alene her dying wishes will be seen to and agreeing it's time to spruce up the classroom. He sees no reason to debunk her happier schemes and can recount with nostalgia the times when he, as a child, spent late summer days there with her, helping her unpack fresh-smelling notebooks and wash the huge window that had precisely 96 panes of glass. But he leaves the hospital in a welter each evening, right after her early dinner. He is almost grateful for the traffic on Northern Boulevard, which gives him time to compose himself before he gets to Carl and Clara's and can sit down to a welcome glass of beer with his uncle.

Their new house, just a short drive from the hospital, is in the same middle-aged neighborhood as Clara's old one, a Great Neck enclave built in the 1920s. Each house features a generous setback in front and a half-acre yard in back. Though there are stained glass windows in both bathrooms and fancy parquet flooring downstairs, there is nothing showy about the house. "It's not ritzy," says Clara. Most of the nicer features, like the slate roof-tiles and copper downspouts, were standard fare for the time and place. "Quality," says Carl. "This house is not going anywhere."

Lewis smiles at the phrase, one which always bespeaks his uncle's approval. Nothing Carl has ever built or bought would be "going anywhere." Privately, Lewis doubts that many of the structures Carl condemns are going anywhere either. A house with aluminum siding on it wasn't necessarily falling down, it just looked shabbier. Redwood shingles or not, Lewis and Catherine's tiny house in El Cerrito, their first mortgaged home, must have looked shabby to Carl, because he surely gave it the royal sneer. "It's not the house," Catherine told him at the time, "it's the location. He wants you closer to New York."

Each night after supper, the three of them go out walking the grid of wide clean sidewalks, past the half-timber houses shielded by neck-high hedges trimmed flat as a table on top. Their unhurried strolls are soothing to Lewis after each long sad hospital day. Indeed, they seem expressly designed for the purpose and he wonders aloud if they do this much walking ordinarily, when it is just the two of them.

"Always," says Carl. "Always we walk."

"In summer we do," says Clara. "We walk when it's nice, Lewis, and it's usually nice in the summer."

"Always we walk," says Carl.

Easy enough for Lewis to resolve the contradiction. They walk together when the weather is good, Carl walks regardless. He still walks with a negligible hitch (never present, Lewis recalls, when he *ran*) and still gives the same straight-faced response when asked to account for it, "Frozen toes."

"But frozen toes in July? In August?"

"Yes in July. You know this."

Television makes Carl restless. He watches a little to keep Clara company, Huntley Brinkley and every now and then a movie. He is more of a reader, but he reads in short installments, half an hour to an hour. In between he is up and moving, walking it off.

Unless he has changed. He is almost 70, after all: balding on top, graying on the sides. Fond as he has always been of his uncle, Lewis has seen him less frequently. It was a part of growing up—taking the train in from Connecticut, walking up to Carl's midtown office—but those days were getting to be a long time ago. Back before college and graduate school, before distances and marriage, children and jobs. In Great Neck this week, Lewis has discovered he might be getting a bit older too. Twice he has fallen asleep in a chair, in the garishly lit hospital room where his mother is dying.

The three of them talk easily on their nightly rambles, which has been a nice surprise. Carl and Clara welcomed him absolutely, insisting he stay with them each time and taking pains to perfect his comfort in the airy guest room overlooking Carl's gardens. Still, he is not the youth they once knew, he is a man with a family of his own, and that can be a tricky transition in relationships. In fact, everything has been easy, every conversation easy and natural, even with Aunt Clara.

Carl seems not to have marked the years that have passed since Lewis graduated from college. Back then he was bent on hiring his nephew. You could come home, he would always point out, as though Lewis had gone to Maine and then to California simply because he could find no work in New York. The dialogue from those days has not even been rewritten, as Carl tries to hire him now.

"How much do they pay you?" he says. "I can double it, easily."

"What would I do to earn it, though? I'm a teacher, Uncle Carl. I don't know the construction business."

"Management. From the office."

"I don't know management, either. I don't know anything, Uncle Carl."

"This is the bullshit."

"Carl!" says Clara, the shortest sentence she has ever spoken, on the heels of her longest silence. This much has changed radically.

"No, my dear, it's the bullshit. This kid knows plenty."

"Also, he's not a kid anymore. Are you, Lew?"

"That's a tough question," says Lewis, with what he hopes is a disarming grin. He has always joked his way past Carl's aggressive generosity rather than argue against it. A joke, a hug, and then wait for Clara to issue the cease-and-desist order. Together they might pry from Carl the dismissive wave which meant that Lewis was stubborn, Clara was an intrusive busybody, both of them were sadly misguided...but for now he would let it go.

"The job stays open. The offer stands. That's it."

To Carl it makes no difference that his nephew is a scholar with no interest in real estate development. Lewis is the right man for the post, no questions asked. That's it.

All week they have spoken a good deal about the family. Carl Barry married into this family after one premature funeral—Clara's first husband, Ben Weiss—but in time to attend the next two, her son Philip and her brother Jules. Now there looms another. Alene is only 59. One year ago she was a vibrant and to all appearances healthy woman, far younger than her years.

Untimely death has not been the focus, though. This has been more a time for filling in blank spaces on the blotter. Despite his lifelong reputation as the relentless inquisitor, Lewis has never gained access to a few dark corners. Jules' strange and angry wife is never mentioned, though looks are exchanged whenever Jules' unexpected death comes up, as though she might have poisoned him. Carl says yes, absolutely, she did it; Clara says I doubt that but I wouldn't put it past her.

Lewis knew his cousin Philip well in a way but the topic of Phil, who clearly was never exactly normal, has been off limits since his suicide. Really, the topic was always off limits. So Lewis is just learning—this week—about all the doctors and the harsh drug treatments that could not stop his breakdowns. He loses count of all the depressing hospitals Philip endured before opting out.

The grandmothers have been overlooked. Neither of them were talkers. Ask a question and get a snack, that was the deal. They knew how to feed a child, not talk to him. But who were these grandmothers? Kenny's mother Ruth left Kracow while in the womb, so she was born here, in Brooklyn. Alene and Clara's mother Ida left Minsk as a child and came over on a boat before the war: "Not that war, the first one." Grandma Ida went to work in a candy store.

Question: How did she manage to live selling candy? Answer: She found Sid Wohl, a tailor, and married him.

Clara could provide this information and she had tales to tell of Alene, pegged early on as the family beauty, and of Jules, Ida's pride and joy. Pronounced a goner four or five times, she refused to die until her only son finished medical school. He would be, Ida told her attending physicians, "a real doctor."

Families were complicated, family histories riddled with secrets and surprises. Aunt Clara was one of those surprises. Typecast as a non-stop yakker and a bigtime kvetcher, she emerged this summer as an articulate, balanced authority. A *resource*. Had Clara been so badly misjudged or had Alene's cancer, on the heels of all the earlier tragedies, sobered her up and rendered her stalwart?

"Tell him," says Carl, as they tramp through the warm twilight on what will be Lewis' last night of this trip. Unless Alene declines precipitously, he will not come east again for another ten days.

"You tell him," says Carla.

Carl waits her out, content to point first at his wife and then his nephew—pointing back and forth as if drawing the line of connection that will overcome her resistance.

"All right," she shrugs, "I'll say it for you. Lewis, he wants me to say that he is changing his will. He wants to leave Number 1200 to your mother."

"That's very nice, but it makes no sense. Even if she wasn't dying, Mom would have no use for an apartment building in the city. And she really is dying, you know that."

Carl taps his temple with his index finger and clucks, which Clara translates as a reference to Lewis' lack of common sense, or worldliness. "He is accusing you, Lew. You're guilty of innocence!"

"In that case, I guess it's a good thing he didn't give me that job," says Lewis.

"Didn't give, nothing," says Carl. "The job is yours. That's it."

"Lew, you won't ever take anything from him. He calls you a refusenik. Did you know that? So he leaves it to your mother, then you inherit. It's a trick. Your Uncle Carl believes he is tricking you."

"No trick," says Carl, sharply. "No one tricks this kid."

"Carl, please. He's not a kid."

"He knows what he is," says Carl.

The apartment house is not real to Lewis. *History* is what has always been real for him and last night it struck him that Uncle Carl, who lost a wife in Europe, also had two grandmothers. He had a mother, a father, and uncles of his own, none of whom were ever mentioned. What were their stories? How would there be time enough to ferret out those secrets and surprises, especially when Carl was the only soul who could tell them. It had taken him so long, so much work, just getting the chapters of Carl's story he had.

Saying goodbye at LaGuardia, saying thanks, he starts for the gate with his duffel, a box of Clara's peanut butter cookies, four portraits of Franklin, and a headful of unanswered questions.

1945

They were walking behind the convoy in loose formation when the shooting began. There was no cover, nowhere to go, so they turned and waded into the storm of bullets, toward the source. Karel's first thought was the usual: finally we are dead. This is craziness and we are dead.

Then as most of them reached the trees, he revised his thinking: this is becoming a fair fight. They have an army, we have an army; they have weapons, we have weapons.

Still, it *was* crazy, and not so fair a fight when one considered the Nazis could see them coming. It was an ambush, plain and simple, and all he really saw before getting hit was the curtain of green and a galaxy of dangerous, exploding stars.

Stretched out on a damp cot under a canopy of mildew-spotted canvas, Karel was fully aware that these conditions were luxurious beyond imagining. A bed of sorts, a roof of sorts, and clean bandages? He had it pretty good.

He had to savor that irony and wonder about this one: living in the forest, cold to the bone and always hungry, hunted like an animal, he had gone unscathed. They were like a small herd of deer turned out in a park for the pleasure of someone's "civilized" shooting party, yet he went unscathed. Now, finally absorbed into a proper army, a confident triumphant army at that, he was clipped by a German round.

Big Boris stopped by to offer sympathy and more importantly hot coffee, for though he now sported a Russian Army jacket, Karel was still considered "one of Socrates' men." The general sat on the end of Karel's cot and made a show of examining the messy ankle. The original cloth bandages had just come off and it looked (usefully, thought Karel, who was enjoying the benefits of soft bedding) a lot worse than it felt.

"So finally you found the one bullet with your name on it."

"Or it found me," said Karel.

"Better a foot than a brain," philosophized Boris.

"It's true I have two feet, but only one brain."

"This is a minor matter, Bondy," said Boris, swinging Karel's foot back onto the crude bolster. "In a few days, you will forget it happened."

"Yours is a soothing and cheering presence, Commander Socrates. And this coffee is not bad at all."

"Delighted to hear you say such a thing. That something is not bad?"

Once before, Karel was certain he had been hit, surprised to find he was not. This time it was the exact opposite. Inside his boot, inside the wool sock, skin and flesh and bone were shorn by what he perceived as a bee sting.

Just prior to the sting, when the battle had leveled off into neutral positions, he had exclaimed to Ladislaw almost gaily, "Why the hell are they shooting at us, if the war is over?"

"Not at us, Jew," Lado grinned, "at you. I am an innocent bystander."

The reason they were firing, of course, was the hope of evading capture. Captured, a Nazi trooper might enjoy prisoner-of-war status. He might be treated decently. On the other hand, he might be subject to summary rough justice and this was a gamble better not taken. Safer to disappear into the woodwork; climb into civilian garb and start weeding your garden; pretend you had been pulling out those damned persistent weeds for six years, nursing along your peas and beans while the cruel war raged at a distance.

The war was over the way a football match is over when victory is out of reach yet several minutes of playing time remain. The larger outcome may be knowable, but a thousand smaller outcomes are yet to be reckoned—plenty of senseless suffering lay in store on both sides. The Russians would lose a dozen men in this meaningless engagement. Perhaps Boris could score the match a tie, since the trees yielded up as many Nazi corpses in the aftermath.

Some of those corpses were still drawing breath when first encountered. There were many soldiers for whom killing was by now a habit, and others who felt justice demanded it. War was war. Then there were the pragmatists, faced with issues of convenience and inconvenience as the army moved west.

By the next day, Karel's wound no longer looked worse than it felt. It felt like bloody hell. The good news that day was that his toes did not hurt, or if they did, that familiar sensation was drowned out by nerves raging nearby in his ankle. Soon it would become a real challenge trying to rank these regimes of pain, each of them so far from his brain geographically.

He refused to ride in the caisson. Once he was able to walk, he insisted on doing so. It was awkward and he hated being one of the slow ones, but he could tell the wound was healing. It would heal a lot faster, Boris scolded him, if you rode.

"The trouble," he told Jaro, "is that before, I knew exactly how to limp. Now I don't know which foot to favor."

"You have two working feet," said Jaro, "which is two more than many million Russkies and many million of your Jews have. Give thanks to God and stop complaining."

Complaining? Karel had been in rare high spirits all that morning, or so he believed. Not only was he was keeping pace better every day, he was able to joke about the whole business.

"If you mean I am not among the dead, then yes, surely, thank you, Yahweh. Just admit that my two working feet are working very poorly this week."

"Limp evenly, that's my advice. If you go unevenly, you'll throw out your back."

"How in hell do you limp evenly? The whole point of limping is that it's uneven."

"All right, you'll see. By tomorrow you'll be complaining that your back hurts."

"My back hurts already, but I promise, Jaro, I will only complain about your advice."

1982

Clara pronounces herself pleased with the turnout. Which is exactly what she calls it, as if this is a successful yard sale rather than her little sister's funeral.

She has always been slightly jealous of Alene, who was not only younger but also livelier, prettier, and more gifted temperamentally. Perhaps unfairly—for Clara has also always loved Alene—Lewis can imagine his aunt wondering right now how many of these people will "turn out" for her own funeral, when the day comes.

The Family Circle, an assortment of rarely-glimpsed aunts and hard-to-categorize second and third cousins, accounts for 60 or so, and almost that many from the old days in Brooklyn show up. Then there are all of Alene's friends and colleagues from the years in Connecticut.

Even Kenneth is there. Lewis' father galvanizes the congregation when he materializes at the back of the Temple. "It's Kenny!" someone whispers, and dozens of heads turn toward a man most have not seen in decades. They revered him once, when Kenny and Alene were the golden pair, with looks and charm and what seemed, even to them, like perfect love. Perhaps it gives a jolt of youthfulness to the aging company to see him and recall those retrospectively joyful Depression Era days.

Kenny does not make the trek over to Jersey, to the family plot. The magic was all in his entrance; his exit was dimly lit. In fact, very few of the 200 who crowded into the synagogue to pay respect will choose to cross the bridge. Lewis guesses 30 at the cemetery, heads bowed in the blinding sunlight as his mother's coffin is lowered into the tan rectangle so cleanly chiseled from the earth.

Looking out across the gravescape he sees a bountiful harvest of headstones, a varietal crop ranging in size, slant, and stone. There are thin slabs of black slate, thicker ones of gray granite, towers of engraved white marble. Here in the family plot, however, all the graves are marked with footstones, laid nearly flush with the grade. From the access road they were barely visible. Had groundskeepers not clipped the lawn close as a putting green, the footstones would be obscured by grass, as they must be in winter by snow.

Alene's gravesite (where Lewis will find, when he returns the next day, only a cheap plastic stalk bearing a number, not even her name) will eventually be distinguished by the same honed-slate tablet as all the others, her dates engraved in the same font. Apparently the same stone-yard has been on retainer for half a century, for here are the old ones who blazed the trail from Belarus and many stems and branches of the generations since. Here are the ones Lewis knew: his cousin Philip, Phil's father Ben, Uncle Jules who died so young. It is odd how that phrase always attaches to Jules, dead before his time at 46, yet never to Phil, who died even younger.

For whatever reason—that Alene's decline was so gradual and inexorable? that her illness was so ravaging the end seemed merciful?—Lewis has yet to cry today. Even as he gazes down at Jules' marker, where the day of that funeral he could not stop crying, his tears stay locked inside. But Carl Barry moves slowly among the footstones, weeping openly.

Though he is known to all as a hard-nosed stoic, Carl's eyes have been swollen all day and here at Forest Grove they overflow. He knew few of these dead, felt a deep connection only to Jules. Nonetheless, as people embrace (in the beauty of the lilies, quite literally), the scene might be mistaken for a happy gathering of the clan were it not for the steady sobs from Carl Barry.

"They are all here," he says, compressing his nephew in a fierce embrace. Lewis extricates himself one limb at a time, like Harry Houdini, just so he can return comfort to this uncle who seems so uncharacteristically vulnerable. Indeed the word "invulnerable"—a word learned from *Superman* comic books!—was one he still associated with Carl. When they met, Lewis was a young child and Carl was a man in a suit, with a thick accent and an air of total command. Now Carl is this small, sad, *vulnerable* figure. "They are all here," he says, again.

Earlier in the day, Carl had dispensed one of his indelible dark homilies. This was hours before the service, when just the immediate family came to view the coffin. Lewis had not given one iota of consideration to the choice which Fred, his mother's husband, made in that regard. Whatever they may have cost, the few caskets he has seen were all ugly. Maybe they were required to be ugly.

But he did recall Carl's reaction to the coffin at Uncle Jules' funeral. Under a veneer of phony opulence, he insisted, the coffin was a piece of junk. The piece of junk had cost "plenty," nonetheless, and Carl delivered his judgment on the Bockelman Funeral Home: "This is the making of the money."

Lewis noted the contradiction. His uncle made lots of money, pots of money, and therefore must believe "the making of the money" was permissible. "Never in time of death," was Carl's response, never when people were at their weakest. Beyond that, the judgment did not go to profit but to excessive profit. To greed.

This morning's verdict was directed at Fred, not at the men in their professional mourning clothes. "This is the saving of the money," declared Carl, convinced that the money in question belonged to Alene, whom he loved, and that Fred was bent on doling out as little of it as possible. The casket he chose did not meet Carl's standards. It failed to honor Alene properly.

Now as the casket is about to be lowered, Carl steps forward in turn. Eyes blurred by tears, he brushes a hand over the top and then retracts it quickly, as though stung by spiders.

The three of them reprise their evening constitutional, filing past the barbered hedges of the hushed enclave, wordlessly for once. A dog barks from inside one house; radio voices float through an open window; sprinklers hiss in a few yards. It has been a long summer for Lewis and their chatty perambulations of July and August seem part of another era. Strange to realize it is still calendar summer.

Silence feels right. Lewis has lost his mother, Clara her sister, and Carl seems to have experienced Alene's death as loss itself, the disappearance of the world's remaining riches. Or such is Lewis' interpretation of Carl's grim pronouncement, "They are all here."

Then, out of the silent darkening blue, deposited as solidly as a boulder on the road in front of them, comes one more of Carl's indelible sentences: "I never liked him."

Though there is no context, nothing that leads toward or away from his abrupt avowal, it is obviously Fred to whom the statement refers. Fred he never liked. Apparently "the saving of the money" indictment was neither chicken nor egg.

"*Never,*" Carl reiterates, in case he has failed to make himself clear. Not another word is spoken until they are back inside the house.

1945

Jaroslav had gone north, hoping to locate his brother in Danzig. After his "visit" to Lindauer, Karel had ridden south, toward the border near Jesenik. It was warm for late October and Karel was constantly tempted to shed some of his impost. He had the horse now but there were still hours of walking and between victuals, water, knapsack, ground-cloth, maps, and the Ruger, he was lugging 15 kilos.

Just as "east" had once been a fearful mystery and "north" a shapeless destination upon leaving Krakowski's farmstead, *south* was merely Karel's latest undefined itinerary. True, he was pointed toward home, but he did not think of himself as going home. The future was a blank page. He had found Lindauer; the war was over. What came next was the unanswerable question.

"After the war" was a phrase one heard constantly back in '41 and '42. For Karel, the phrase had long since lost all meaning. In its original sense—of a life, or a way of life, simply resumed once the insanity subsided—it would never come to pass. That much was clear to him before Terezin and crystal clear at Auschwitz-Birkenau. Still, you had to keep putting one foot in front of the other.

He spotted the jerry-rigged tent (essentially a scrap of canvas propped on sticks) in a copse of beech trees a short distance from the rail line. This close to the tracks, one saw stragglers everywhere. All of Europe, he guessed, was populated thusly, with soldiers who had deserted or been cut loose from prisons, guards and petty officials fleeing their histories, bandits, hobos, fast-footed youngsters blazing their way, Jews and Gypsies who had come through alive. The arteries flowed with every soul imaginable, the saved and the damned alike.

Karel was one of them and the young man he found under that canvas was another. The salient difference was the young man's unbuttoned German Army blouse. Peace or no peace, a Nazi was still a Nazi.

Even with a pistol and bayonet on the ground beside him, though, this particular Nazi posed no present threat. He lay sprawled and motionless, like someone sleeping off a drunk, until Karel's footsteps roused him. He opened rheumy eyes and smiled weakly. In a soft halting voice, he thanked Karel for answering his prayers.

"I have had no food and the dregs in my canteen must be poisonous. The water tastes like mud mixed with tin."

Karel had no trouble imagining such a flavor, having experienced it daily at A-B. Still, he was not here to answer a Nazi soldier's prayers.

"You will help me?" said the young man.

"Help you?" said Karel. "Why would I help you, after you killed my wife and my children? Killed my parents and my cousins—"

"As God is my witness, I did not do this. No wives or cousins, honestly. I shot at the Russian soldiers and to tell you no more than the truth, I am sure I missed them all."

Sapped by the effort at communication, he trailed off coughing, or just possibly laughing at the idea of missing so many shots, because he did resume a moment later in that vein. "I was a terrible fighter, the worst. I never wished to fight, I am an artist."

"You are a criminal."

"No, please, I am like you, a citizen forced to take up arms by my country."

Karel's hand flew up and slapped the feverish youth hard across the face. "Your country is the country of Hell. You took up arms to promote the great state of Hell on earth and you expect me to help you?"

"Yes, please help me," said the young man. Perspiration was arranged on his forehead like a line of tiny, transparent bullets.

So, Karel smiled to himself, I am being given a *test*. Multiple choice, no less. Choice number one is to execute this person, who would so recently have done as much for him. Execute him, perhaps, with his own gun! Choice number two is to simply walk away and let death make its own bargain with this admittedly insignificant cog of the German Army.

One of these must be the right answer, given that choice number three, to help the fellow, must surely be the wrong one. And yet the war was over, was it not? Had not his visit to Lindauer's estate signaled the end of the end of it, so to speak? What if this sick child actually had been an artist and a victim of sorts himself, if such were possible for anyone wearing the German uniform.

Karel reminded himself of the ingredients that may have gone into the weave of those German trousers. He asked himself what might transpire if this Hitler youth was the one standing and Karel the one lying on the ground. Would the boy be a hapless marksman then? It seemed much more likely he was a half-clever charlatan, an avid Jew-killer who had concocted a sob story in hopes of saving his wretched skin. The landscape might be teeming with pacifist Nazi "artists."

As he continued along the siding, Karel tried to shake off the entire troubling incident. Whatever it meant or did not mean, it was over. Right or wrong, he had made his choice.

The boy's name was Heinrich. Like Heinrich Himmler, which might have hurt his chances even as Heinrich Mann, absurdly enough, might have helped them. The real problem was that he had a name at all and that Karel had been obliged to learn it. Still bothered by what had happened at Lindauer's, he had been adamant with this lad. Do not tell me your name, he had instructed, or where supposedly you studied art, or what your poor sad mother liked to cook. *Do not try to convince me you are human.*

Though the boy complied, his name was stenciled onto the cloth cover of his battered canteen. Karel filled the canteen once to bathe the boy's face and neck, and give him drink. He filled it a second time to leave behind a supply. He also left a packet of biscuits. Doing so, he rationalized, would serve to lighten his own impost.

Heinrich Seidenberg may or may not have heard Karel's parting lecture, but he did manage to stand up. Though he was far from stable on his feet, it seemed possible he could survive. Youth was on his side and they were still in German territory.

"Go home to Hell and tell them," Karel had railed at the frail soldier, who at the time was mainly concerned with staying upright. "Tell those shameless strutting fiends that a Jew has saved you. That the one you tortured and robbed and murdered—*that one* saved you. Tell them someone was human and it was not you."

"I shall tell them," said Heinrich, nodding.

"Tell them who is human and who is sub-human. Say that even a filthy rat in a rain-barrel is better..."

Suddenly words failed him, left him. Analogies, metaphors, accusations: all were thunderously unequal to the task. However emphatically he put the case, words were inadequate. This too would be a legacy for "after the war," that words and ideas had been rendered useless. Coherent thought had been rendered obsolete.

"I shall tell them, sir," said Heinrich, glassy-eyed and nodding. "I promise you this."

Karel had been casting about for his night's shelter, for an abandoned train car or lorry, a bat-infested barn. The matter did not concern him greatly. If he found no indoor accommodation, he would sleep beneath the sky, as he had in weather unimaginably harsher.

But the noontime encounter stayed with him. The miles he traveled, the people and places he passed and now the coming of twilight, had not put sufficient distance. Who would grade him on this test? He could not cease wondering if he had done too much or not enough; wondering if he had done right or wrong.

Above all, wondering whether he had been played for a fool. What if he were to come across another Nazi straggler, one not sufficiently quick-witted to declare himself an artist and a scholar? One who stood behind the standard lie of ignorance.

Karel had wanted the lad to survive—that was the problem. He could admit this to himself or he could deny it. He could tell himself that he simply wanted his lecture to be absorbed, his telegram to Hell delivered, but the truth was he liked the boy. Astonishingly, bizarrely, he discovered he had *nothing against him*.

Which made it just as astonishing to Karel that he had come within a hair's breadth of riding away as the boy lay suffering in the mud.

1987

The City. People here called New York "the city" as if it were the only one. Though his family had moved out to Connecticut, Lewis knew his way around the city. For one thing, he had always paid attention when he went "back to the old country" with his father. And even when he was eleven or twelve, they let him train in alone and make his way to the ballpark or to his Uncle Carl's midtown office. No one, of course, would allow that now.

For decades, the office had been located in the once nondescript but increasingly posh neighborhood now known as Lincoln Center, where Carl had "built" (before his first visit to a construction site, Lewis had pictured his uncle swinging a hammer) several high-rises. "That's one of mine," Carl would say, as if Lewis didn't recognize 658 or 715 or 1200. Carl always identified the buildings by their number.

This year, though, Carl had taken on a major rehab uptown,

near the Lenox Hill Hospital, and shifted his office there temporarily. His real base of operations shifted to a hole-in-the-wall delicatessen on 76th Street. But Lewis, cruising on automatic pilot after a nostalgic stopover at Compo Beach, long accustomed to finding Carl at Allegro, has forgotten about the change of venue for their lunch. And having provided himself the traditional half hour cushion, he is unconcerned when the train makes a lengthy unexplained stop in Stamford.

The cushion is almost gone by the time they chug in to Penn Station and he hustles up to 61st Street. Only as he reaches for the door pull and sees his reflection in the glass door of Allegro does it hit him that he is 15 city blocks from where Uncle Carl (who is never one second late for anything, and intolerant, to say the least, of anyone who is) will be waiting. Worse, Lewis is already winded from running this far.

Though there are a dozen bright yellow taxicabs in sight, they are not moving much faster than the parked cars. Might as well lie down in the gutter as get in one of those cabs. So Lewis begins to run again. Sweating from the exertion and the anxiety, he weaves through foot traffic, marking his progress, 69th Street, 70th Street... With luck, cheating the lights, he could be less than 20 minutes late.

Then he turns an ankle. Dodging around two wide ladies and their wide, voluminous handbags, he catches the edge of the curb and the ankle folds over. He cannot afford to stop, though, and begins alternating an awkward limp with stretches of outright hopping, in a painful potato race uptown. 74th Street, 75th...

Finally he is there. He sees his uncle pacing back and forth in front of the deli. Hands jammed into his jacket pockets, Carl is pivoting in such a tight arc that it looks as though he is rehearsing an Arthur Murray dance step, this way and that way and this way...

No, it looks more militaristic than that, more like marching, stern and staccato. Carl's jaw is tightly clamped, as if he is biting through a steel rod. While Lewis has been treated to small samplings of Carl Barry's temper, he has never been the target of it. Until now.

"Nobody does this to me," are Carl's first words. His eyes are clouded with fury, his voice clotted with it. "Nobody."

"I'm really sorry, Uncle Carl. First the train broke down and then—"

Carl dismisses the train's mechanical shortcomings with the half-wave of undiluted disgust. Impossible as it seems, his eyes are brimming with *hatred*. He is almost unrecognizable, a different person. Gone from the outset is any chance he would notice the obvious strain, the effort, and excuse Lewis on those grounds.

"—there was unbelievable traffic."

Carl may or may not believe in the unbelievable traffic, but he is offering neither sympathy nor mercy. Lewis doesn't dare trot out the ankle sprain. *Bullshit*, is how he imagines his uncle's response to it.

But apparently Carl has finished responding. He has nothing else to say as Lewis follows him into the deli. The white-jacketed proprietor greets Mr. Barry Sir by name, trails him to the table, and pours two tumblers of ice water. With evident pride, he recites Mr. Barry Sir's order ("brisket on rye, black coffee") while Mr. Barry Sir maintains radio silence. If such non-responsiveness is rude, the proprietor is happy to overlook that aspect. "And for the young man?" he says.

"The same, thank you," says Lewis, "except I'll take cream with the coffee, please."

Carl sips his ice water, the blank whites of his eyes cast up balefully above his new half-rims. When their coffees arrive, he pushes the sugar shaker farther away as though it is an object of scorn before draining his first cup of black coffee in two long draughts. The deli man refills it almost before it touches back down on the table.

And now, with a second, softer wave of disgust, Carl sweeps the intolerable offense, the entire episode, off the table and off the face of the earth. Abandons his anger completely; would not know anger if you spelled it for him. Poof.

"So!" he says, brightly. "You are here!"

Somehow it's over. Lewis' awful lapse has been expunged.

Five minutes? It can't have been longer than that; Lewis is still perspiring.

"Yeah, I'm here. I really am sorry, Uncle Carl. Obviously, I should have caught the earlier train. The only reason I sprained my ankle was because I was racing to make up time."

He is content with this slight misrepresentation, with leaving the impression he has just sprinted from Penn Station on a bum foot solely because the train betrayed him.

"I lied to you once, Lewis. *Just* once," says Carl, jarringly.

Lewis is confused. He is the one lying, why is Carl the one apologizing? What happened to "Nobody does this to me"?

"*You* lied?"

"My ankle. I told you was a football injury. You don't remember?"

"I do remember, but that must have been thirty years ago."

Carl's right ankle is slightly off kilter. A bone-spur bulges slightly and the skin is stretched livid across it. Long ago Carl told him that this happy accident accounted for his "Moravian Twist," a long curling ribbon of a kick that always bowed in mid-flight. Though everyone could achieve this to some extent, Carl's version had twice the arc, nearly scribing a semi-circle.

"It was a lie. The truth is I took a bullet. Not much, or I would have lost the foot like it was a shoe. That happened to many, believe it. So I was lucky."

"Why would you lie about that? The bullet wound makes a much better story."

"You were a little kid, why scare you? And listen, this was a Nazi bullet. I should tell you the Nazis got me?"

"You're telling me now."

"Yes, now I will tell it."

Lewis smiles at the undying pronunciation: I vill tell it. "Is it really why your kick curves so much?"

Carl shrugs. The origin of the Moravian Twist is not the point. "You want to hear the story or not?"

"Are you kidding me? Of course I want to hear it."

"Then be quiet and I will tell it. Not the bullet, which was nothing. I will tell you Lindauer. You eat."

1946

The road to Borva, the only road into the village, had fallen into such disrepair that the mare moved like a disjointed machine. She was an old girl and it was a rough descent from the abandoned fire-watch where they stayed overnight.

If they passed through this village without stopping it would not have interrupted their progress for long. There were a few shops on one side and row-house residences on the other. These were joined in snug continuity even though the landscape opened up for miles around, over a prospect of green fields. Freestanding at the far end of town, like an afterthought, was a small unadorned church.

At the moment, a single representative of this teeming metropolis was in evidence. Square-set in the doorway of his shop, assessing the lowering sky, was a large bald man in a blood-stained apron. He wiped his hands in the folds of the apron and addressed Karel quite casually, as though they were old acquaintances. "Rain, for sure. I felt it in my elbow last night."

"That tavern is closed?" said Karel, setting aside the subject of elbows, and indicating a shop-front displaying a flagon of beer on its painted sign.

"Today it is. Kaberle's wife is giving birth."

"A child," said Karel, absently.

"Well, yes," laughed the butcher. "Not a calf!"

The genial fellow seemed taken aback when his jest failed to extract so much as a smile from the stranger on horseback.

"I am surprised to see someone arrive here by horse," he said, and this time Karel did smile at the notion anyone would arrive here by any means.

"I am in no particular hurry," said Karel. It struck him that he was in the exact opposite of a hurry, whatever the word for that might be.

"Perhaps not, but surely to find care for a horse in these days..."

This concern Karel dismissed with a shrug. Not only had he

found it rare to cover five kilometers without encountering a farm, it was also true that during these years in which farmers were so essential to survival, he had developed a sixth sense for locating any farmhouse within range.

"You don't favor old horses? Not even for your butcher shop?"

"Please," said the butcher, drawing back in mock horror. Locally famous for his relentless good nature, he was glad to see the stranger closing the distance between them a little.

"Where can a citizen of —?"

"Borva. You are in the village of Borva."

"—of Borva, find something to eat on those days when the tavern-keeper's wife is giving birth?"

"Step inside," said the butcher, bowing Karel into his own establishment. "You need go no further for your excellent bread and excellent cooked meats."

"Excellent," said Karel, reproducing the man's favored adjective with only the faintest charge of sarcasm. Inside, in a glass display case, were blocks of beef, both cooked and uncooked. Dangling from above were the carcasses of rabbits and chickens. Karel ordered four sliced beef sandwiches, two for now and two for later on.

"We can use this rain," said the butcher, as he went about deftly composing the sandwiches. "Last year's barley crop was so thin that there has been talk of ditches."

"Irrigation? Here?"

"Just talk, so far. But the brewery is our lifeblood. You'll see it when you continue on, not far beyond the church. They managed to keep it going through the war, but only at half speed."

Karel took two sandwiches out to the stoop to eat them. They were indeed excellent and the ale, even if brewed at half speed, might justify irrigation. But the relentlessly sociable butcher pursued him outdoors and kept talking.

"You were in the war, of course?"

"Of course," said Karel, his tone again skirting mild mockery.

"May I ask with whom?"

"With whomever. We were Russians, Czechs, Poles. One Hungarian."

"You are a Jew?"

"If I say yes, will I be murdered in my sleep here in Borva?"

"Let's say instead that you are eating kosher without bothering to ask. I am also a Jew. Klima."

"To eat kosher, Klima, is not to be Jewish," said Karel, leaving aside the question of finding a rabbi anywhere in the region. "To be despised and murdered is to be Jewish."

"And to survive, no? No one seems to have murdered you."

"So you say."

"So I observe," said the butcher, unable to suppress his natural smile. His face, his whole round head, shaped itself around a smile. "Borva is a very quiet place. Fortunately for us, the war didn't come here, though naturally some of our young men went to fight it. I was not young and stayed put. No shame in that."

Karel nodded. If the man required permission to go on living with himself, let him have it. At least he made a good sandwich.

"I have been looking for a place the war didn't come."

"To live?" said Klima.

It was a harmless question, essentially an expression of surprise. To reside, was what the man meant, but it recast itself in Karel's hearing: to live meant *merely* to live. To *not die*. And as for shame? Not to have died with the others might be a source of pride, but it was also a source of shame.

"And to work?" the butcher went on, filling the broadening silence. "Might you be the new manager at the brewery?"

Karel shook his head no and took a swallow of ale. "Come now. Would your new manager arrive by swayback mare?"

The butcher was unstoppable. If Karel wasn't the new manager, then who was he? "You were injured in the war?" he asked, pointing at Karel's leg.

Karel was surprised to hear his limp was noticeable, especially on a warm day when there was no pain. The ankle was no longer a problem and you could hardly call sore toes a war wound, unless you identified tight shoes as the enemy.

"Halfway between here and the fire-tower," said Karel, keeping his ruminations on shoes to himself, "I saw a house. A stone house on a bend in the river, with a small orchard. Do you know the one I mean?"

"Fein's Castle."

"Hardly. This was not even a large house."

"We just called it that. Bert Fein was the last German in these parts. That house was his fortress, until he left with the peace. But Bert was not a bad fellow."

"I will take his castle."

"Suit yourself, I'm not the tax collector. No one goes to the house. Some peasant families who grow sugar beets upriver will be your closest neighbors."

"It seemed quiet."

"Here in town it's quiet. Out there it's *silent*. Bert hated the war, you know. Hated everything about it, thought Hitler was a madman. He was deeply ashamed—"

"Sell me two loaves of your excellent bread," said Karel, tired of probing all the facets of shame, "and I will go take his house."

"We—my family—are the only Jews in Borva, but there were no collaborators here, no sympathizers. We are all good Czechs. I'll introduce you around, if you like, some evening at the tap-house."

Earlier, when Klima supplied his name, the stranger had not responded in kind. Now he made no response to the notion of socializing. Not interested. Not eager to know anyone—or perhaps, considered Klima, not eager to be known! These days, of course, any new face could belong to a Nazi in retreat or a collaborator seeking cover. If such was the case with this fellow, though, he put up a hell of a good front. He could not have acted the victim more convincingly.

Back outside, the air was so charged it shimmered. Klima set down a bucket of water for the horse and Karel watched as she drained it. He was sure she would like the clear water of Fein's riverside and the high thick grass in his orchard.

"Before the war," Klima was going on, "Borva moved slowly. Like a turtle, my brother-in-law liked to say. Then the war put our turtle on his back. All the young men were gone, the crops went bad. It all hinges on the brewery, you see. There's nothing else."

"It's good enough for you," observed Karel.

"True."

"So it's good enough for me, too."

"You'll tire of it. I tire of it myself at times, though I won't be going anywhere else. Not at my age."

The butcher was all right. A nice man. After tightening the saddlebag strap and mounting, Karel tossed the fellow a soft salute.

"Good luck," said Klima. "I hope you encounter no German ghosts at Fein's Castle."

"Luck to you too," said Karel, shaking the reins.

1987

Over the years, Lewis had worked at crowbarring the details out of his uncle. It was never easy. Carl's news releases came years apart and they were always muted, never more than the bare minimum. Each time he managed to gather in a fresh nugget, Lewis was left torn between guilt over badgering the man and fear the story would be lost if he left him in peace.

He never mistrusted the facts. While it would have been easy enough to distort such dramatic events, or simply misremember, Carl's expression always said otherwise. That combination of faraway concentration and pained reluctance made plain how searing the memories were. Lewis had no doubt they would remain intact as long as Carl's brain was intact, yet even that reassurance implied its own limits. At 74, Lewis realized, Carl was the oldest person he knew.

On the afternoon when Carl finally told him about Lindauer ("You want to hear the story or not?") there had been nothing to indicate this might occur and nothing to indicate why it did. Lewis had not even broached the matter.

Curiously, though, just before Carl opened up, Lewis had seen him as "Karel," seen him in that context for some reason—maybe it was the dark flash of fury—and mused on the person his uncle would have been had the Nazis never come to power. Had Europe not been ravaged, the Jews not slaughtered, Carl would be a man developing real estate and tending his vegetables 4,000 miles to the east. Far from being his beloved uncle, Carl would be a man Lewis never even met.

Had some sort of telepathy brought forth "the rest of the story" that day? Hard to believe it was pure happenstance, a random set of neurons coursing through Carl's brain while he brushed his teeth that morning, or as he paced outside the deli with steam pouring out of his ears. If the impulse had bubbled up at a time when Lewis was home in California, would Carl never have told it? To Lewis or to anyone else?

Lewis recalls all the times Aunt Clara's face would appear at the kitchen window, curious—or nosy—about what she and Alene called The Inquisition. Lewis "interviewing" Carl. Clara has always professed ignorance about it: the European family, Terezin and Auschwitz, the partisans—and certainly this new chapter, with the S.S. officer Lindauer. "Auschwitz at least I have heard of," she would say.

Lewis believes her just as much. Her face proclaims, through indifference, the truthfulness that Carl's face proclaims through intensity. For Clara (who after all has lost a husband, a son, a brother, and a sister—none of them to the Nazis, all to bad luck) the past is happiest when irrelevant. This intentional distancing or outright disposal of the past, a condition which extends through every branch of Lewis' family—whether owing to death, divorce, or madness—seems to him more than unfortunate, almost tragic in its quotidian way, since "the past" is no more and no less than the lives they have lived.

Officially the war was over. Or maybe better to say *unofficially* it was. There were hundreds of fronts, after all, and a thousand versions of the truth going around. For a time, absolute confusion reigned and you answered to anyone holding a gun. You were never sure who was in charge, or what the objectives were; not even where the national boundaries now lay.

And this state of confusion provided a kind of grace period for the settling of debts.

"Provided by whom?" asks Lewis.

"Provided by these circumstances, all right?"

"And by debts, do you mean money? Valuables? Land?"

"I mean Lindauer," says Carl, his jaw so firmly set that the words barely escape. "This was the man who looked into Milena's beautiful eyes and condemned her to the gas."

Undoubtedly, he had touched her. They all pretended to be appalled, repulsed, by these sub-human Jews, yet were appallingly eager to touch the flesh of the sub-human Jewish women. Lindauer had touched her and then murdered her. He had thrown away the unlived lives of her terrified children as though they were insignificant pests, barn rats. Lindauer was the very man.

And how smoothly Sturmbannfuhrer Lindauer transformed himself into the good and gentle Herr Lindauer, tucked in behind the demure fuchsia hedges of a hillside villa with its splendid prospect of the Spree Valley. Lindauer the country squire. Even a very recent past could be clouded in those wild west days, with so much disorder to deal with. The Russians, the Americans, the British: each of them left countless Lindauers unpunished.

No doubt he had regaled them with the necessary fabrications. Presented freshly minted papers, laid out a fictitious trail of innocence. Auschwitz? My God, everyone heard those stories, he would have said, shaking his head in disbelief, perhaps bowing his head in profound sorrow that some of the stories may have contained a grain of truth. But the Lindauers? The Lindauers have always been an honorable family. On my late wife's side, he might well have confided, there was even a Jewish ancestor. And may I offer you a glass of something, he would have said, with the intonation and manners of a perfect gentleman.

Now, greeting this shabby stranger at his door, Lindauer presumed the situation called for more of the same, the glass-of-something and the posturing. Not that he would fawn. Karel could read on his face the equipoise between the pragmatism of manners and a barely contained superciliousness, could detect the unspoken challenge: how dare a vagrant such as yourself disturb a true aristocrat such as Herr Lindauer?

Lindauer tried German, which Karel refused to speak, vowed in fact never to speak again. Karel tried Czech, which Lindauer seemed not to know. Although Karel's English was crude where Lindauer's was perfect—British-sounding, to Karel's ear—it was in English they were forced to communicate.

"Now what exactly can I do for you?" Lindauer said, a second time.

Karel had stood mute the first time, unable to find the words even though he had rehearsed them many times. He could only stare at this man—this fraud, this sadist—who went on humoring him with his my-good-man rubbish. Karel was not clean shaven, his jacket was torn, he had not slept well for several nights. In truth, he had not slept well for seven years. In Herr Lindauer's eyes, he could only appear insignificant, one more pest to be exterminated.

"To begin," Karel finally said, "open safe."

"If I had a safe—which incidentally I do not—why exactly would I choose to open it?"

"So to empty out," said Karel.

"Am I to understand, then, that you are you a common thief?"

"Open," said Karel, lifting the pistol from his belt. "Then we exchange."

"An exchange! Now this becomes interesting. I am at a loss, however, to imagine what we might be exchanging."

"You have for me some things, and I have for you."

"Sounds a delightful bargain. Out of curiosity, again, might I inquire what it is you could possibly have for me?"

"I have for you five bullets."

"Just five, sir? Why not empty your pistol?"

"Give credit where due is credit" was a favorite maxim of Uncle Carl's, but it was strange to hear it dropped into this emotional account. Credit where due is credit: even with a loaded Ruger angled up to his nostrils, the Nazi could sneer. But sneering alone, Carl spat out (perhaps retracting some of the credit), does not make someone an aristocrat.

"One bullet for each in my family," he explained.

Lindauer went on playing the fool, the bystander who could form no connection between himself and anyone with a grievance. Granted, the war had featured much injustice and engendered much suffering for all involved. Still, what could this have to do with a country squire on a remote estate so far from any of the fronts?

He spread his arms in a gesture of bafflement and self-acquittal. He smiled indulgently, as if to indicate a limit to his patience for this rude intrusion. Karel shot him in the right knee.

1946

From Fein's Castle, one caught musty whiffs of the river below. Through gaps in the hillside foliage, one saw it threading its way between the green tangled banks.

The house was strangely intact, as though its owner had gone off on a simple errand from which he would soon return. No signs of mice, or looting, no disorder on shelves stacked with crockery or in drawers storing silverware. The floors, narrow strips of russet fir, seemed freshly oiled. It was a well-made, unpretentious country house, whose creator had permitted himself a few flourishes, such as the candelabra-style chandelier depending from a chip-carved tie-beam. Bookcases lined the parlor, in the middle of which was a low table with a chess board painted directly onto its oak surface.

Something about the room reminded Karel of his own parlor in Praha, his and Milena's. Even the woman who had sat for a large oil portrait looked vaguely familiar, with her dark hair piled high and a hint of merriment in her sea-green eyes that rendered the picture more witty than formal. Fein's wife? His mother? Karel took the painting down and placed it in the pantry, face to the wall.

Unlike the house, the small jerrybuilt barn had been badly neglected. The grain bins contained nothing but droppings. The pump had lost prime while gaining a hornet's nest the size of a melon. A heavy oak branch that had come crashing partway through the roof years ago was still resting there, with a number of crisp brown leaves still clinging to the twigs.

Meanwhile, thunder had been building, approaching, and suddenly the leading edge—the butcher's forecasted downpour—began slapping the roof shakes so heavily it might have been raining stones. The breach in the roof quickly became a spigot. The mare became agitated, backing and whinnying. Trapped in the barn, Karel stood at a window and watched lightning etch the orchard.

Lightning had always frightened him, ever since the incident his mother called a bad dream. "Karel's bad dream," she called it, euphemistically, because it was not a dream: he had seen it happen, in Pribram. A twig-legged fawn stood drinking in the pond, as heedless and contented as a fairy-tale creature.

Then came a shimmer of lightning and a distinct sizzle, like the sound of a match doused in a glass of water, and the animal dropped as though shot. Karel couldn't move. Transfixed, he had watched it float on the surface, the carcass slowly circling, before he could make his own thin legs start running.

He knew a storm this violent would pass through quickly, so he settled the mare and waited. The downpour pinpointed half a dozen additional roof leaks by the time it slackened. Even before it stopped completely, though, the sun was burning through.

The high grass soaked his shoes as he walked back to the house. He boiled water for coffee, drank a cup, then gathered all the bedding and carried it down to the river. By then there was a sunlit mist over the water and he washed the linens while standing in the stream, only mildly fearful of (or superstitious about) any stray lightning charges hiding in the trees.

Karel would have walked to the village, except there would be supplies to bring back, the remaining basics of a larder. So he rode, and coming over the bridge on the roan he felt like a figure from the distant past, a pilgrim from another century. He saw two automobiles parked on the road, plus a boxy green delivery van the butcher was unloading.

Saluting Klima, he continued on to the tap-house, where he took a corner table and ordered the meat, its provenance unspecified on the chalkboard, and dumplings, with a tankard of the half-speed ale. Apart from the bare necessaries uttered by the proprietor, the young father Kaberle, no one addressed or even acknowledged him.

This was not the case an hour later at Klima's establishment, where the butcher hailed his entrance loudly: "Good afternoon, my Jewish friend!"

Before Karel could conjure a response, Klima was calling out his next stentorian greeting, this one to a stout, florid woman coming through the doorway. Determinedly sociable, he went on to introduce the two of them, or rather present Karel to Ludmilla, whom he designated "my very best customer."

"Her son lost a close friend to the Nazis. And Rudi himself was nearly taken, was he not, Ludmilla? Nearly taken for a Jew."

"Yes," said the woman. "Because Samuel was Jewish—Samuel, his friend—and this took place in Frydek-Mistek, where they would not have known him."

"Terrible things did happen," said Karel, bowing to the woman, who appeared puzzled by the gesture.

"He is a good lad, Rudi is, no mistake about that," said Klima, as he handed Ludmilla a package that had already been wrapped in paper and bound with string. A standing order, perhaps, from his very best customer.

"Rudi is in Ostrava now, studying," said Ludmilla with maternal pride. She freighted the word 'studying' with accents of high achievement and universal progress. Karel bowed again as she left the shop.

"Don't be too hard on us," said Klima. "As I told you, the war was felt less here. And who knows why?"

"Your God must know why."

"My God is your God, remember. And look what a sly and subtle force this God of ours can be. True, the war was far away. Equally true, Borva was a happy and prosperous spot. You see what it is now. A ghost town."

"We are living now on a ghost continent."

"Does that make us ghosts?" said Klima, slapping his considerable belly to indicate a too too solid fleshly component. "You and I?"

"Speaking for myself, I would say yes, it does."

"Two years ago, the river flooded us. The water in my cold room stood waist high and my wares, beautiful salami and sausages and cheeses, went bobbing away like dead fish."

"I must be missing your point."

"I haven't made it yet. For days, I went around in a state. You know: woe unto me, so many days of work lost, so much money lost, my cellar beginning to sprout mold. And that's when we heard Samuel was taken."

"And you thought, thank heaven for a little mildew."

"Yes. So the point of my story is that the war was elsewhere and also it was not."

"Now the prosperity is elsewhere. Unless they irrigate your fields."

"So much has changed," said Klima, uncharacteristically morose, or perhaps just sentimental. Too distracted in any event to register Karel's gentle teasing. The business aspect of their transaction was completed and he barely noticed when Karel slipped away.

He kept to himself. On Fein's private strip of the river, trout came so eagerly to the bait that it seemed they loved nothing better than to be hooked, cooked, and eaten. With the flour and salt and the sack of potatoes he had purchased, with the fruit trees in yield and the woods flooded with mushrooms, he would not be going hungry.

He fished every day, though the river drew him in other ways as well. The water was never warm yet somehow it always warmed him. Each morning he would sink down and let the current envelop him. After years of deprivation—not enough to drink, not enough to bathe—the simple ceaseless bounty of water was luxury enough.

Another luxury was the storeroom in Fein's cellar, piled

two deep and three high with with crates of wine. Europe was infested with looters of every stripe, yet this impressive cache sat undisturbed. Less surprisingly, the same was true of Fein's library. Karel found a treasure trove there: the Russians, Balzac and Zola, Goethe and the brothers Mann—but also the works of Jirasek, Herben, Arbes. He held these volumes gratefully, turned the pages reverently.

The painted chess board faced him with a serious temptation. Chess was a particular taboo. The Kornfeld brothers—Isaac and Isador, his chess partners—were dead. It seemed disrespectful, a secular sacrilege, to play and so he had not. Here he restrained himself from even touching the pieces or scheming future moves in Fein's interrupted game. He left it as he found it, *in medias res*.

Each evening, he opened a fresh bottle of wine and drank while frying his catch. Though Karel was no connoisseur, more a man who would take wine when beer was not on offer, he could tell these wines were good. After finishing his meal and washing up, after an hour of reading, he would strip and pick his way back down to the riverbank. He knew the racing stream, coupled with the wine racing in his brain, would help him sleep.

He would dry himself in the vestibule and then sit by a token fire—a handful of kindling, a few of Fein's dirt-caked birch logs—and read his way toward each night's oblivion.

1987

"May I ask," said Lindauer, struggling for dignity in the face of his pain, "that you leave my house at this time?"

"No. I ask, at this time, you put uniform."

"I have no uniform."

"Get it. Put it."

Pearls of sweat on his face, blood soaking through his trousers, Lindauer braced himself against the mantel, examining his wounded leg as though he found it an interesting specimen. Looking up, he fixed Karel with an expression of complete disdain and said,

"You are nothing but a filthy Jew and a madman." Karel shot him in the left knee and Lindauer dropped to the floor, screaming.

"Uniform," said Karel, though it did seem problematic how the Nazi would fetch it—without a leg to stand on, was Karel's mordant thought.

Two faces loomed in an arched portal, old folks: a man in a loose-fitting brown jacket, a woman in a long yellow apron. Servants, no doubt, who had heard the shots and heard their master's scream. Quaking with fear, they withdrew quickly when Karel waved the pistol.

Leaving Lindauer for the moment, he set out to explore the house. It was vital this monster not be in his smoking jacket and slippers, but rather in full regalia, right down to the polished jackboots. Either that or helplessly naked—why not hoist the fiend on his own petard?

Finding the safe was easy. Karel simply began taking down paintings and there it was, behind a bucolic scene of a Rhine River castle. The safe wasn't even locked. Karel raked through money, deeds, and letters, including two letters of commendation from the Reich with fancy purfled edges and high-flown encomiums.

In a dressing room upstairs, he strewed clothes haphazardly; in a large walk-in closet, the same. Only at the bottom of a paneled trunk in the back of the closet did he find any part of Lindauer's well-remembered costume, and it was only the cap. Sturmbannfuhrer Lindauer had saved the cap, could not bring himself to part with it. It had the piping, it had the wings of Satan embroidered above the brim, it would have to do.

He brought the cap back downstairs through the vaulted great hall and set it on Lindauer's head, insultingly askew. Lindauer snatched it off and sailed it as far across the room as he could manage. He was still evading justice, refusing to confess, as though by denying facts he could disprove them.

"What have I done to merit this barbaric treatment?" he said, speaking formally, grammatically, though his pain had to be extreme. And the pose was impressive in its way, even if honesty might have served him better. Karel was uncomfortable killing in

cold blood and honesty, or humility, might have chilled him and made it difficult. It was Lindauer's hideous posturing that kept his fury in focus.

"What you done is murder my wife."

"I served my country. That is all."

Karel shot him twice more, left shoulder, right shoulder. "Murder my wife, murder my children, everybody. And every day laughing! Enjoying."

Karel was certainly not laughing or enjoying. He was shaken by the ugliness of the moment, Lindauer rolling back and forth on the thick carpet. Had he really expected this would be easy? It was justice, yes, but it was also murder. This was not the field of battle.

Exodus 21 came back to him, restored him to purpose: eye for eye, hand for hand, life for life. Murder not merely justified but murder as justice, precisely. Still, he was distressed by the suffering he was obliged to inflict.

Once he went with his grandfather to hunt down a predatory fox. The fox had been taking chickens and had to be shot. When it proved to be wounded, and lay whimpering, Karel could not watch the end. He never forgot the cry of that animal in the awful moments between injury and release. Now here he was, causing the same agony.

In a way, he could understand why the Nazis called it a mercy shot when dealing death with a swift report from the blind side. But theirs was a mockery of mercy, for they were killing the innocent, where he was killing the guilty. Lindauer was a killer driven only by the Devil's mandate, a predator who lacked even the fox's justification of hunger.

Nonetheless, Karel was weeping as he assigned the fifth bullet.

Five, because he had understood from the beginning that just as they had murdered Mila and Benno and Lucie and Helena, so too had they murdered him. Five bullets.

From the wall safe and from an armoire in the attic (a lumber room with no lumber), he took bundles of notes and a wooden box stuffed with jewelry. He came down a back stairway into the kitchen, where the two faithful retainers stood frozen, hands in the air, pleading for their lives. Hating to think they might take him for a common criminal, Karel thrust a fistful of bills at the old man and instructed him to take the automobiles.

"They are yours to keep or to sell off," he said, speaking in Czech, which they may or may not have understood. Falling back into his own language served to calm his nerves. His hands were still trembling. "Your master has left you the autos and this bit of severance pay, in his last will and testament."

"A fine man," dared the woman, tentatively, in German. Clearly she was as confused as she was frightened.

"One of nature's noblemen," said Karel, though he doubted irony was her strong suit.

He filled a leather bag with the remaining money and some of the gold and pearls. Among the stabled horses was a quiet old roan that suited him; he liked the way she met him with a lively eye. Karel knew he wanted no part of the automobiles, without knowing why this was so.

He would have a few more hours of light, time enough to reach the border and the small inn at Klovidan. His plan, his only plan, was to sleep indoors that night. To eat a good meal, drink all the pilsner that would fit inside him, bathe until he looked human, sleep between sheets.

Carl's face has been as firmly closed as a vault. He has been in a sort of trance, narrating from behind a mask. His voice clotted, his tone dirge-like. Lewis wonders if Carl even knows what he has been saying.

Yet from inside this flat blank mien Carl did manage to convey any number of strong emotions. Fury above all, but also sorrow, regret, sympathy, disgust. And *reluctance*, if that can be accounted an emotion. It certainly seemed to be one, as Carl was speaking.

But reluctance to do what he did after the war, or reluctance to relive it now? It could even be reluctance entrusting Lewis with this confession, after so much time. Among other things, he has just confessed to murder.

In any case, the spell has been shattered. Lewis is sure there is no chance of getting Carl to annotate the facts he has just published. The wonder is that he put the facts out there at all.

"Thank you, Uncle Carl," is all Lewis can think to say.

"It needed doing."

"I mean thank you for telling me."

"You asked."

Despite the solemnity of the moment, Lewis can't help laughing at this. He reaches across the table for both his uncle's hands. "True! I also asked thirty years ago. And twenty years ago. And ten."

"So I answered."

"Ecclesiastes."

"Not Ecclesiastes. Exodus."

"Ecclesiastes. A time to tell and a time to refrain from telling."

"Exodus 21. A life for a life. I was only sorry he had a name."

"But you knew his name."

Is Carl confused? Has his mind wandered to the tale he shared years earlier, about a young German soldier whose name he tried to avoid learning?

"I knew he was Lindauer. Sturmbannfuhrer Lindauer was what I knew. Thief, rapist, liar, killer. *Nazi*. That guy got what he got. But the old man said to me *Kurt* Lindauer. Because, you see, the old ones believed he was a human being."

1946

By any objective standard, Karel's existence here was a healthy one. One evening as he was working the molasses into Grandfather Bondy's spruce beer recipe, he conceded that a fly on the wall might call it idyllic. To describe it as such would not, objectively speaking, be inaccurate.

It would also be laughable, and somehow Karel could laugh, though he questioned his sanity when he went on to consider it might be even more idyllic if he had a dog for companionship.

There were dogs nearby. Their lively discussions traveled down the river to him at dusk, a notice delivered each evening as he sat on the small tiled terrace. The dogs served as a reminder that even Karina had been taken from them as they "packed" for Terezin. At that fraught and disorienting moment, with their lives in such disarray, he had not properly mourned her loss.

Karina would love the life at Fein's Castle. For her, the place would be more than an idyll, it would be the *ideal.* She would have limitless opportunities for sniffing and foraging, she would never be confined, and her master would never leave for work. Karina always whined when she saw him reaching for his hat; now he did not even own one. True, the world had been tumbled to ruin by something calling itself "National Socialism" but to sweet dumb Karina the arrival of a newspaper signaled nothing more tragic than half an hour's boredom.

He had not forgotten how often it was the dogs that frightened them, the dogs one needed to outwit. Ludvik Baderle had lain all night in an earthen latrine, swimming in a piss pit, and still they got to him in the morning with the dogs. And they executed him on the spot because they did not care to touch him. His first day out, Karel had slogged in that brook for hours, hoping to frustrate their noses. These days he felt so clean he wondered if a dog could smell him.

They terrified Milena, those dogs pacing the platform at Bohusovice. Enormous black shepherds on short taut leashes expressly designed to improve the mood for carnage. Those snarling beasts were mostly for show, a device to frighten the women and children, and they were effective enough at that. When he told Mila this was their chance, likely their only chance, she gestured toward the dogs and dismissed the notion out of hand.

She looked impossibly beautiful to him at that terrible moment. In her faded green-and-white checked smock, with her hair loose and lively. So beautiful, and as unconcerned as ever. "What are you thinking, my love? That I can outrun those dogs? That you can, while carrying the children in your arms?"

"A dog is only a dog, Milena."

"Not those dogs," she laughed, touching his face tenderly, as if to say poor Karel, always so foolishly self-confident. As if to point out there were other obstacles, for holding those taut leashes were vicious men with guns and without a speck of conscience. "And where would we go? Where do you propose we end up after your one-hundred-meter dash? For now, we are safest obeying."

"Please, Mila. Don't be so naive."

"Please don't be so cynical. Look, at least we are all here. Our parents are here, and my brothers. Whatever happens next, we begin with family."

Begin and end, he said to himself, for it was already too late. At once all the pretenses were dropped and they were being herded down a dusty roadway toward the fortress. The charade was over and now the only consideration was to get them penned up as quickly as possible. Many of the suitcases they had been urged to pack wisely, giving careful consideration to what they would need once "safely relocated," were simply stranded on the platform.

And yet Lucie, who had sailed up into his arms as they walked, was greatly relieved as they passed through the gateway to this place, this prison that had been so deceptively represented as their new "home." She was glad to feel safe from the dogs.

He slid into the current and began wading upstream toward the canine chorale just as their concert was winding down. Either the dogs made a peace each night or they were ushered indoors around this hour. All he heard now was the rush of water, in crescendo when it crashed over boulders. Closer to the beet fields, though, he heard someone singing.

He left the water and climbed the embankment. Moving along a stony path, he discovered that the sound was singsong speech, a volley of excited voices coming from the peasant colony. Soon enough he saw them below, four young women splashing in a deep pool where the river swooped around a sandbar. It struck him that he had become skillful at moving through the trees invisibly, like a Red Indian in America.

Three dresses dangled from branches, a fourth was spread flat over a low bush like a tablecloth. Twitching within him, a vestigial fragment of youthful mischief, was the teasing impulse to give them a fright. Let out the Wolfman's howl, or feign a madman's laughter and scatter them like chickens.

He was sobered immediately by the memory of the Silesian women they tried to save, the women ploughed into a hole in the ground. The way these voices had come, faintly at first and then with increasing clarity, was so much the same. What a difference, though, between that catastrophe and this scene of joy, of radical freedom. Between the nakedness of those poor women and the nudity of these.

One of the girls might have spotted him. At least she was staring directly at the bluff where he had just pronounced himself invisible. Karel fixed his gaze on a strip of moonlight spread like pale paint on the sandbar. This was Little Boris's trick for ensuring perfect stillness: lock your eyes on a fixed object or a specific spot. Little Boris had a trick for everything.

When Karel dared to unlock his eyes and look again, the girl had ducked her head in the water and was wringing her hair on one side. She had not seen him after all. Standing in the shallows unselfconsciously, breasts and flanks pale blue in the moonlight, she was as secure in her privacy as he was in his invisibility.

Suddenly, one of the other three, the tallest, let out a shriek. Something had moved under the surface. A *snake*—more likely a stick—had brushed against her and now in a flurry of splashing, a chaos of gaiety, they flailed and scrambled to the sandy patch where their dresses hung. Karel had been crouching for so long he felt a cramp snatch at the back of his leg, but he had to keep still. Fortunately, this was another discipline he had mastered.

A prisoner of stillness, he was at the same time a privileged audience, for their dressing proceeded like a beautiful dance, an inadvertent performance that might have been entitled Youth and Grace. The absence of intent only made the choreography lovelier, just as the absence of self-consciousness perfected their bodies. Slim backs, small breasts (with one almost comical exception) and smoothly muscled legs all disappeared by portions into the cotton smocks.

Karel knew he could choose to look away. In the camp, he had always looked away; it was a matter of principle to do so. To look at these girls seemed a different case. Looking was not only the natural reaction, it might be the correct one. If this was a gift given him as spectator, was it not also a gift given them? They would not always be so lithe and careless. Not for long would they take such simple pride in their bodies, or feel so thoroughly in command of them.

He watched as they fiddled with one another's hair, lingered over misaligned buttons. They tugged at one another playfully, giggled, hurried away. Karel was weary and suddenly chilled by the dark wind. Any erotic provocation he felt—and he could admit there had been some—gave way to a more familiar, lazy desire to be back at Fein's Castle.

To make up the fire. To be dry and warm. To slide beneath Fein's soft duvet and sleep.

1990

Lately there had been a number of articles about reparations, about the ways in which a few venerable European businesses were owning up to past transgressions. Lewis had followed this issue closely and was calling Carl specifically to discuss it. Not that Carl would care about bullion, or real estate in Brno, but surely he would be interested that all those "other" Nazi crimes—the art and money stolen, the properties seized—were finally being addressed.

Far from taking an interest, Carl doesn't want to hear a word of it. All he wants to discuss is Lewis' impending visit, an event which will only be real to him, apparently, after Lewis recites the itinerary five times.

"I have for you something nice," Carl says—this too for about the fifth time. His tone, Lewis cannot help thinking, is that of someone offering a bribe, a sweetener to clinch the deal. Lewis needs no such incentive. He knows it has been too long. He has blocked out the time and the car is already loaded.

Rachel is off traveling with friends—she is a *grownup* now, she keeps insisting—and he is to deliver the boys to Catherine, in Madison. She is still saying this is a trial separation, Lewis is still wondering why they are separating at all. So half the trip is for bonding with Matt and Sandy ("Road trip, Dad!") and the other half will be for brooding over Catherine once she begins receding in the rearview mirror.

"I have for you something nice."

When Carl says it again, he is probably imagining that Lewis will try to guess, play the game, but Lewis flashes back instead to a parallel construction, the revelatory unforgettable "I have for you five bullets."

"Do you remember telling me about Lindauer?" he says. "About the five bullets?"

"Lewis, please. Do I remember?"

"You said it was justice. Justice precisely, quote unquote. That's how you thought of it at the time."

"I think of it the same exact way today."

"Well, so I don't understand why you don't feel that way about this whole reparations business. Isn't that all about justice, precisely?"

"Enough with your justice," says Carl. "I have for you something nice."

"That's great, Uncle Carl," says Lewis, caring as little about the something-nice as Carl cares about the reparations. All Lewis can see is the villain Lindauer, the man who for reasons actual or symbolic had become the focus of all Carl's fury, sprawled and bleeding on the floor. "I'll have something for you too."

He did intend to have something, but settled for paltry last-minute gifts, fancy preserves and cookies picked up at Gold's on his way through Connecticut. He only hoped Carl hadn't gone over the top with *his* something.

Which, of course, he had. "It's a car," says Carl, and for a moment Lewis is confused. He has just driven across the country and arrived in, yes, a car. Why is Carl bothering to identify it as such?

"I'm talking about a real car, Lewis."

"What do you mean?" says Lewis, though he has begun to realize that a "real car" could be the something-nice.

"You know what is a car? English speaking word for automobile?"

"The word I understand," says Lewis, inadvertently adopting his uncle's habit of inverting grammar, object first, verb second. "But I have a car."

They are standing on the flagstone path to Carl's front door, scant moments after Lewis emerged from that very car, which he now points out, in broad jest, for his uncle. A car I have! It's that old gold Corolla, parked alongside Carl's big low boat of an Oldsmobile like a poor relation out at elbows.

"Please," says Carl.

This is his dismissive. Roughly translated, it means don't give me any such nonsense. So what if this lesser breed of transportation has just come from California without so much as a hiccup, it is simply too small and too old—barely six years!—to qualify as a real car. By the time Carl produces an envelope, Lewis is willing to play the guessing game: the envelope will be stuffed with cash, however much cash a real car costs.

"You're lucky you weren't robbed coming out of the bank with this," says Lewis, blushing at the extravagance of the gift.

"Let me tell you, the robbers were lucky," says Carl, as if a small elderly man might spell big trouble for armed and desperate criminals.

Whenever Lewis visits, there is an envelope. Years back, the envelopes were generated spontaneously, at the last minute, and as such were somewhat circumscribed. As Lewis would begin to leave, Carl and Clara would go around the house dredging up money—opening drawers, going through purses and pockets—so it was never too extreme. For all Lewis knows, today's envelope could contain $10,000.

To say the obvious thank-you would legitimize the gift, which he is not ready to do. So instead he changes the subject, takes a shot at re-opening a discussion of the reparations issue. Carl's glare does his talking for him: reparations, bah humbug.

"Think about this for a minute, Uncle Carl. Why *not* take it?"

"Take what?"

"For now, I guess, take an interest. Who knows? Every week, it seems there's a fresh story out of Europe. Car companies apologizing for using slave labor—"

"Apologize!"

"Make amends. Pay up. The Swiss are looking into millions in gold—"

"Now? Fifty years after, they are looking into it? Lewis, please."

"It stinks, I get that. But look at it this way. If they do have a lot of your money, or your family's money, why on earth would you want them to keep it?"

"So they can choke on it. What else?"

"And it isn't just money involved. Houses are being repossessed. There are keepsakes, jewelry, *photographs*. Do you know anything about 'Canada'?"

"I only know everything about it. This was Pollak's job, what the kapos called Canada. Every single thing we owned, they took, and to hell with *looking into* it."

No surprise that Uncle Carl would disdain the notion of compensation. Needless to say, there is no way to compensate for one slain child, for one parent or one sibling, much less six million. To try and put a price on those stolen lives would be grotesque. But wasn't it equally grotesque to allow property stolen from the Jews, with half a century's interest already accrued, to remain in the hands of the thieves? What if they didn't choke on it? What if, instead, they used it to treat themselves to fancy yachts and mansions on the Black Sea?

But Carl is finished with the topic. There is nowhere for Lewis to take the conversation. And perhaps Carl is right, or at least being logical by his lights. To consider accepting anything—call it compensation, blood money, or more palatably reparations—would be to entertain the possibility of forgiveness. Lewis is pretty sure his uncle is not the man for that job.

That evening, he asks after Clara, who is in Boston visiting Madeleine's family. It is good news that Clara felt well enough to make the journey. "She is back in the pink," Carl assures him.

Then, systematically as always, Carl inquires after Lewis' children: grade of school, serious interests, recent accomplishments. He is pleased to hear that Rachel will be studying history in college, pleased both boys are playing "soccer."

"They must remember to enjoy," says Carl, having taken in the summaries of youthful success, as well as a second glass of Courvoisier. "Excel, yes, but also enjoy."

This is Carl's mantra, albeit there is scant evidence he has remembered to enjoy his own life. Sometimes it seems almost a matter of principle he not enjoy it too much, or at least never confess to enjoying it.

"Here is to your late most lovely mother," says Carl, raising his glass. He never forgets to toast Alene. She too is always a topic.

"And to my Aunt Clara, in absentia," says Lewis.

"You will see your Aunt Clara tomorrow, bubula. For now, with all the driving you did, and in the tiny car?—better sleep. And do me this one favor. Don't start telling me with morning coffee that Goebbels's grandson is on his way over here bringing flowers and candy."

"I promise not to mention it. Even if I see the item in tomorrow's *Times*."

"A basket of fresh fruit from Goebbels! Apologies from Heydrich for what happened. What *happened*, Lewis. Do you see? Like nobody *did* this."

"Don't get yourself worked up, Uncle Carl. It's late."

"Rhine wine from Hitler! The milk of human goodness!"

Carl sets his glass down so heavily Lewis is surprised it doesn't shatter. Maybe it was actually his third brandy, or his fourth? Lewis is fairly certain he has had just one himself.

"It would be poison, you know. The candy."

Lewis is smiling as they stand and hug, partly at Carl's attempted shift to humor, more so at his pronunciation. It vood be poison.

"You're right. Probably it would, in some way or another."

"So that's it. A good night's sleep tonight and then tomorrow we shop for your new car. I know the right place to go, believe me."

1946

Karel found himself waking earlier, craving the brightening air. He would walk straight out the door, bare skin to the wind, and start down the hill. By now he knew every extrusion along the steep path, each twisted root and sharp edge of schist. Familiarity had remodeled these obstacles into a crude, irregular staircase. He did not mind that the water was getting colder. The chill only made him eager for a pot of hot coffee and with it some decent cheese and warm bread. To brew real coffee was still almost thrilling. He would read as he ate, mining the riches of Fein's library. There was no news of the wider world here; most of what he read dated back 20 years, if not a hundred.

Willy-nilly, with no particular purpose in mind, he had begun sketching hypothetical projects, scratching down hypothetical specifications. These structures would never be built, they merely provided exercise for the mind. Even in the real world—had the real world survived—no one was about to underwrite steel hinges fastened into glass or an arena with a retractable roof. Karel was simply amusing himself.

The same was true with regard to chess. While he never actively decided to set aside his resistance, it had moved aside on its own, freeing him to maneuver the pieces on Fein's painted table. Soon he was playing matches against himself, Bondy v. Bondy, as if one could be ignorant of one's own strategies. To mitigate this problem, he would make a careless or illogical move and then abandon the game for the nightly sequence of cooking, eating, and cleaning up. He would bathe, and read, and only then return to the haphazardly realigned board, hoping to find himself freshly engaged.

In truth, he was getting fed up with his own company.

"It's the recluse!" said Klima in his usual hearty manner. Once again it had been weeks since Karel's last foray into the village. "I began to wonder if you had moved along and left us."

"No. Here I am."

"Or killed yourself!" said Klima cheerfully.

"No. I found I wanted a game of chess."

"Well, that's a good sign, if killing yourself was the alternative."

At this, Karel's mind flashed back to the night Pavel was dying while at the same time craving a cigar. The butcher was right; even the smallest desire was a proof against death.

"Yes, but then what if I can't find a game?" said Karel, placing an index-finger pistol against his temple.

"Someone must have built you with leftover stones from a wall, you hard bastard. I have no idea why I like you."

"Your problem is that you like everyone," said Karel. Though he tried sounding stern, he was secretly touched by the butcher's solicitude. "You are a good Christian Jew."

"Kaberle is your man for the chess. He plays. He never could defeat Bert Fein, so he may not be in your weight class. Then again, they say Fein had been a grandmaster."

"They say that, do they? I will say that his chess set is beautiful. Do you know where those pieces were carved?"

"No idea. Never laid an eye on them. The closest I came in my life to chess was listening to Tomas mutter on about Bert's bloody knights and pawns."

As he watched Karel step inside the tap-house a moment later, the butcher took a few lumps of sugar from his apron and fed them to the roan.

Two men stood at the bar, sipping from tall steins. The landlord sat in a chair by the window, rattling a newspaper into form before smoothing it flat on the table.

"Busy?" said Karel.

"Never a moment's peace," said the landlord, who could not have appeared more idle. The two men at the bar constituted his entire clientele. "What can I get you?"

"I would like to have a basket of your bread sticks, a glass of the ale, and a game of chess. Can I place such an order?"

Tomas Kaberle was amused at this flurry of words, this outright repartee from the famously silent man. In each of his prior visits, "the recluse" husbanded syllables as if he was paying a tariff on each one uttered.

"Maybe later on. The shift changes in half an hour and it will be busier. So we'll see."

Not long after that, certainly less than half an hour, Kaberle put on his hat and strolled out the door. No one came to replace him. If the shift changed, and business flooded in, there would be no one present to attend to it. Fortunately or unfortunately, no such business materialized.

When he returned an hour later, Kaberle was amazed to find the recluse still there. Karel had moved to the bar, where he sat with two empty steins in front of him. Clearly he had drawn them for himself and in payment had sprayed some coins on the oak slab. Nothing was spoken as Kaberle, with great deliberation, repositioned his hat on its peg. The clock ticked loudly in the empty room.

"Exactly how much of your half speed piss do I need to drink before you'll give me a game?" Karel said, as the innkeeper flapped a fresh white apron, very much in the way he had flapped his newspaper earlier.

"One more, I'd say. But I'll join you for this one."

Kaberle was no slouch, and Karel was far from sharp. Really, he had not played in years and soon discovered that competing against himself had provided better exercise for his fingers than for his mind. In very short order he found himself toppling his king in surrender.

"You see the strategy," said Kaberle. "My ale is so strong it addles your brain."

"An easy enough task," said Karel agreeably, concealing his pleasure in having lost the game. Losing it meant they would play again.

1994

Aunt Clara's latest illness is far worse than Carl had let on. Lewis arrived with offerings suitable to a quick recovery—sourdough bread and See's candy from the San Francisco airport—only to find her bed-ridden and gaunt. It is mid-October, Indian Summer on the Island, but all the windows are shut and the bedroom smells of death.

"She is always cold," says Carl, explaining the windows.

Lewis notes the irony, for Carl has always been the cold one, his toes forever cursed by those infamous tight shoes. Carl seems oblivious to the odor, whether from having imbibed it by increments or from a need to deny the gravity of the situation. But his grief seeps out. These two people had lives before they met, disparate histories, yet time has accumulated and by now they have been together 40 years. Carl trembles when he bends to kiss her waxen forehead.

Once, as a young child, Lewis was invited to punch his new uncle in the belly and did so softly, reluctantly. "No, really punch," said Carl, so Lewis punched harder. "That's it?" said Carl. "This is the biggest punch you got?"

He then hit his uncle so hard that his wrist bent back (and would be sore for days) but Carl's belly was like wallboard. "Are you a Superman?" Lewis said, thinking for the first time about Carl's invulnerability.

"Sure I am. Me and Nietzsche."

The boy did not know who Nee-Cha was, nor did he believe his uncle could be a literal Superman. But he knew this man was hard to hurt and impossible to kill. Behind this latter notion was Carl's claim that he survived the War "because I have nine lives, like the cat."

Nine was a lot, no question, but given his uncle's age and his aunt's condition, Lewis now fears Carl could be down to the last one or two. When they step out into the yard, the vegetable garden yields up corroborating evidence. Stalks of dry drooping corn that went unpicked, wasted tomatoes that split open on the vine. The green peppers have gone to red.

By way of denying the unspoken charge of neglect, Carl plucks a clean head of cabbage and presents it to Lewis. There are lettuces still coming in, this kind and that. Carl points to something he calls a winter lettuce and Lewis agrees it is impressive. Mainly, he hopes they won't be having Carl's boiled cabbage for dinner.

"This is where I come," says Carl. "Every day."

"To think."

"To *not* think."

Lewis can see it, Carl standing in the garden not-thinking. Not even moving, just staring off into the mysterious distance only he sees. In the family, Lewis was always considered closest to Carl, a special connection, early acknowledged. Of course no one is close to Carl Barry in the usual sense of the word. Lewis' gift has been his patient faith that his uncle's reluctance was less an end in itself than a prelude to important utterance. He has never taken silence for an answer. Consequently he could, in Alene's phrase, "always worm a little information out of Carl."

Still, there are deep wells of information unplumbed, great swaths of time unaccounted for. While he knows there was a family in Europe, a family that did not survive, he knows almost nothing about them, and nothing at all of parents, siblings, or friends. Carl was around 40 when he came into Lewis' life and apart from the War stories—the camps, the forest, Borva, *Lindauer*—those 40 years of earth have scarcely been turned over.

The banal metaphor jars Lewis. It makes him visualize the heaped bodies that lie below the soil of European history, the mass graves of the Holocaust.

"Can I ask a question?" he says, absently flipping the cabbage from hand to hand.

"Such as will my cabbage survive being treated like a toy?"

"Sorry about that. No, a question about the past. You know I teach history?"

"Lewis, I am not senile."

"Of course not. I just meant I am in the business of facts. Just the facts, as Sergeant Friday used to say."

"Who said it?"

"A cop on TV, no one real. How about for each fact you supply, I trade you half an hour of power weeding?"

"Oh, it's a quiz show. With prizes."

"Exactly."

"I don't need these prizes. I can do the weeding."

"We can do it together. Get more done, have more fun."

"Better make up your mind, are you the historian or the bad poet?"

"A TV cop, Uncle, just the facts. So here's the first question: what was your birth name, in Czechoslovakia?"

"Bondy. You know this. I am Karel Bondy."

"What was your wife's name? I don't mean Aunt Clara, obviously. Your first wife."

"She was Mila. Milena Molinova. To me, Mila."

"That is such a pretty name."

"She was a pretty girl, believe me."

"Of course. And your children. I am sorry if you mind my asking, but I never heard their names."

"I don't remember."

"You don't want to say. That's okay—"

"Not I don't want to say. I don't remember."

"You don't remember their *names*?"

Caught off balance, Lewis has slipped from delicacy. He can't help taking Carl's shrug of denial for a lie. At the same time he encounters for the first time a notion, a revelation, that Carl's nameless murdered children are *related to him*. Cousins by marriage after the fact? Whatever the designation, they are *family*. His cousins were murdered.

"Do you remember their faces?"

This is virtually an insult, but before Lewis can retract or soften it, Carl is shaking his head no. Is this because he remembers them all too vividly or because, perhaps more terribly, he truly does not? Carl turns away, as if seeking comfort from the colorful profusion of his nasturtiums, which unlike the vegetables have thrived on neglect. But is he staring at the flowerbed or staring past it into that mysterious distance?

Carl is past 80. He lost them half a century ago and was left without a single photograph to remind him. Maybe he really can't recall their names and faces. Lewis is wise enough to close the inquiry regardless, even though a solitary fact is all he has to show for it. Karel Bondy he did know; he used that question as a starter, a solenoid to get the train of memory moving. It only moved as far as Molinova, one station, before screeching to a halt. So much for Sergeant Joe Friday and the facts.

"You are cold, bubula," says Carl. "We should get you back inside."

For Lewis, who is not cold and who has just spent nine hours enclosed in airplanes and cars, going back inside the fetid house is the last thing he needs. The sun brightens and is somehow brightened by the rainbow of blooms, the breeze sweetens the grape arbor as they pass by...but the matter is not open for discussion. Carl is already holding the back door open.

"Good idea," says Lewis. "We'd better check and see how Aunt Clara is doing."

1946

He and Kaberle had by now styled a limited, wary friendship, whereby they drank together without a hint of cheer, joked without laughing, and competed without admitting the outcome mattered. One time they played the ten-second chess, "black lightning" as they called it in the capital where according to legend it had driven men to madness. But those souls must have been near the edge all along, Karel and Tomas agreed. At stake in their own matches was nothing more dire than a stein of half-speed ale.

The brewery men, the workers, took notice of this new social strophe. "So, is he better than the German?" they would ask the innkeeper, after the recluse was gone. And Kaberle's stock answer was, "Of course he is better. He is Czech." The men would laugh, then slide back inside their closed circle, rekindle their harmless crude jokes. They might nod to the outsider now, or make reference to him ("Did he beat you again today, Tomas?") but no one addressed him directly. He was Czech, but he was not one of them.

One afternoon, two officials from the brewery came in, men in suits, with a young woman in tow. Her frock was shapeless, loose at the waist, yet somehow it managed to imply a supple form. Her face was almost ordinary until one noticed the sparkle in those almond-shaped eyes and a quicksilver smile which delivered a small jolt to the male heart each time it occurred.

Tomas did not fail to register Karel's curiosity. He leaned over and whispered that during the war this young woman, Pavenka, had been the "bride" of a German official in the district.

"He was killed?"

"No, he simply left. And left his pretty wife behind."

"He was neck and neck with Herr Fein?"

"That guy was no Bert Fein. He was a genuine son of a bitch, in fact. But you are right, quite a few were neck and neck. There were not so many Germans around, but all of them scattered like cockroaches."

"Yet she stayed."

"She is Silesian. Doesn't speak a word of German, according to my wife."

"She is plain."

"Do you think so? I find her extremely attractive—just don't tell my wife I said so."

"She is both plain and attractive," conceded Karel, who had never so much as glimpsed Kaberle's wife, much less confided in her.

Karel's grudging compliment, even the fact he noticed the Silesian girl, seemed a departure to Tomas until he realized this was his first look at the recluse in the presence of a woman. That could alter an equation, especially if the woman in question was Pavenka. Women who had consorted with the enemy were sometimes treated harshly, banished or worse. Not Pavenka. And it was no accident she was keeping company with two of the wealthiest men in the district.

No accident, either, that she was as aware of Karel, a new face and one that had tilted her way, as he was of her. Those almond-shaped eyes missed very little. She caught him glancing over and unabashedly returned the favor. For an instant, their eyes engaged and Karel had the sense she might break free and come strolling right over to their table. Something bold about her, for sure.

Before anything of the sort could happen, he snapped his gaze away, so he did not see one of her consorts spin her round, muttering crossly about her crazy ways. He did hear her derisive laughter, whether aimed at her present company or at men as a species. This Pavenka was a dangerous woman; she had cracked a sort of code.

"Tomas, can we start this game over?" said Karel. "I have lost the thread."

"I see that," said Tomas Kaberle, with an amiable smirk. The recluse was human!

That night she came to him in a confusing dream. "How are you, Karel?" she said, solicitously, tenderly, as though they were long acquainted. And they were, for she was his wife.

Or she was and she wasn't. Her voice was Milena's, yet when she began to undress she was the girl from the tap-house. Karel watched the shapeless smock collapse to the floor and pool at her ankles. Watched as she—anything but shapeless—stepped free of it and raised her slim arms to unclasp the same amber earrings she had worn earlier in the day. She was Pavenka.

"Please," he said. "You must leave."

"You asked me here," she replied gaily, and she was Mila again. His hands came to rest on Mila's hips and he spoke her name.

"No, Karel, I am not your wife," said Pavenka.

"Then leave."

But he liked the smell of stale beer on her breath and her cool satin skin. His hands found her breasts and this served to disengage him from the conundrum of who she was or wasn't. He was engaged instead like the idler wheel, the gear which both turns and is turned, until his dream world swirled and bloomed, releasing him into a dizzy oblivion.

Fog had pooled on the terrace and filled the pathway down. A gray haze covered the river like a blanket. Karel waded through the haze and sank down into the fast current. Even with his feet set on the bottom he had to paddle to stay in place. A pine bough riding on the slipstream brushed against him as it spun past.

The fog was burning off by the time he came back up the hill. Roof tiles were pumpkin-colored in the spreading sunlight, apples were bright red in the orchard, and he could not help thinking what a beautiful place he had found. Beautiful and so estranged from the madness. What could explain it? He thought of Lado, and of Blake's poem: "Did he who made the lamb make thee?"

Swaddled in one of Fein's soft robes, drinking coffee on Fein's well-made terrace, Karel suddenly, involuntarily, emitted a self-mocking growl. What a perfect fool he was, to be considering such idiotic inquiries, to still expect some kind of sense. Nobody made the goddamned lamb. Nobody made the tiger, either, except for Mr. and Mrs. Tiger on a jolly night.

But trying to make sense of things was just a reflex, an old habit of mind, vestigial and useless. It had stolen up on him, as had the girl Pavenka. The world would don its disguises and play its tricks. Meanwhile, the mare was whinnying her impatience. Whoever made her had included breakfast in the grand design.

A few days later, he stood on the bridge with Klima. Sliding between the sidewalls of the stone-lined raceway below, the river flowed two meters below the high-water mark. There were brown patches all through the pale green fields. If the butcher's elbow was correct again, if his latest weather report proved accurate, this would be the first rainfall in nearly a month.

"Late afternoon," declared Klima, "if not sooner. This one will be a thorough soaking, an old-fashioned autumn downpour."

Apart from the change of seasons, were not these more or less the same words Klima had spoken on the day Karel arrived in Borva? Wasn't this the same forecast?

"If you are right," said Karel, "then the rain ushers me in and the rain ushers me out."

The butcher mimed astonishment, as if he had caught Karel with his fist in the till. "You are leaving us? Leaving our peace and quiet? Our delightful irrelevance?"

"I am, my friend."

"Well, it's too bad, it really is. But it's also good that you have set aside the dark demons that chased you here."

"Nothing has been set aside, Josef. I am running low of money."

"I didn't see you spending much."

"You took it all. You and Tomas," said Karel.

"Why do I know you are lying?"

"Both of you should be aware that there are crates of wine, untouched, in Fein's cellar. There are good chamois hides that would rot and good silver going to waste."

"He leaves us a legacy, no less!"

"Any largesse is a tribute to your peasants. They destroyed nothing and they stole nothing."

"Bert was always good to them, I am sure that's why. Maybe you should bequeath all this fine wine to them?"

"A good idea, except we won't be going back that way."

Beyond the Catholic Church with its wide stone steps ascending to the heavy-hammered wooden doors, the sky had broken in half. As though applied with broad parallel brush strokes, a dark band of charcoal pressed down on the orange fire of the sunrise and an unearthly glow, straight from an illustrated Bible, overspread the fallow fields. They watched together from the bridge as the strange glow gave way to an even stranger daytime darkness, and then the rain began. Klima felt vindicated, even if his elbow was off by a few hours.

For now, it was a soft warm rain. Karel didn't mind it and the roan clearly welcomed it. Her ears were up, her nostrils busy. She seemed pleased to feel it on her face and pleased to be going. Ready for something new.

1998

Far removed for so long from the world where he had grown up, Lewis had few meaningful connections back east. His friends had scattered, some as far as Sao Paulo, some as close as Palo Alto, but no one was still in New York or Connecticut.

Except Uncle Carl. Lewis has tried not to lose touch with Uncle Carl. He would never come east without visiting Carl, but between work, the children, the divorce, and of course the distance, he has rarely found time to make the trip. He can hardly believe he once drove it, boomeranging back and forth across the country like Kerouac and Cassady.

There was little he could do to improve the situation. He would call, but the telephone did as much to widen the distance as close it. His uncle was not a talker, especially when it came to the phone, and their conversations often made him angry. At best they devolved into rote exchanges that gave him little pleasure.

Maybe nothing gave him much pleasure. Cousin Maddie reported that he saw no one and lately had taken to picking fights with her. "He's surly, Lew, do you know what I mean?"

Admittedly, Carl was somewhat combative with Lewis as well. "So where the hell are you?" was always his first question and "California" was never an acceptable response. Lewis offered it as a joke, of course, but it was a different sort of joke to Carl, who understood California to be the place where the crazy people lived.

Over the phone, at least, Lewis could whitewash his life. He could not bring himself to tell Carl that ever since the final separation he was living in an apartment, while Catherine stayed in the house. The divorce went unreported, as did the economic strain it caused them. On top of all that, Lewis and Marta Sorenson had been seeing each other—been a couple?—for a year now and Carl, kept in the dark, would still ask after Catherine.

The problem began on their wedding day, when Carl pinned the two of them in a corner with his hard look and, poking Lewis in the chest, intoned with slow emphasis "Until death will part you." While Catherine was hearing a boilerplate benediction, an injunction to treasure forever what they were so privileged to have, Lewis was hearing a reference to the tragic end of Carl's first marriage and a command to let nothing destroy theirs.

Meanwhile, Carl might be threatened with a third marriage. According to Maddie, who Lewis checks in with ahead of time to get some sort of "intel" on the situation in Great Neck, the candidate is a shameless gold-digger with two worthless sons and a large mortgage on Park Avenue she can see Carl paying down. As Maddie puts it, with characteristic indelicacy, "She'll marry him, poison him, and live off his fortune."

Nor would the job be difficult, Maddie adds, given the pharmacopeia on Carl's nightstand. The "vast array of meds" she mentions is news to Lewis; apparently Carl can whitewash over the phone too. At a bare minimum, Maddie alerts him, the gold-digger is in a position to hasten the end. "Too much of this one, too little of that one, the wrong one at the wrong time—you know."

"Is she living there, at the house?"

"I don't drive by to check, Lewis. I'm in New Rochelle, you know, and I'm not exactly invited. I offer to come—Can I bring, can I do—and he says no thanks, everything is under control. *Her* control, is what he doesn't say."

Maddie is building up to the part where she says her mother must be spinning in her grave (Clara has been spinning for several years now) but before she can say it Lewis slips away without even having to lie: he was cooking, he smells something burning, he has to get off the phone.

It does smell that way and it is burnt in part—the part that has stuck to the pan. Somehow, the rest of his re-heated curry, the part that is not stuck to the pan, isn't even hot. He discovers this only after carrying his plate to the table and digging in. Abandoning the unappetizing pile of poorly repurposed food, he drops two slices of rye in the toaster.

He wishes the boys were with him tonight, wishes they were flying east with him tomorrow. On the other hand, this is bound to be a tricky visit, whatever is really going on with Carl. Cousin Maddie is not necessarily the most reliable source. She has just told him, in the same breath and with absolute certainty on both counts, that Carl never sees another soul and that a certain Mrs. Goodman is trying to marry him. So who knows.

And who knows which would be the larger problem, between loneliness and a flawed companionship. This is a riddle not unfamiliar to Lewis. He just feels badly that he knows so little, that he has let things slide to that point. It does make him eager to get there and see Carl face to face. Eager to meet the lady in question and perhaps start sorting out fact from fiction.

Given the "vast array of meds" dispatch, Lewis is immediately heartened by Carl's apparent vigor. His movements are brisk, his voice is strong. Mrs. Goodman's poison campaign has yet to take effect. In fact there is hope that Maddie's black widow may turn out to be nothing more than an older woman seeking company. If she proves innocent of any Machiavellian plots, she may be the best thing for Carl.

"You look all right," says Carl, releasing Lewis so as to appraise him at arm's length.

"Uncle, you took the words out of my mouth. I was about to say the same about you."

"So, good. We both look all right. I have fresh coffee made. Come."

At his first logical stop, the bathroom, Lewis scouts for signs of a female interloper. There are plenty of likely items in the bathroom, but they could easily have been Clara's, still lying undisturbed. He had never taken notice, much less inventory. Skimming the labels on a row of vials, he sees the prescriptions have all expired—leftovers from Clara's final year.

In the kitchen, the old Glenwood stove lives on, as does the dented aluminum percolator, occupying its traditional spot on the right front burner. There are no fancy new accoutrements to signify regime change. Everything looks the same.

"Will I be meeting Mrs. Goodman today? Or tomorrow?"

"Meeting who?" says Uncle Carl.

"Your girlfriend. Mrs. G."

Lewis had called last night, still early enough back east, and got Carl to mention his new friend. She was "an acquaintance" in one sentence and a neighbor in another. How old was she? Maybe 65 in one sentence, maybe 75 in another.

Today she has ceased to exist altogether. Carl dismisses her—the notion that she is a girlfriend? the possibility Lewis might meet her? the woman's very existence?—with his crisp backhand wave. Gone is Mrs. G.

"I thought she might be here."

"You are who is here."

"Yes, and it's been too long," says Lewis, willing to set Mrs. G. aside for the moment.

Carl insists on doctoring Lewis' coffee for him, how much cream, how much sugar, and he does this deftly enough, correctly. He remembers. But then he brings to the table a tray of pastries straight from the freezer—brings them *frozen*—and there is something odd in his demeanor. Not odd enough to prepare Lewis for what Carl says next:

"Do you know that I dreamed last night of your mother?"

"You did?"

"At the dam. This was one of our naughty afternoons at the dam, before you were born."

Lewis is at a loss. Doubtful Carl has dreamed of Lewis' mother. And naughty afternoons? Before Lewis was born, Carl and Alene were continents apart and a decade away from meeting. It is obvious that Carl is not himself and Lewis wonders if he has missed hints of similar disorientation in their admittedly out-of-synch telephone exchanges.

"You know the place, my golden boy, because you were there many times later on. We would fish there, Benno, you must remember. You would always listen for the Convent bells to ring."

A few years back Carl could not recall, or was unwilling to speak, the names of his murdered children. Now Lewis feels a slight shock run through him at the thought that "Benno" must have been Carl's son. These memories of fishing and of Convent bells ringing could be perfectly accurate, except it seems he has the past and the present radically tangled.

"The Convent bells, Uncle?" he says, in case the word itself, *uncle*, can restore them to their proper relationship. But it doesn't:

"Your mother was such a beauty. To you, of course, she was simply Momma, and to the baby boy his Momma is always beautiful—"

It is the telephone ringing, not the Convent bells, and with the sound Carl's face changes. The ringing has tripped a switch; he knows exactly what to say to his caller. "Yes, Trudy, hello."

Presumably this is Mrs. G., calling him back to Great Neck and back to the present. When he turns to Lewis a moment later, he understands perfectly that his nephew has just arrived from San Francisco, not his son, from Heaven. As proof of this, he trots out his standard witticism: "So tell me, Lewis, has the Golden Gate swung shut yet?"

It is possible Lewis has just experienced his uncle's first lapse of this kind, more likely there have been others. In fact, he now recalls that recently Carl reported having a problem with a hotel key—he had lost this key—and it emerged that the hotel was located in Karlovy Vary, in what was then Czechoslovakia. The room had been rented in 1930-something.

Carl caught himself quickly that time and quite nimbly spun it into an old age memory thing, or a test. He called it that, "a little test," leaving it unclear which one of them was taking this test.

That was over a month ago, sometime shortly before Carl took a fall in his driveway. According to Maddie, only Mrs. Goodman has seen him since he left the hospital. "He's at her mercy, Lewis," Maddie reported, stopping just shy of suggesting the scheming harridan had bowled Carl over.

As Carl described it at the time, the fall was of no significance.

"No fall is insignificant when you are eighty-six," Lewis pressed.

"*This* fall was insignificant," Carl insisted, neglecting to mention he had gone to the hospital. So he fell, big deal. He wasn't hurt, he wasn't even scratched. Where was the significance?

Lewis allowed himself to be convinced and let go of it. In fact he had forgotten it, and now that he is here he can see for himself that his uncle does appear unscathed. Still, he knows now from Maddie that they kept Carl in the hospital for several days. What about that?

"This was a very stubborn doctor," says Carl.

"Were they doing tests?" says Lewis, imagining what the very stubborn doctor had to say about his very stubborn patient. "They must have felt they needed to do some tests."

"Test what? I told you, I wasn't injured. I got up, I went home."

"You were home when it happened, actually, and you went to the hospital. I can understand why they took you there, but if you weren't injured, why would they keep you in there so long?"

"Observation, is what it said on the piece of paper they gave. Is that what you want to know? Well, let me tell you, bubula, I was observing them too and that outfit will not be getting my business next time around."

1947

It was eerie to find the capital intact. To see, in the Quarter, sunlight spread over the stuccoed walls of Josefov as uniformly as a fresh coat of varnish and see, behind the Pinkas Synagogue, the jumbled eruptive headstones untouched in the cemetery.

But the people were gone, and with them all the old cafés and shops. The apple seller had abandoned her post in front of the Old New Synagogue. Was there anyone here who Karel even knew? Behind every familiar door he encountered a stranger.

Floating through the narrow twisty streets, he was overcome by a sense not just of his irrelevance but of his outright insubstantiality. He was a citizen no one wished to acknowledge, a witness whose testimony no one wished to hear, and a plaintiff to whom no justice was available. None, that is, beyond the small measure of rough justice he had himself exacted in keeping with Higher Law. Exodus 21.

Leaving the Quarter that morning, he drifted back through Old Town Square, where someone said there had been some damage. "Someone" had better eyesight than Karel, who saw no more damage than that which a bad windstorm might have caused. The worldwide shock had glanced off Praha, leaving in its wake a limp complacent gratitude that the disruption had been so minimal. "It could have been worse" was a line universally rehearsed here and while this sense of relief might typify the state of mind in much of liberated Czechoslovakia, Karel knew the places where it could *not* have been worse.

He walked to the Bridge and listened, as he had so many times, to the dirge of deep horn notes from barges gliding underneath. There were flowers, a million blooms along the Vltava embankment, which struck him as a stage set, a grand illusion. President Benes had sent forth a hundred gardeners to proclaim his safe return.

Then at the stroke of noon, at the café on Kampa Island, a mirage appeared in the form of Jaroslav Heyduk. Aimless and distracted as he was, Karel could easily have overlooked him, for this was a Jaro neatly barbered and restored to hitherto unglimpsed pre-war dimensions, big-bellied and barrel-chested. Restored to the corpulence whose loss he so comically lamented. "Never say fat," was his standby line of self-defense. "I was *corpulent* before the war, never fat."

They had fought side by side in the forests, ready pals from the start through nationality, personality, and circumstance. One such circumstance was that Jaro understood no Russian, so that Karel became his operational manual. Every task, every order, came filtered through Karel. Take first watch, gather wood, clean the guns. If Karel told him to stand on his head in the snow, Jaro might have believed the order came down from Big Boris.

He was a good soldier, a good man—and a good Catholic. Assigned by the occupying Nazis to a barrel factory in the north, he "called in dead" (like calling in sick, he explained, just a touch more dramatic) and made his way to the ragtag partisans under Socrates' command. His reward for such virtue was to spend the rest of the war in discomfort, deprivation, and extreme danger. Twice he was wounded.

The second time was the charm there, as Jaroslav spent the last months of the war as a guest of Uncle Joe Stalin. Only now did Karel learn how his friend had landed in a Moscow hospital after an infection took hold in the leg wound. Jaro never reached Danzig, first because of the hospitalization, then because word came of his brother's death. So he stayed in Moscow and was given soft jobs ("Armchair jobs," he scoffed, "work you do sitting down") until the Russians too tried sending him to a barrel factory.

"Believe it or no, I still don't understand ten words of Russian."

"A remarkable accomplishment, Jaro. But the real question is why do you keep fleeing your obvious fate?"

"Barrels are not my fate, Karel, merely one amusing detail of my saga."

"Your saga, yes, of course."

Recalling Jaro's way with a tale, and with any details that might attach to it, he was belatedly suspicious of the second barrel job, in Moscow. He was only surprised that Jaro had not concocted a beautiful Muscovite nurse, who dressed his wounds tenderly and communicated in the language of love to compensate for his lack of parooski.

"The road of life has its twists and turns," Jaro grinned. "Who could know that a German bullet would be the shape of my luck!"

They had long since agreed that no one came through, much less in one piece, without the sort of luck enjoyed by that one cottage skirted by a flood, the one hen spared by a fox.

"I am so happy to know you had such luck—and so sorry about Milos."

"My poor little brother. But what about you? What shape did your luck take, Karel? Where have you been all this time?"

Karel shrugged. This was his third day in Praha and already he was eager to leave. He had stopped over in Brno and experienced the same feeling there. A city might be his fate, just as barrels might be Jaro's, but he wished it could be otherwise. Who but highly civilized city people could dream the murder of an entire race? In the countryside, there is always work to be done.

"I had nothing that needed doing, so I did nothing."

No sagas forthcoming from Karel Bondy! Jaro shook his head in recognition. No one does "nothing" for a year, albeit some people are gifted at *saying* nothing.

"It can't be the truth, not with you. Anyway, I hope you got that out of your system."

"Almost," said Karel, as the waiter brought them each another tart and another coffee. He was not sure why he said it; what it was that was "in his system" and how he could have almost got it out. Like the butcher of Borva, Jaro seemed to think reality evaporated if you left it out in the sun long enough.

"That's good to hear, because I have an idea and it concerns you."

Jaro announced his plan to open a shop. His family still had their business from before the war, dry goods, but he wanted something of his own, something different. "I thought about hardware, you know, with all the work going on now. Or supplying concrete. But maybe better a café, like this one. A pleasant place where people come to pass a pleasant hour."

"Why not? Good idea."

"The thing is, we could be partners in it. It would be grand, just like old times—you tell me what to do and I do it!"

"I tell you what Big Boris tells me. He was in the newspaper, you know, as some sort of high mucky-muck in the new Kremlin. Maybe now he tells Uncle Joe what to do."

"Or clears out the palace with one of his cosmic farts. But I'm serious about this little business idea, Karel. About doing it together."

"How serious can you be? As of one hour ago, you thought you'd seen the last of my handsome face forever."

"Yes, well it turns out I hadn't. And I am such a fast thinker that I have already begun drawing up our partnership papers. You know it would be grand, Karel."

"It would, my friend," said Karel, and he meant it, even if any such undertaking was out of the question. Still, who was there alive on this earth that Karel loved or trusted more? Here was Jaro (in the flesh so to speak, corpulent to be sure, if not perilously close to being fat) with a lovely invitation back into the world.

"I have my eye on a place in Suchdol, a small building on a lively corner. It was a bicycle repair shop, with two nice flats above. You know Suchdol—very idyllic. The sun shines all day long on this one street corner."

"Even when it rains?" said Karel, caught up by the word *idyllic*. It took him back to the house in Borva, where one day he wasted an hour ruminating on the definition of an idyll. "What could be more perfect, Jaro."

"It's a magical little spot. And the flats you could rent out, or live in, or one of each. At least agree you'll come look it over with me. If you are interested, we would go fifty-fifty, straight down the line."

"I am interested, for you. For myself, I won't stay around Praha very long."

"Don't tell me you have had problems..."

"Problems?"

"You know. There have been a few incidents. I know I haven't seen any signs saying Welcome Home Jews."

"No one has bothered me," said Karel, though he did now recall the expression on the concierge's face when he tried to stick Karel in a cramped attic room. The hotel was full, or so he explained until Karel came stomping back to the desk and suddenly the hotel was not so full.

"It's been a very few incidents," said Jaro, "and it's bound to get better."

"I won't know if it does, because a week here will be enough for me."

"Enough for what?" said Jaroslav, though he saw the gesture, that flick of the hand, and the sour smile that always accompanied it. There would be no accounting, only the cast-iron decisiveness that summarized it.

"The truth is I nearly didn't come here at all. I knew it would be changed..."

"But it's not. Praha is still Praha. Listen, man, I saw Hamburg—blown to smithereens, a wasteland like you would not believe—and they say Dresden is worse. Praha was safe inside a bell jar! Barely marred."

"You are right, in a way," said Karel, withholding the trailing clause, *but then again, you are not a Jew*. Jaroslav Heyduk of all people did not deserve that reproof, however true it might be. It was only natural Jaro would join the ranks of the could-have-been-worse. "Let's just say I have adventure on my mind."

"Meaning Palestine, after all?"

"Too hot."

"Too much sunshine? The warm sea too delightful for your cold toes? Oh, how I miss hearing your nightly complaints about those metacarpals."

"Metatarsals, Jaro. Who knows, maybe I grew attached to foul weather."

"Not me. Ice in our beards? Ears that might break off like soda crackers?"

"Such lovely days and nights, we did enjoy."

"Where will you go, then, for this terrible weather you crave? Siberia?"

"There's a thought. More likely the U.S., though. New York."

"The U.S.? Are you sure it's cold enough there for you?"

"I hear the people are very cold."

"Well then! That recommends it highly."

It was warming, uplifting, to be with Jaro and almost inconceivable to be with him in peacetime, leaning back at a café in the sun and bantering. One table over, a pretty young mother was laughing at her baby's efforts to convey a cookie to his questing mouth. Karel shook his head at the notion that such moments were possible. It was like waking into a dream.

"I have a cousin there," he said. "An older cousin, who went over in '32, started making steel. He has a business supplying stock for the government."

"He is a rich man, this cousin?"

Karel shrugged again. He remembered Jan from old photographs, pictures that were no longer extant. He did not know whether Jan was still living in New York or still running the steel plant in New Jersey. For that matter, if he was still alive. Jan might have come back over to fight the Nazis. He also might have been run over by a bus in one of the News, York or Jersey.

If alive, Jan was the only one who was. Of all the aunts and uncles and cousins, only Jan might still be breathing—except for Karel himself, of course. He sometimes forgot to count himself as he scrolled down through the extended family of casualties. He and Jan might bring the total breathing in and breathing out to two.

"Visit me over there, Jaro. I'll send you a steamship ticket and a nice new suit. They dress well in New York, I hear."

This was a lovely old joke between them and it started them laughing in the old way. For all the filthy trousers and reclaimed greatcoats they had draped themselves in, there was always the everyday comedy of Jaro dabbing melted snow on his moustache to "comb" it with his fingers. Of Jaro straightening his "lapels."

"We want to look our best for the Borises," he would say on those frigid mornings in the forest, forever frustrated to have no mirror for his self-improving ablutions. "They dress well in Moscow, I hear."

1999

Can it really be Uncle Carl on the phone? Or is Matt just pulling his leg, handing him off to a telemarketer as punishment for obsessing over his failure to call Carl.

All week Lewis has been saying it—he owes Carl a call, he needs to get in touch—instead of doing it. Finally at supper last night, Matty pre-empted him ("Hey Dad, hadn't we better check in with Uncle Carl?") and Sandy chimed right in with "Oh yeah, didn't we mean to get to it like *yesterday*?" Teenage humor.

Now Carl has beaten him to the punch. Carl, who never calls, has called. Amazingly, he has undertaken to dial the number. Without exception, all previous calls flowed east.

"You won't believe this, Uncle Carl, but I was just this minute about to pick up the phone and call you. Matty was just reminding me."

"You're right, I don't believe it."

"How are you, though? How have you been?"

"Depends. When are you coming?"

"Soon," says Lewis, who has no plan, only the usual bobbing raft of good intentions. "As soon as I can manage it."

"Soon? What comes soon is Anno 2000, Lewis. The end of the world, according to my television set. Better come first and say goodbye."

The good news? Carl is not merely lucid this time, he is downright jocular. His anger is so soft that the invitation is more prominent than the indictment he always folds into it.

"One minute into Anno 2000, they'll all be proven wrong, Uncle. The hoax will be exposed."

"What if they are proven right? Why not come first? Besides, I have for you something."

"What sort of thing?"

"The sort of thing given hand to hand, during Anno 1999."

"Something that won't keep, then. Is it a cake, or a loaf of bread?"

"Stop guessing and come see what it is."

"The problem is I have a hundred papers to grade—no exaggeration, a hundred five, actually. And then it's Christmas, you know. Chanukah—"

"I know Christmas, I know Chanukah, which by the way ended a week ago. So I will expect you on December the 26?"

"Let me figure things out and call you back on the weekend. We'll talk on Sunday."

But Carl rings back an hour later. After all these years, he has discovered that dialing the number is easy. The bad news? He is no longer lucid, no longer based in Anno 1999. How strange and unsettling it is, when just one hour earlier he had a firm grasp on the eighth day of Chanukah.

"Did you know this?" he starts out. "That every time the train arrives, Pollak is unloading six cases of horsemeat? Meat for the *dogs*. We are lucky getting one egg a week, two crusts of bread, and the dogs are eating meat. You knew this?"

"Which train do you mean, Uncle Carl?"

"The supply line, second Wednesday. Pollak sees everything. He sees the bill of lading, you understand? Pollak can tell you exactly how much whiskey the bastards consume, how much wine. The point is they want us weak and they want the animals strong."

"These provisions are going to Terezin or Auschwitz? What year are we talking about? Roughly."

There is a pause, dead air. Maybe Mrs. G. has entered the room? Lewis hears nothing and can only guess at what has interrupted Carl's headlong rant. And once again he could never have guessed what would come next:

"Roughly nothing," says Carl. "I told you what year exactly,

Anno 1999. This is the purpose of my calling. You forgot this already?"

End of fugue. Something tickled the switch in Carl's mind and turned the pages of history. Relieved as he is by Carl's return to reality, or present day reality, Lewis is disconcerted that the ground keeps shifting underneath him. It has been this way for the last six months, maybe longer. It is one reason calling has become so fraught. Matty more or less nailed it with his baseball analogy: if you look curve, Carl comes in high and tight; if you look fastball, he drops a slow curve on the corner.

"No, Uncle, I haven't forgotten. And you won't forget we have a plan to talk again on Sunday, right? I'll call around noon, your time."

There really are papers to grade and there is Marta. "Next time you see this legendary character, I would like to meet him," she has said. "He probably won't live forever."

Marta has no idea her existence is a secret and that to produce her in the flesh would constitute an admission the marriage has failed—a decade back! But conveniently for Lewis, Marta's daughter Karen is due to give birth "any minute now," which clears the coast well into Anno 2000.

On Sunday morning, Lewis calls as promised to announce he has made arrangements. He will make it to Great Neck before the end of the world.

"Too late! You missed it!"

"No," says Lewis, assuming they are in the same joke. "I get in the night of the 28th."

"Don't tell me no. I was *there* when it ended."

"Whatever you say, Uncle Carl."

Lewis is cautious, unsure which way this call is tilting. They are not in the same joke, the Anno 2000 joke, if Carl is talking about the A-Bomb or the Holocaust.

"I say come anyway. So what if the world ends, you can still buy me a nice lunch."

And there it is, the slow curve on the outside corner. With it Carl has revived a routine they began over thirty years ago. Carl is "worth," as Maddie always puts it, millions. Carl owned the bloody restaurant. Yet his then penniless college freshman nephew once tried to grab a check. Once! Forever after, it was, "So, Lewis, you are going to buy me a nice lunch?"

"You will bring the children? And your lovely wife?"

"Rachel is in London, I'm afraid. She is a little hard to bring anywhere these days."

"So bring the rest of them."

"They're teenagers. They have all these complicated plans."

"Your wife is a teenager?"

"She really is, at heart!" Lewis says, hoping to hide behind the deflection. "Catherine would love to see you—"

"I would love to see her."

I would love to see her too, muses Lewis, before confessing that Carl will once again have to settle for just him. After all, someone has to stay home and keep an eye on the children.

"Teenagers, they were, a minute ago. You said teenagers, with complicated lives."

"All the more reason to supervise. But listen, Rachel plans to come see you on her own. She gets home in May and she'll be coming through New York."

"If the world doesn't end."

"End again, you mean. Because it already ended once, right?"

"If you say so."

Carl's tone is one of indulgence, as though he is the one tending a delicate case. Good will is evident and humor is present, though as usual Lewis can't tell from moment to moment who is humoring whom.

1947

The best of it was the weather, a week of bright cool days, like links on a chain. Such days were made for walking and walking was still Karel's main occupation. He rarely had a specific destination in mind, he just kept moving. He had no desire to be here; that had not changed. The problem, also unchanged, was that you had to be somewhere.

Such purpose as he did have, the business of re-entering the world officially, was thwarted to the fullest measure of each bureaucrat's ability. Papers could not have been processed less efficiently had inefficiency been the stated goal. Within each agency there raged a conspiracy to increase exponentially every shred of meaningless paperwork. It would have been maddening to stand in those stagnant lines, sit for hours in crowded outer offices, except that killing time was not the worst thing. In a way, it was Karel's primary objective—other than to keep moving.

He vowed that as soon as this was done—transcripts, licenses, identity papers, passport—he would leave the capital behind forever. The tension was too visceral, between Praha his home and a Praha which could never be home again. Every inch of the city was colored by memories; they were hung like paintings at every street corner. And the memories, designed to delight, were all impossibly sad.

This puzzled him. When one's aged mother leaves this earth, or when a treasured friend dies, memories are what one is left with. Memories are the part you cannot lose, the part assigned to provide comfort. Why didn't it work that way now? He was tempted to revisit the taverns and theaters and bookshops and parks where in theory those sweet recollections lingered, yet each time the prospect alarmed him. The most glancing thought of Mila squeezed his heart in a vise. Not for anything would he risk standing alone at that curve of the river above the Vranska dam.

Walking along Panska one afternoon, he saw that the offices of Pikorny-Kovy had been displaced. On the ground level, where shops had operated—flowers, news, wine—now stood a shiny new bank. The levels above, both of which they had occupied, boasted an assortment of financial counselors and estate attorneys. He was curious whether P-K had gone out of business or merely relocated, but did not permit himself to research the matter.

The answer would come to him by chance, when he was hailed in Kampa Park by none other than Petr Kovy himself. Greeted with enthusiasm, no less, as though time had stood still, nothing had changed. The big cheese had not even bothered to change his clothes in the intervening years. He wore the same shiny black suit he had on in 1942 or, for that matter, 1938. Maybe he owned a dozen of them, identical. Underneath the matching black fedora, which he doffed, there were, however, barely a dozen strands of hair. So time had taken a toll on Kovy after all.

"Bondy, it's wonderful to see you. A wonderful surprise."

"Hello, Petr."

Karel's salutation was hardly friendly, yet it did subsume a level of credit. Kovy could have put his head down and ploughed right past him. This was a small courage, perhaps, but it did take courage to say hello.

"Forgive me if I am curious where you are working now."

Poor Kovy was nervous as a cornered cat. This was a brand new world and for all Kovy knew Karel might pitch him headfirst into the Devil's Millstream. At the very least, Petr had to know he was sailing blindly into poisonous disdain. Nonetheless, his nerves propelled him forward, his words spilling out past a smile tight as a stove bolt.

"Because, you see, we will soon be expanding—getting back to full force, you see. And naturally, we will want to have the best men come on board."

"Naturally," said Karel.

Kovy was determined to stick with this version of events. The firings had been a business decision, and a difficult one at that.

Now, with business happily picking up, P-K might once again make use of Karel's exceptional talents.

"What do you say?"

"Say, Petr? I say that, although still alive, I am also still a Jew."

"Please, Bondy, you must know that was not my choice. You must know that."

"Must I?"

Petr was hardly the only one wearing blinders. Pick up a newspaper and you would find no hint there had been an occupation, or a war, much less the annihilation of a people. The new politics were much discussed. Old Masaryk was deified, young Masaryk applauded, Benes appreciated—even as Moscow's broad shoulders loomed over every proud headline. The arts were huffing and puffing, with the poobahs blissfully pretending that 90 percent of the talent in Praha had not been Jewish. It was simply a fact that very little had been smashed here; nothing, that is, beyond the soul of the nation.

Such big thoughts did not stay with him. They were just faint shadows projected onto idle moments in the course of his relentlessly idle days.

"You are not with Anderle, are you? Or the Brothers Novotna."

"I am still fielding offers," said Karel, amusing himself with this absurdity. He could be an impoverished full partner in Jaro's dream café or, apparently, a well-paid slave again at Pikorny-Kovy. For sure, the offers were pouring in!

"I don't doubt you have been," said Petr, pressing a business card into Karel's hand. "So think about it. And keep me posted, yes?"

His most pleasant hours were the ones he passed with Jaro. They would meet each morning for coffee and rolls, meet again in the evening for pilsners and a skewer. One afternoon they took the tram to Suchdol to look into Jaro's business venture and Karel was delighted to find the place exactly as described in Jaro's prospectus. The neighborhood was pretty, the corner shop with its large welcoming windows on two sides was charming, and the rent was suitably depressed. Wholeheartedly, he could recommend Jaro take the plunge.

"If you manage to fail, it will still beat hell out of Poland."

This was another old standby, one more that could always make them smile. They would recite it in fun but knew the bedrock of truth underlying it: wherever they went, whatever they did, could only be an improvement on the death camps and frozen forests of Poland.

"At least admit you are tempted."

Karel was sufficiently moved by Jaro's need to win him over that he was willing to lie a little. "Tempted, yes. But temptation is sometimes there to be resisted."

"Not this time, surely."

"Listen, Jaro, for you this is perfect. For me, not so much. You see how it is, my friend."

"Yes and no. And speaking of temptation, do you remember the girl I mentioned, my sweet little Tamina? Well I also meant to mention that my Tamina has two very nice sisters, Eva who is one year older and Jitka..."

Jaro trailed off. He had been planning to advertise the sisters, each of whom was indeed quite lovely in his lifelong bachelor eyes. He did not know that Jitka was also the name of Karel's mother, but he knew the nuances of his friend's expressions.

"Maybe Miss Tamina will complete the picture. I will be happy for you and for her too!"

"Will you stand up for me if we marry?"

"I will if you marry this week."

Had he wished for a life stripped of pressures he once thrived on—of the need to work, compete, produce—Karel could have stayed on in Borva. He had too much energy for Borva, though, or for Suchdol. He was no longer tired, or no longer exhausted by his anger. These days, the anger was pushing him towards work.

"Jan has cabled back," he said. "My American cousin."

"Well then, there is proof he is alive, at the least."

"Alive and quite well, it seems. Business there is good for him. And he has two children at university, in the U.S."

"Will he hire you?"

"It's not like that. But he would welcome me, you know. Help me get two feet on the ground over there."

"I'm sorry, Karel. I cannot picture you in the U.S."

"Hell, I can't even picture the U.S., outside of their Hollywood movies. But Jan says it's okay, it's good. A crazy place, but fun."

"Crazy but fun? Sounds like you. Well, at any rate the crazy part."

"Listen, you made the craziness a little fun. A little bit, once in a while—all we could hope for. You were a help to me, Jaro. And I am honored you would want me in your wedding."

"You helped me too, for sure. Who knew that stealing cigarettes from the bad guys would be the high point of my life?"

"Or of your life to date. But let's hope we accomplished a bit more than that."

"Sure we did. It's just that sometimes it was like, you know, being lads again. Playing games."

"Cold hungry lads, playing dangerous games."

"I'll confess that to me it has already begun to feel like the good old days."

In spite of his unqualified admiration and affection for Jaroslav Heyduk, Karel was forced to confront the words. Not for the first time, they bubbled up unbidden: *Of course, but you are not a Jew.*

2000

"He won't know you," says Mrs. Goodman. "I'm sorry to be telling this to you, but he won't know who you are."

"He might," Lewis insists.

The emotional truth is that Lewis cannot resist the impulse to contradict this woman. The medical truth is that Carl has not spoken since the second stroke and has been on I.V. nutrition for a week. It is not being called a coma, it just looks and acts like one, as Carl lies there, wasting away. When they turn him in the bed, his body is the size of a child's.

"Look, I understand, you were fond of your uncle—"

"He's not dead, Mrs. Goodman. I don't think we should speak of him in the past tense."

"Fine, you *are* fond of him, in the present tense. I'm just saying, he doesn't know you are here."

"Probably you are right."

"Probably? Fine. He is going to jump up out of bed and start complaining about the soup. Start with his nutty stories. I can't wait to hear it."

Lewis steps to the window and looks down on Carl's gardens. In the flowerbed, the knee-high weeds and the late blooms are kept from collapsing only by the extent to which everything is tangled together. While it might almost be called pretty, the overall effect has gone beyond neglect to abandonment. When was the last time Carl stood at this window? Is he anxiously pondering, right now, within his cone of silence, the lost sequence of greens—lettuce, kale, peppers—in the vegetable bed?

When Lewis turns back, Mrs. Goodman, blessedly, has left the room. Shoes squeaking, the hired nurse enters. "Eight hundred dollars a day," Mrs. Goodman had whispered, "*out of pocket.*" Maddie's version is still that Mrs. G. is after the money. No one has seen the will, if there is one.

The nurse stays as long as it takes to attach a new tube and ping it twice—a dollar a minute?—remarking cynically that she hopes the patient enjoys his "lunch." But her negligible ministrations seem to rouse the patient. He mutters a few sounds, not recognizable as words, and his head swivels one way and then the other as though his neck feels stiff. Lewis lowers the rail and frees his uncle's hand from the bedding. There is no response. Carl's hand is limp and cool. His face is a pale green, the color of hospital walls.

Probably the woman is right, Carl does not know he is there. Probably his uncle will die soon; maybe he is dying this very minute. Keeping Carl's hand in his, Lewis wonders if either of them, the quick or the dead, will know the difference at the precise instant it occurs.

Karel has a sensation of such strange broad light that it could easily be celestial. What a joke, if Heaven really exists and he is winging his way there right now! If Mila is waiting for him, with the children. His chest thickens and tightens, so heavy it feels ready to implode at this new thought he might see them again. But the voices were not theirs. At first he heard the voices clearly, then less so, as though the speakers were walking away, or in a different room all along. There had been Mrs. G., unmistakably, and another woman, and a man who could be Lewis. But why would Lewis be talking to Mrs. G.? Confused, suffocating inside the dense robes of a drug-driven oblivion, he is drawn back down into the well of dream.

As usual, he has forgotten where they arranged to meet. Clearly he will be late, but just how late depends entirely on where he has to go. The one important event in a week crowded with work, and he managed to lose track of it!

Then it comes back to him: they are to meet on the Bridge, at the statue of Nepamuk. If he starts running immediately, he will be nearly on time. Mila wouldn't refuse him over a matter of two or three minutes, would she? She does love him, after all, doesn't she?

From Reslova, he sees the wide sweep of the Vltava and inhales the aroma of its familiar rich poisons—sulfur and coke from the power plant, mash from the brewery. Above the rush of flavored air, he can hear flags snapping on the barges.

He was telling her the truth when he insisted that theirs was the finest country in the world. This is less a matter of experience than of simple logic—"not big, not small, not rich, not poor, just a free and beautiful place"—and at the same time a matter where logic has no standing. Or so he had proclaimed. Obviously, he was somewhat in jest when he swept the panorama that day and assured Mila that all this was hers. Theirs.

He sees her approaching from the short side and sees that she is hurrying too, running late. This is a first, Milena late! And what a mitzvah it is. A rush of relief suffuses his body, followed by a flush of joy at the thought he might actually beat her there—not be the late one, be in the right, be loved. She even joins in the act by speeding up, holding her skirt high so she can match his finishing kick. It could be a scene from a sentimental film, except they are the opposite of solemn as they run, they are two souls overcome by the lovely hilarity of life.

He will listen to her excuse (an unruly student? a silly last-minute staff meeting?) and be delighted to need no excuse of his own. Milena looks so beautiful and laughs so richly that it can only be true she loves him and true therefore they will start a life together just as soon as he can complete his degree and be on the job full time.

Surely, the rest will take care of itself.